The Lost Girls

Also by J.M. Cannon

The Quiet Wife

The Lost Girls

J.M. Cannon

embla books

First published in Great Britain in 2025 by

embla books

Bonnier Books UK Limited
HYLO, 5th Floor, 103-105 Bunhill Row, London, EC1Y 8LZ
Owned by Bonnier Books
Sveavägen 56, Stockholm, Sweden

Originally published as *The Flash Girls* by J.M. Cannon in 2023

A CIP catalogue record for this book is available from the British Library.

ISBN: 9781471419010

This book is typeset using Atomik ePublisher.

Printed and bound in Great Britain by Clays Ltd, Elcograf S.p.A.

Embla Books is an imprint of Bonnier Books UK.
www.bonnierbooks.co.uk

FSC www.fsc.org
MIX
Paper | Supporting responsible forestry
FSC® C018072

Corpse

Marble eyes. That's the rumor.

A woman's corpse has been found with eyes like a doll.

Anna thinks it sounds just strange enough to be what she's after. The location is right. So is the body's estimated age. This could be the end of all her searching, yet still all she feels is a sinking sensation in her stomach.

She stands at the Pineapple Fountain. Waterfront Park isn't as empty as she thought it would be. It's September in Charleston, and the post-Labor Day tourists are quite different than the pre.

Gone are the parents pulling around their sunburned kids—enter the elderly. The park hugging the end of the French Quarter is all retirees. Men in bright polos with shiny Rolexes scratch their necks while walking with their wives.

She sees one in pink, two in blue, and the farthest wears yellow. They all glance around, somewhat bored; it's clear they just want to golf.

Anna lights her first cigarette in four years. The next minute is all silica sting and headrush. It distracts her enough to forget about the body waiting a few blocks away.

She looks out to Charleston Harbor. In the distance sits Fort Sumter. Beyond that, the Atlantic.

The city is sunny, but low over the ocean dark clouds have appeared. They aren't a blanket; there's space between them. And they move at the same speed in formation, like a squadron of bombers flying in from the sea.

The Atlantic blackens beneath their shadows, and in another minute, they've made it into the mouth of the harbor. They're moving as quickly as any clouds she's ever seen. The tourists start to notice, and one by one, their chins tilt up.

Soon the clouds are very close, a minute away maybe less, and Anna can see the harbor ripple as it's pelted with rain.

The sun vanishes. The city begins to darken.

The tourists turn from the water and start to shuffle for safety, as if this were an air raid. Anna only shifts so she's under a palm branch and keeps smoking.

Nine hundred miles away, a hurricane swirls, building strength. This little cluster of storm clouds, Anna thinks, is one of its scouts.

The hurricane's current trajectory puts Charleston in its eye. But three days from landfall, residents are confident that will change.

Initial hurricane models *always* change.

Though Anna's not so certain.

Already the clouds have passed over the city. The sun is back, baking the moisture on the pavement into more humidity. The tourists look cautiously towards the ocean expecting more clouds, but upon seeing none, they chuckle and pat their damp clothes.

Anna frowns.

She's not all that superstitious, but something about the little storm and the smiling tourists shaking it off sits wrong with her. The sun shower now has the feeling of a warning. One that's going unheeded.

Get out.

Her anxiety grows as the sun warms her face. The sunshine, the gentle breeze—typically they lift her spirits, but something about it feels like a trick, like it's the perfume rising from a carnivorous plant.

A bigger storm builds off the coast. One big enough to sink the entire city. But no one seems to mind; the media has cried wolf too many times, they say. But behind her brews another system: the doll-eyed corpse found in a cobwebby mansion.

The disturbing rumors about the body's condition have already drifted through the streets. Anna is wasting time staring towards the sea, but for this story, she needed a cigarette.

She quickly turns from the harbor and starts walking into the French Quarter. She passes a fence that uses real cannonballs as post caps. The iron balls dimple the concrete on which they've been placed.

Anna stops and stares. She can almost *feel* the weight of the iron just looking at it. Maybe because it's the same heavy sensation of dread that sits in her stomach.

Friends

On Church Street, there's only one news van and a few reporters loitering outside the old mansion.

The police presence is light, too. There are just two squad cars with their lights off and the county coroner's van. They're all parked neatly against the curb.

The street isn't blocked off with crime scene tape as Anna had pictured.

She figures most of the police force is busy preparing for the worst-case scenario with Hurricane Charlie.

The scene is calm, apart from a small posse of press and curious neighbors idling near the mansion's door.

Anna makes her way to them.

"Hey, Justin," she says to a man of about twenty-two. He turns to her, his eyes widening at the sound of his name and then narrowing as he realizes who said it.

"Oh, hey. I didn't think they assigned two of us to the story."

Anna smirks. Justin's the newest reporter at *The Charleston Journal*, fresh out of college. He's overly ambitious for his position and doesn't want to share the authorship spot on an article.

"Bruce texted me. Two minds, ya know?"

Justin only grunts. He has acne-scarred cheeks and wiry stubble—the look of an overzealous honor student who's spent his entire life getting good grades and never learning to groom himself along the way.

Anna is lying. Their boss, Bruce, asked her to go out to Lowe's and interview the manager about the sale of plywood, screws, and electric lanterns. Then go to the parking lot to get some panicky quotes from the people buying these things.

It's the kind of hurricane fluff piece she has no interest in.

There's a *body* here. One whose history she might know. She was pissed it was given to the kid, but she hasn't done a good job making friends at work. In part, she realizes, because she does things like this.

But Anna has a plan: She'll just say the manager was too busy for an interview and make the quotes up from preppers on her own. It's the same recycled garbage for every storm anyway.

"Do you think it's her?"

Anna thinks she's overheard a question meant for someone else and stares at the orange brick of the colonial, wondering if the body inside is, in fact, that of Sylvie Platt.

It isn't until she senses someone's looking at her that she realizes Kate Doyle, a reporter for the local Fox affiliate, is asking *her*.

"Wh-who?" Anna stutters, playing dumb.

"The Platt girl. She lived just two blocks over. I think she even walked past this place on her way home from work. Isn't that crazy? I mean, what if she was here the whole time?"

"Yeah, crazy." It's all Anna can say. Kate is prepped for the camera. Her blonde hair shines, and her sunglasses must have cost three hundred dollars.

Anna looks her over. Kate's never had to worry about someone asking who her family is or where she's from. She's self-confident, not self-conscious.

She's traveled outside the country, has friends in different states, and knows her wines.

Anna just wants a fraction of the normalcy she has for her own life. To blend in, and laugh with friends, and have witty remarks at the ready.

Her heart plummets when she sees that Kate is giving her the stink eye. Anna realizes with a little horror that her eyes have not left Kate's face the entire time she's been thinking this.

This is why, exactly why, you are not normal, Anna thinks, looking away with a grimace. But she doesn't dwell on her faux pas. She thinks of Sylvie as her eyes scan this mansion left to rot.

Sylvie Platt—5'4", brunette, valedictorian, and nineteen years old when she went missing.

Anna's best friend, her *only* friend in the whole world. Vanished for four years. Does her corpse sit inside now? Anna's eyes are wide and staring. They look crazed. This could be the end of everything.

The end of all her searching.

Suddenly, there's a gasp and the light clack of heels moving on pavement. The crowd around Anna has taken a step away from her. She surveys their faces.

Disgust.

Embarrassment.

She's about to ask what they're worrying about when Justin says, "Anna, your nose."

She throws her hand up to her face and when she brings it back, it's bright with blood. This isn't just a little nosebleed; they never are for Anna.

There's a wet tickle on her lips that she didn't even notice while lost in thought. The blood's already been flowing, racing off her chin to puddle on the pavement.

Nosebleed

A gusher. Now? Great. Anna's peeved but not surprised. She digs in her purse and takes out a packet of travel tissue. She tilts her head back, twists each tissue into a tusk, and sticks them in her nostrils. Then she begins wiping the blood off her face.

She's a professional at this point.

Nobody in the small group has come to her aid or even asked if she's okay. This, too, is unsurprising. Her nosebleeds leave her looking like a leper. Each one is a gusher, and people back away as if they might catch the Black Death.

She's tried to explain it's just HHT—a genetic disorder of the blood. It can cause serious symptoms in some people—seizures, strokes, but for the most part, it just gives Anna horrible nosebleeds.

She finds a light post several feet from the mansion's entrance and tilts her head back against it, giving gravity a chance to stop the flow.

Justin knows her condition—most people in the office do—and he walks over to her with his little notebook flipped open.

He doesn't mention her nosebleed. "Want me to catch you up?"

"Sure," Anna says nasally.

He sighs as if speaking to a child, but Anna is a couple years his senior. "The building is owned by the Robinson family. Has been for about eight years. They bought it expecting, with the money they had, that they'd be able to grease some palms and make some wild renovations. But look at the place. Zillow says it was built in 1784. It's on the historical register. Rumor has it they contributed to some city councilmens' campaigns, expecting an exemption for renovations but never got it. The place has sat empty since they purchased it in 2015."

Anna looks up. The mansion's windows have been covered up with plywood that has been painted to look like bricks.

"Nice paint job, right?" says Justin. "The Robinsons tried to make this place an eyesore when they didn't get their way. They put standard plywood on the windows, and then vandals would graffiti it. Looked ugly as hell. Eventually, the city made them put these up instead." Justin points at the brick-painted boards.

Anna is a bit bewildered. "How do you know all this already? Didn't this get called in an hour ago?"

Justin smirks, and Anna looks towards the crowd and thinks she sees Kate do the same. "I grew up on Clifford Street. Everyone who lives around here knows the story."

Anna tilts her head just a tiny bit farther back in a nod. So, Justin is rich. His attitude begins to make sense. He must see his place at *The Journal* as a stepping stone. He was probably pissed he didn't immediately get an internship at a bigger paper somewhere else. Anna thinks he seems smart, but perhaps not smart enough to comprehend just how dead journalism is. The few spots there are at the top media firms have become incredibly competitive, and all for peanuts.

"What are they saying about the body?"

The entire group turns to look at Anna. She blushes, and her eyes dart away. Of course, Anna knows. It's why she's here. She'd gotten a tip from a freelance friend who heard chatter on the police scanner.

"Female. Teens or early twenties . . ." says Justin. "The detectives seem a bit shaken up about the condition of the body."

"Shell-shocked," Kate adds.

"Because of the eyes?"

"It's not just that." Justin shakes his head and laughs. "They say she's all dolled up."

"How so?"

"I dunno. The only other thing we got from the police was that the body was embalmed."

"Embalmed? Like professionally?"

"Again. No clue. That's all we got."

Anna has to control her expression. If she were to show how excited she was, she'd look like a psychopath. No one here knows her connection to the case.

Justin keeps talking. "A body . . . embalmed, with marbles for eyes. It's like this young girl was taken to the taxidermist."

Anna slowly brings her head back so it's level and stares at the mansion. Her tissues itch, and she takes them from her nostrils. She almost wants to smile. If she were alone, she would.

An embalmed body with marble eyes. She knows in her gut that this is the beginning of the end.

He will show his secrets—few serial killers can resist not doing so. They all long to be caught.

The crumbs will finally come together, and the man who's been playing this sick game for seven years is ready at last to reveal himself.

There are tears in Anna's eyes, even as the hairs on the back of her neck prick up one by one.

Sheets

After another five minutes, Anna's nosebleed has stopped completely, and two men come walking out the mansion's front door holding a stretcher with the bulge of a body under a white sheet.

Anna watches the two men. There's no strain in their expressions or the muscles of their forearms as they carry it. The body is obviously light. They look completely unbothered and easily heft the stretcher up into the back of the coroner van and then slam its doors shut.

She couldn't get an exact read on how tall the dead girl was by looking at her sideways body. She wasn't noticeably short or tall.

The reporters had been quiet while the body passed, but as the detectives step outside the old mansion, there's a commotion of questions.

Anna stays in the outer ring and watches. This is the part of the job she could never do.

It was another reason she's been assigned to do a fluff piece at a big box store today, and not the homicide case. The thought of following someone and blurting out question after question like a seagull hoping to get a scrap makes her cringe.

The reporters remind her of pigeons cooing for food or students bobbing up and down with hands in the air, hoping it's them that the teacher calls on.

Anna picks at her fingernail and keeps her eyes on her feet. She can hear the generalities—"We don't know much at this time. It's best not to speculate until we have more facts."—and the reporters stop with their questions, knowing there'll be no more bread.

While everyone begins to leave, Anna hovers. Justin nods instead of saying goodbye, and Kate widens her eyes at her feet as she walks by her, making a big show of stepping around Anna's tiny pool of blood.

She isn't bothered by being ostracized—she's plenty used to it.

Anna's attention is still on the scene. She notices there's a teenager talking to one of the detectives. The girl is wiry thin and heavily pierced. She has dyed red hair, and despite the heat, she wears a sweatshirt.

Anna heard that the body was called in by some trespassing kids. The cops probably gave them immunity for a little trespassing fine in order to get the details about the exact circumstances they found the corpse in.

When the detective finishes speaking with the kid, he pats her shoulder and steps away.

That's when Anna follows. He doesn't head towards a car. He crosses to the other sidewalk and is soon walking casually. One hand in his pocket. A little sway in his stride.

Anna knows it's Terry. When Sylvie first went missing, he was one of two detectives assigned to her case. Anna was hard on him, hounding him and the rest of the police force when they gave up looking for her.

They aren't friends, but it's worth a shot to talk to him. Anna checks her face on her phone's camera screen to make sure there isn't any blood she missed and then walks up quickly behind him.

"Hey there," says Anna.

Terry stops and turns. "Anna Klein. I thought I saw you hovering. Why didn't you say hi?"

She can sense his sarcasm. "That's what I'm doing now."

"Well, you're wasting your time. Unfortunately, all I could say I said back there."

"You mean all you would say without a bourbon in front of you?"

Terry narrows his eyes at her. He's fat and bearded, and Anna knows he's the kind of guy to think he's more of a man because of it.

"That could be the case . . ." He scratches his beard with a thumb. "But I really do need to be home. Hurricane prep and all . . ." He goes silent, and so does Anna. First one to speak loses.

"Alright," Terry concedes. "But only if business isn't all we talk."

"Deal."

"Before I have bourbon, I've got paperwork. Meet me at Crooks Distillery on Main at seven?"

"Seven." Anna extends her hand to seal the deal.

Terry takes it and shakes it lightly.

He keeps walking while Anna stays in place. His palm was warm and clammy, and she wipes her hand off against a brick wall.

Compared to Terry's sweat, she preferred when her hand was covered in blood. But there is too much at stake now to pull any stops.

In two days, this town could be flooded, and she isn't going to let the answers to all her years of questions slip beneath the surge.

B&E

It's only a couple minutes before Anna's back at the mansion, and at the very moment the house comes into view, the last cop is pulling away from the curb.

Everyone has already gone. There is too much to do for both journalists and the police.

A single piece of yellow crime scene tape stretches across the big oak door and ripples gently in the wind—the only evidence that all the commotion had even happened.

Anna doesn't look over her shoulder as she makes a beeline for the back of the mansion. She walks confidently, like she's there for a job.

She knows neighbors could be watching. They, too, didn't get the answers to their questions from the police. Surely their heads are swirling, knowing there has been a dead body next door—someone who was likely murdered.

Anna goes down an alley narrow enough for just one person to walk. There's a six-foot brick wall at the end of it.

It's not the easiest climb for someone who's 5'1", but she's driven by something different today. Without hesitation, she pulls herself over and goes tumbling into the backyard.

The yard is little more than a large patio with a patch of overgrown grass and a stained fountain. It's small and secluded, and Anna looks around at who could possibly see her.

There are a few windows of surrounding houses that look into the backyard—too many for her liking. She can see where the teenagers broke in because a plain blonde piece of plywood sits newly installed in one of the first-floor windows. It is not painted in a brick pattern like the others. She walks around the house and finds a low cellar window on its west side.

It's covered with more plywood. This piece is about eighteen inches high and thirty-six long. She could fit through the opening easy, if she can get it off.

She lies on the ground and positions her right heel so it's in the middle of the board, and then she kicks.

The plywood doesn't have much give, and it was louder than she thought.

Part of her is screaming to leave, that this is a foolish idea from the get-go, but it's silenced as she kicks again.

Again.

And again.

She gets smart about it and kicks in a rhythm like that of a hammer. Plenty of people have been barricading windows for the hurricane, and no one would think twice about the sound.

She's about to give up when suddenly her foot hits nothing but air. The plywood leaves the frame and bangs into the basement below.

Anna is immediately hit with dank cool air. It pours from the window, like the house has sprung a leak. It smells of rot and salt and cold stone.

The ancient cellar of a seaside city.

Anna stays still on the ground. She's petrified, staring into the black mouth she's opened as she inhales its breath.

Again, she wants to leave. But this time something different unsettles her. It's not the fear of authorities or the trespassing or possibly losing her job. It's that she feels like something in the house *wants* her to come inside.

And by slipping into the cellar, she is only falling into its trap.

Abandoned

In the end, the decision is easy. Anna turns so she's on her stomach and shimmies backwards through the open window and into the cellar. The drop is farther than she thought it would be, and she stumbles when she hits the ground.

She sighs as the bruising pain leaves her heels and then takes out her phone and turns on the flashlight. She can see immediately that it wasn't the screws in the plywood that had given way. She had kicked it so hard that the rotted wood had separated from the window frame entirely. Although that's not the only thing that catches her eye. The plywood is double-sided, and sandwiched in the middle is what looks like yellow spray foam. To guard against mice, or water, or intruders, Anna can only guess, but she doesn't give it another look.

She surveys the cellar. It's all brick.

Brick walls and brick columns and brick floor. Some of the stones in the floor are no longer set, the mortar has crumbled, and they wobble under her feet.

The room itself is nearly empty. There are the rotted pyramids of empty wine racks and some flattened carboard boxes for tools and renovation equipment, but that is all. The sights so far aren't as unsettling as she'd thought they'd be.

So far, no pentagrams.

She feels better about this. Her imagination has been running amok, but the plain room and branded boxes are a reminder that this isn't some haunted mansion—it's just another abandoned building.

The cellar doesn't twist and turn and maze into the earth. It's a square in the ground, and Anna quickly makes her way upstairs.

She comes out into a narrow butler pantry that is even emptier than the cellar. The cupboards are doorless, and she can see into the glass cabinets. The entire room holds nothing but dust.

The kitchen is much the same, and the theme continues throughout the first floor. The rooms are void. It looks clear that this place was purchased with the intention of being completely remodeled.

What most unsettles Anna is the pitch dark that lingers at the edge of her flashlight's beam. The windows are boarded up with wood, and there's not so much as a stray sunbeam peeking through anywhere in the house.

It's a dark dungeon in the middle of the city. Anna thought she'd be able to hear traffic or sirens, but the house is deathly silent. It's not warm, either. The sunlight is blocked by the brick and the wood over the windows. It is not the South Carolina humidity that has slipped through the cracks and down the chimney, but an Atlantic breeze.

In just a T-shirt, Anna has chills.

In the living room, a pipe runs out of the floor and into the ceiling. It's thin and painted white to match the walls. The wood floor around it is softened and stained black. The rot emits a musk that Anna quickly steps away from.

She's still not as calm as she thinks she should be. She knows the police were just here and they would've checked every nook and cranny. But what if they missed something? A hidden door somewhere, and the man who turned a girl into a doll just stepped out of his hiding spot.

Something thumps upstairs, and Anna freezes.

She stands as still as she can, taking quiet breaths. Listening. This is an old house—damn near ancient by American standards—and old houses make all kinds of noises. But now that a few silent seconds have passed, the sound isn't what scares Anna. It's the lack of it.

She thought it strange that she couldn't hear the street through one panel of quarter-inch plywood, but now it is more than that. There is no noise whatsoever, this house is so quiet her ears ring. She can hear her heart ka-thunk, ka-thunk as if she was wearing a stethoscope.

Anna moves quickly to fill the air with the sound of her footsteps. She exhales noisily and starts up the stairs.

She enters a hall with half a dozen closed doors, three on her left and three on her right, but what catches her eye is the room directly at the end. It sits doorless, like an invitation, and she walks to it slowly, as if entranced.

It's there that she loses her breath.

The room is not empty like the others. There is a curtained bed, a wardrobe, and a set of chairs around a low coffee table.

On the table are circles in the dust where plates and glasses used to be. It seems like the police likely only just took them into evidence. Anna leans over to glance at it with her arms neatly at her sides, as if she was an observer at a museum.

She walks to the bed. The blankets aren't dusty like the rest of the room. They're twisted and coiled around like someone had just gotten out of bed. Someone had slept here at some point while the house had still been abandoned. The thought is terrifying.

Not even the homeless of Charleston would find much comfort in this cold mausoleum. The lack of light alone would mean purchasing lanterns and walking around like some specter.

No. It takes a disturbed kind of person to stay in a lightless, soundless place like this.

Anna walks to the wardrobe. There is nothing inside, but it is noticeably less dusty. There must've been clothes in it up until today when the police took them into evidence.

Why, she wonders, didn't they take the blankets?

She runs her fingers on the cold clothing rod. Was this filled with men's clothes for who might've been living here or women's clothes for this dead human doll? Anna doesn't think of it too long.

She shuts the cabinets and turns to leave. She's disappointed.

Anna didn't find a clue like she thought she would. All the more reason to meet with Terry to try to get something out of him about the body.

As she turns back towards the hall, she's shocked still. Written on the wall that she still hadn't turned to face are several lines of text in red paint. She mutters along to herself as she reads it.

The apple of an eye despite that goodbye
See all I say true, I promise not to lie
I am had by all, but not by some

Called a name but not my one
I am a beginning. You, with just a little skinning
The apple of my eye, and it is there where one can find me
What am I?

Anna stares at it for a long time. This message was intentionally left. It had to be. And her assumption is right—the killer wants to be found.

The only problem is that this still isn't an admission of murder.

Three girls have disappeared under the exact same circumstances. Each was walking home alone at night when out of an alley or from behind a car, their picture was taken with a bright flash.

When they turned to look, they saw a hooded figure. Their face wasn't visible. Nor did they ever speak to the girls. They only stared.

Each girl was then stalked for the next couple weeks, and each girl eventually vanished from the face of the earth.

But that was exactly the problem—there's never been a body. Not until maybe now.

A body changes everything.

Anna switches to her camera, takes a picture of the riddle on the wall, and leaves the room.

Neat

Anna had searched the rest of the rooms and found nothing but dust. She knows she saw all there was to see.

Now, she sits at the bar at the distillery while the bartender pours her a whiskey. She doesn't like the taste, she never has, but she doesn't like herself, either.

She's a half hour early, but by the time she was done scouring the mansion, it was too late for her to go home.

Luckily, Terry isn't late, and by the time he walks in, Anna has a confident buzz.

He sits with a groan, and the bartender doesn't ask what he wants before putting a glass in front of him and pouring a double of bourbon.

"You a regular?" asks Anna.

"Let's just say I didn't have to amend my schedule to be here. Every evening before I go home to the wife, I stop in for a double. It washes down the day. Especially a day like this one." Terry nods at the bartender and gives him twenty.

"And what kind of day was that? Are those rumors true? About the body."

Terry holds out his hands. "Whoa, slow down. Remember how I said this wasn't going to be all business? I come here to decompress, and today, I just wanted some company. I'll speak in abstracts, but nothing for the record."

"Fair enough."

There's a silence until Terry nods up at the TV. "Can you believe this crap? It's like the whole thing was made up for views. Hurricane Charlie for Chucktown. How do you people stomach selling fear for a living? That storm's targeting us deadeye now, but there's not a chance in hell it's still that way come landfall."

Anna only became interested in journalism when Sylvie went missing, but she's already gotten used to the amount of hate the profession gets from certain types.

Terry keeps talking. "You've got good folks scared and moving and putting off work all for a sprinkle. It's one of many reasons I hate journalists. You . . ." He has his first sip and glances back at Anna. "You I can stand. You don't quack out questions like the others."

"Maybe not in public." She smiles. "But other than the eyes and the embalming, I heard the body was a female. Teens or twenties. Is that all true?"

"If it'll get you to quit talking, yes. When there's a case this twisted, those kinds of facts are going to be impossible to keep from the public."

"Why did the police leave the house so soon? Is this not being treated like a homicide?"

"It's being treated as suspicious. At the very least, we're looking at desecration of human remains."

Anna suddenly has a plan to get what she needs, and she sets it in motion. She takes a sip of her whiskey. "Really? Just desecration of human remains, even with that fucked-up riddle on the wall?"

"Who told you about that?"

"And what about that little tea party in the bedroom? Whoever did this was obsessed with this corpse. What, for one second, makes you think he didn't kill her, too?"

"You need—" Terry starts, but Anna interrupts him.

"Hannah Greenwood, Tess Gibson, and Sylvie Platt. They were all murdered, and your police department is going to finally have to admit it."

"Look, can we start over? I'm here as a courtesy to you, Anna. In case this *is* Sylvie Platt. I know she was your friend. But don't get ridiculous," Terry scoffs. "Those other two girls were drug addicts. One had a boyfriend with a history of hitting her so hard she'd get concussed. The world isn't as sinister as serial killers. The answer is simpler than that. They're runaways. Overdosed in the woods. Buried by their boyfriend. Take your pick. Now who told you that stuff about the house? Did that leak come from my department? Or did you break in?"

Again, Anna ignores his questions. Terry is not in the same jurisdiction as where Hannah and Tess went missing. He doesn't know the details. The stalking. The panic in their stories. She's learned to keep her mouth shut, though. She's been belittled for being crazy by the other departments. "You don't think Sylvie was a Flash Girl, but she was. They all were."

He pauses and hesitates. If there's something he wants to say, Anna thinks, he doesn't say it. "Let me clarify something for you. There's no such thing as the Flash Girls. If you try to paint some serial killer connection, you're scaring people for no good reason."

Anna's not going to fight him on this. She's been around this block before. "Okay, but what makes you thinks it's Sylvie's body? Do you have something?"

"We don't know who the body is. We only just found her."

Anna thinks she can sense him lying, but she could just as well be wrong.

"And please don't take advantage of me being polite. I'm not saying this on the record, and I'm not even saying this is a confirmed homicide. But we have a suspect."

"What do you mean?" Anna leans forward in interest.

"I mean stop sticking your nose in this or you'll blow the whole fucking thing, Anna. Don't go exploring on your own. Don't try to figure this out yourself. Let us do our job."

Anna knows he's referring to the early days of Sylvie's disappearance when she took it upon herself to investigate. She interviewed neighbors, chased leads, and trespassed once or twice. She was always getting in trouble with the police department back then as a vigilante. He's telling her not to do it again.

"You just want me to take your word for it? How do I know you're not just saying this to keep me home?"

Terry sighs and has another sip of his drink. "Alright. You heard about the young woman who was killed a couple weeks ago in Orangeburg?"

"Of course. I didn't write the story, but I read most of what we print and everything on homicides."

"Sure you do. So, the girl gets stabbed to death, but in the process she's able to drag her nails down his arms and gets him deep."

Anna knows what he's getting at. "So, you have his DNA? I heard she was found without fingers. That whoever killed her clipped them all off."

"Right. I'm not going to cross a line and give you privileged information, Anna. But when I say this, I mean this." He looks her dead in the eye. "We've got them. Quit your worrying."

She keeps staring at him even after he takes his attention to his drink. "If what you're saying is true, then you have to know it's Sylvie."

"Look. What I'm saying is we don't know."

Anna turns to her drink and has a sip. He's been polite, she doesn't want to push it, but at the same time something feels off. Like maybe he's telling her all this to stop her from poking around herself, like when Sylvie first vanished.

She needs to know more. She's thought the riddle through and can't make sense of it. Without another lead, she has nothing. "You want to know who leaked all that info to me?"

Terry nods.

"Okay, you answer a few more questions about this case—don't worry, nothing on the record—and you've got a deal."

"You know what, forget it. It was bound to come out."

"Fine. Guess you won't know who took a hundred-dollar bribe."

"A bribe?"

Anna raises her brow and Terry relents. "Okay, ask."

"The body . . . What color hair did she have?"

"Brunette."

"How tall?"

"We didn't measure."

"If you had to guess, how tall?"

"Medium height for a woman."

"What color were those marbles?"

Terry pauses. "Blue."

Lastly, Anna pulls out her phone and swipes to a picture of Sylvie Platt. In the picture, she's on a boat. Her brunette hair falls far past her shoulders, and her blue eyes shine brighter than the sea behind her. Anna shows the picture to Terry with a pounding heart, but he just chuckles.

"Come on, Anna. There are plenty of blue-eyed brunettes in Charleston County. That little picture means nothing."

"Did the body look like her?"

Terry looks again and shakes his head. "I guess your leak didn't tell you everything. You don't know about the body's . . . other condition?"

"What do you mean?"

Terry's face suddenly hardens. His eyes go blank as if looking at the past. "You don't get to know everything. That's not the deal. If you want to know if this is Sylvie, we'll be doing some DNA testing to see if it matches that of any missing persons in the county." Terry's getting mad. Rageful. His eyes flash and his hands turn into fists. "If you're trying to get the jump on your colleagues on this being some would-be serial killer case, you're shit out of luck! Now, who took that bribe?"

The bartender comes close pretending to inspect a row of washed highballs.

Anna waits before she speaks. She wants to press Terry on this "condition," but she's pushed enough. She looks at the picture of Sylvie smiling one more time and puts her phone away. Brunette, blue-eyed, same age and height range. The odds feel like it has to be her.

Anna is elsewhere in her head, and Terry has to repeat the question. "Who took the bribe? I want a name."

"Oh, you know. They were pretty short for a cop. Around my height, maybe an inch taller."

Terry squints, as if he is trying to think of someone who fits the description.

"They were also pretty young *and* pierced. I didn't think you let people like that on the force."

Terry leans back with an empty stare in his eye that quickly morphs back to rage.

"Hey," Anna says. "When we made our deal, I never said it was one of your cops."

"I could have you arrested. Do you know that?"

Anna finishes her drink and stands from her stool. "Come on, Terry. We both know you don't want to work that late tonight." She pats his shoulder once and makes for the door.

Typically, she wouldn't burn a bridge like this. She's now poisoned with the whole PD. After this case is solved, she's done with Charleston. But with the hurricane coming, there might not even be a city left to leave.

Wayward

Anna isn't quite ready to head home. She's been walking from the distillery with her mind racing. *What did Terry mean, the body's other condition?*

It seemed like maybe it wasn't exactly the right phrase. He hesitated before he said it.

Anna shakes off the thought. She needs to put her mind to work, and this won't solve anything. It's Friday night in the city, but she's not staying out to party. Even though she's supposed to.

Her phone buzzes in her pocket, and she pulls it out. Two missed calls and a text asking where she is, but she doesn't even think of responding.

The talk about the body has given her an idea, and she has a new lead to chase.

Her odds feel slim, but she has few other leads to chase, and she wouldn't be able to sleep if she didn't try.

The idea of finding a teenager in downtown Charleston feels like a needle in a haystack, but Anna was one herself once, and from the times she'd visit Sylvie's neighborhood here, she knows where to look.

First, she goes to the spots that are close. An old basketball court that was popular with the local kids near Cannon Street has been turned into a bagel shop, and she remembers the parking lot off King they used to frequent has become an entire megaplex of apartments.

When her feet get sore, she realizes she's being stupid. She needs to go towards the French Quarter and search around the mansion that the teens broke into. They wouldn't stray this many blocks to begin with. Kids often like to vandalize close to home, where they can make a run for it.

Anna busses back to the French Quarter and looks at her watch. *8:30.*

She worries the teenagers will be heading in soon. She has no idea how old the girl was. The older she gets, the more everyone who's fourteen to eighteen looks the same incredibly young age.

Anna decides to check green spaces. The parks where kids can find a place far enough from adults to smoke and drink and have ample warning if the police are going to show up. She sees a few groups of teenagers, but her mark isn't among them.

Finally, she goes to White Point Garden. If there are teens there, they're likely from very wealthy families, but rich kids get bored enough to break into abandoned houses just as much as any other teenagers.

The park is five acres and sits at the very tip of the peninsula that makes up downtown Charleston. Across from the greenspace, by the seawall, two news vans are filming live reports. She can see the anchors under the bright lights gesture out towards the ocean.

Though she can't hear them, she knows exactly what they're saying. "*Here is where models project a twenty-five-foot storm surge is going to first enter the city.*"

She heads into the park where it's much darker.

There are plenty of lights on the path, but off of it and under the live oaks, the area feels almost forested.

Anna hears laughter in the distance and picks up her pace. In between two rows of live oaks is a circle of people sitting.

Teenagers. It's too dark to see their faces, but from their high voices and the rising clouds of smoke, she figures the odds are high.

The only problem is if she wants to see if the girl is there, she'll have to walk right up to them.

Luckily, Anna isn't bigger than most teenagers. If she walks towards them casually, she knows they're unlikely to bolt the way pot-smoking teenagers are liable to.

She tucks her head to her chest to make herself even smaller and starts towards the circle.

She's able to hear some of their conversation as she gets near. It's about the possibility of a looming evacuation order, and every other word she hears is an expletive. She forgets how much kids love to curse. They mutter and go quiet when Anna is just a few feet away.

She's several years older than them. Still, Anna doesn't look like a cop or old enough to be a neighbor concerned about noise or the pot smoke.

Perhaps they think she's looking for some drugs herself.

"Hey," Anna says, breaking the silence. "I'm looking for someone and was wondering if you know her."

"Um . . ." says a boy who's looking at the others, unsure if this authority figure is a threat.

"What's she look like?" says the girl closest to Anna, all chipper.

"She's got reddish hair, dyed. Lots of piercings. She's shorter than average."

The circle goes silent. Their heads turn to someone in the group—a girl with her hood up sitting crisscross with a lit cigarette in her fingers.

"Sounds like me."

Anna can't see her face well enough in the darkness, but then the girl nods her head back to throw off her hood and it's clear she's the same girl from the scene. "I've already talked to the cops today. They said I'm not being charged."

"No, no. I'm not with the police. I'm a journalist."

Suddenly, there's an eruption of yells. The kids are hollering and laughing, and the girl with the red hair jumps to her feet like a lightning bolt and starts to yell above them.

"I told you! I fucking *told* you! I'm going to be rich!" She holds her cigarette between her forefinger and thumb like it's a joint and takes a long drag. Then she flicks it into the air and starts doing a little dance.

"I fucking tooold you," she sings. "I fucking tooold you."

"Ah man," says another a boy who's still recovering from laughing. "That was too good."

"May I ask?" says Anna, curious about the celebration.

The boy points at the girl from the scene. "Dylan's been saying she's got a golden ticket."

"And what might that be?" Anna asks the boy.

"Pictures of a dead body."

The girl is still busy doing a little shuffle, and Anna figures she's high. Suddenly, she speaks. "Really, r*eally* fucked up pictures of a dead body, may I add. A Banksy of a dead bitch! A Monet of Charleston's mummy!"

"Excuse our friend here," says the boy. "She's a little high."

But Anna couldn't care less about the language she was using to describe Sylvie. All she could think was *Bingo*.

Smile

Anna walks away from the circle with Dylan to talk about the photos she took. Anna knew that if there was a body as disturbing as what Terry had told her, the teens that broke in likely would've taken pictures themselves.

"Didn't the cops search your phone?" asks Anna.

"Nope. I said get a warrant!" Dylan yells and lights another cigarette. This girl is a bit unhinged, but Anna likes her. As wild as she is, she had heard that she waited at the crime scene after trespassing in order to tell the police what the teens touched in the house and what they didn't. She could've left a tip and run off.

"And what about these pictures? Can I see them?"

"Hmm, price first."

"Look, there's no way I'm going to offer a price before knowing what pictures you even have."

"Guesstimate price. What are you willing to pay?"

"I don't know. A couple hundred bucks."

Dylan reels back. "*What?* You don't know what I have here. This is true crime-of-the-century shit."

"Then I need to see what I'm dealing with before I pay."

Dylan sets her cigarette in her mouth while she digs out her phone. She swipes for several seconds then turns the phone so Anna can see.

It's a picture taken with a flash in the dark bedroom. There's the body, in a light pink dress. It sits upright in a chair at the little coffee table. Anna doesn't recognize the dress as being one of Sylvie's.

"We thought it was a doll at first. I mean, when we went into this bedroom, we all jumped and nearly booked it. A human-sized doll is maybe creepier than a human."

In the picture, Anna can see a strap on the doll's neck. "What's this?" She points.

Dylan turns her phone and swipes again and turns it back. In this new picture, it's clear what's around her neck—a 90s era single-lens camera.

Anna is awestruck. How did Terry brush her off so flippantly with this evidence? This is the smoking gun. It's the Flash Girl Killer. Anna realizes Dylan is probably too young to know what she's talking about. When no body was ever found, the legends didn't live on. Everyone assumed what the police said about the other girls—runaways, overdoses, boyfriends. Anna's story was sunk.

But this . . . This is undeniable.

"The camera. It was there when you got there?"

"Yeah, we didn't touch anything. In this bedroom at least. When we saw her face, we got the fuck out of there."

"Makes sense."

"No." Dylan laughs a little and takes a puff of her cigarette. "You don't even know."

A breeze comes in off the harbor. It's strong and smells of the cold salt of the Atlantic. Fall is on the way, but so is something else.

Anna and Dylan are quiet for a moment, looking in the direction from where it came, as if through the trees and past the water, they might catch a glimpse of this storm.

"I heard on the news that this storm will hit with more power than a hundred nuclear bombs. Can you believe that?" Dylan laughs, but Anna can tell she's now nervous. "Talk about sensationalism. A hundred nuclear bombs?" she says to herself, as if the thought is amusing. "Were you here for the last hurricane? Hugo?"

"How old do you think I am?"

"Honestly, I have no idea when it was."

"It was in the eighties."

"Oh."

"So, how'd you break into that place anyway? Those plywood boards are on there tight."

"There was no covering on the window. We didn't even break in, so to speak. We smoke in that backyard sometimes at night. If you sit against the back wall, nobody can see you. But the other day, a great big piece of plywood that had been covering one of the windows was just gone. We had to go in."

Anna thinks this over. Maybe this means that the body being found was no accident. Someone knew these kids would poke around the house and find the body if there was an inviting way in.

"Can I see the pictures?"

"What?" Dylan asks, her face is wrinkled in confusion.

"Of the body?"

"Right." Dylan suddenly looks more concerned than she was about the storm. It's the same disturbed expression Terry had when she'd asked him earlier. "Just . . ." Dylan hands her the phone. "Swipe to the left. And I'm watching your fingers. Don't send it to yourself."

Anna grows nervous. Dylan seems carefree about the whole thing, but now she realizes it may have all been a show. She might be high as a kite right now because she's traumatized by this body.

Anna takes a deep breath and swipes.

What she sees is so wrong that at first, she can't quite comprehend it. She can understand now why Terry was able to laugh at thinking the face could be identified with a picture. While it was preserved, the cheeks and forehead were puffy and heavily coated with foundation.

But that isn't the disturbing part. Anna's eyes do a quick scan of the face and then stay fixed on a single point.

It seems impossible. It isn't until Anna sees the twin pins pushed deep into the cheeks that it finally makes sense.

The corpse is smiling wide from ear to ear. Its blue marble eyes stare back at the lens.

Anna turns away quickly.

"Fucked, right?"

Anna can only nod as she takes another deep breath.

"Think it's worth something?"

"Yeah, I don't know. Sell it to someone who sells papers by the cover image. *New York Post* or someone."

"I emailed everybody. All the papers I could think of. Nobody has gotten back."

The concept of talking money for this image makes Anna ill, and she speaks fast. "I don't know. I'm sure you were too paranoid to send the image. Send it watermarked or something. I'm sure they'll bite."

"I didn't think of that." Dylan extends her hand for her phone, but Anna holds it up to have one last look. There's something she's seen that bothers her.

On the body's left cheek is a little smudge of red, and Anna zooms in.

It's not just a random smear. She can make out a few letters. They're tiny, but they're there.

There's a C, and an H, but the rest of the letters are blocked. They lie under the foundation that has been caked onto her cheeks.

There's something written on her skin, and Anna is itching to know what.

"Thank you." She hands the phone back to Dylan.

"Do you want to buy it?"

"No. Sorry."

"You don't think it's worth something?"

"It's worth a lot more than I could ever give you."

Dylan is staring solemnly into space. "I just . . . never want to look at it again."

"I'm sorry. I guess nothing's free."

"Dylan, we're sparking a new one!" shouts one of her friends from the circle. It's like a light switches on in her head. The allure of escaping reality with another hit beckons, and Dylan takes off with a quick "Bye," trotting to the circle.

Anna walks in the opposite direction. A minute later, there is a boom that echoes in the harbor.

She stops and looks behind her. In the eastern sky over the Atlantic, lightning flickers. She hears yelling from the group, and one of them is bounding around and shouting, "End of the world, baby! It's the end of the fucking world!"

It's Dylan. Anna looks away to her feet and starts walking faster.

Death Wish

Before Anna takes the bus back home to North Charleston, she does something she hasn't done in years. She walks alone down the darkest streets of the city.

She heads to one quiet street corner in particular. This is where the photo was taken. Where a flash burst erupted from the mouth of an alley, and just two weeks later, Sylvie was gone.

Anna stares at the alley. She'd do anything to see a flash, but whoever took those photos knows just as well as Anna does that if she ever sees him, she'll try to kill him.

Anna touches the four-inch folding knife in her pocket. She's carried it for nearly four years, and not as a tool for self-defense, but vengeance. Her best friend was murdered, and the idea of that desecrated corpse being Sylvie doesn't fill her with terror so much as it does rage.

A car alarm goes off in the distance, followed by some sirens. She hears a drunken, "Whooo!" from a block over. It's just the sounds of Friday in the city, but she'd kill to hear the click of a camera.

Her phone buzzes again. She's going to have some explaining to do, but she's too stressed to answer.

She takes one last look at the alley before spinning away and walking towards King Street.

Here, she takes the bus north and it's almost eleven p.m. by the time she's staring at her apartment.

She got a good deal on rent with the place. It's an old brick building near the Cooper River, not far from the shipyards. The area is industrial and quiet. In front of her apartment is a massive field. It, too, is soon to be housing.

Her building used to be office space for an old shipping company. Now it's been purchased by an older couple who were banking on being landlords as a retirement plan.

Only two units are livable—the one the couple lives in and Anna's, which is two floors above it. She only has to pay seven hundred a month, but the catch is that the building is constantly under renovations.

She doesn't want to go in yet. She can hear the music from outside.

There's a small party waiting for her in there, and the last thing on this planet that she wants to do right now is be social.

She walks across the street to the field and sits and picks at the grass. She's thinking of Sylvie.

Their entire friendship often plays in her head. But the memories are not cathartic or even bittersweet.

The only thing these memories will ever make her feel is guilt.

December 2010

It's the last day of the semester at the Covenant of Christ. Anna Edwards is eleven years old and stands 4'10". She's tall for her age, but little does she know, she only has two more inches to grow.

Her mom is taking her to school today. It's a rarity, because ever since Anna was old enough to take care of herself on her own, her mom has begun sleeping in on weekdays.

Her mom is usually still snoring off the drinks that it took her to get sleep when Anna starts the one-mile journey to meet her school bus. But today, after much begging, she agreed to be her ride.

She'll take her in their Buick that is worth more as scrap metal than it is as a used car.

Anna's reasoning is sound: it's raining, and she has to bring a diorama for the final project in her history class. It's somewhat safe in a lidded shoebox, but if she were to walk for a while, she'd need to wrap it in a garbage bag. And she looks poor enough at her private school as it is.

"A brilliant kid," her mom huffs as she pours cereal into a bowl. Her cloud of boozy breath reaches Anna, and she wrinkles her nose. The house they rent in North Charleston is little more than a shack. It's musty and hot year round. Anna grew up telling herself that she should be happy her dad was never in the picture. If he was, she didn't know where they'd fit him.

"That's what your teacher said to me on the phone. I hope they're not praising you with the same shit. Then she was lecturing me about needing to come to your conferences. You're not being taught by a bunch of dunces, are you?"

"No, Mom."

Her mother pulls a spoon from the cupboard, shuts the drawer with her hip, and starts scarfing down her cereal. She keeps talking with her mouth full.

"Good. That Mrs. Riley, she seems to have a solid head on her shoulders."

Anna puckers at the very name. She likes her new school. It's only her first semester, but Mrs. Riley has had it out for her.

Although she's an adult, she seems to share the belief that a lot of the other kids have—that Anna doesn't belong there.

"She said you still have a lot of public-school curriculum and habits in you. That as far as scholarship students go, she'd like to see some serious improvement in the way you dress."

"Dress? Mom, we all wear uniforms." Anna looks down at her white polo. It's wrinkled to hell. She has to iron her own shirts, and she still isn't very good at it.

"Well, that could use another iron for one."

"All the other kids have moms who do that for them. Don't you get it? If I stand out, it's because you refuse to do anything for me."

It happens so fast that Anna feels it before she registers her mom's hand flying through the air. There's the sharp sound of the slap, and Anna cringes with her eyes closed in preparation for another.

"Don't you *ever* say I don't do anything for you. I raised you. Alone, all by myself. You wake me up to take you to school early, and you say I don't do anything for you?"

"I didn't mean it like that, Mom."

"How could you . . . say that?" Her mother's face wrinkles into an ugly cry. She is still drunk, and Anna just sighs.

"I'm sorry, mom."

Anna's better off lying, even though her mom truly doesn't do much for her. She only works part-time at the supermarket, and that's to afford booze. The rest of their money comes from a wealthy aunt in Atlanta who feels bad for them and sends a check once a month, but Anna has never even met her.

"Come on." Her mom knocks her keys off the counter trying to grab them. "Let's go."

After a twenty-minute drive into the wealthy suburbs, Anna asks to be let out a few blocks early.

"It's still raining," says her mother.

But Anna is bullied enough as it is. The other students make fun of her for being poor, for her nosebleeds, for having one shoe tied funny. If she gets dropped off in *this* car, she won't hear the end of it.

She has to think.

Anna has begun to notice that her mother is afraid of cops, especially when she's driving. The Covenant of Christ isn't just a middle school. It's grades seven to twelve, and they have a school officer.

"It won't get that wet, Mom, really."

"If you're trying to ditch school, young lady, I won't fall for it."

"You don't want to turn onto the grounds. The school cop has been pulling parents over for not having drop-off lot stickers." It's a lie, but her mom doesn't even question it. She's never heard of drop-off lot stickers, but that's because they don't exist.

A minute later, the Buick peels off, leaving Anna in a cloud of blue exhaust with her shoebox diorama in both arms.

She starts towards the school, and she's almost made it onto the grounds when her luck runs out.

"Hey! Hey! Bleeder!"

Anna keeps walking faster. "Bleeder bitch, wait up!"

When she hears footsteps pounding behind her, she stops.

A girl and a boy flank her on either side and circle her like hyenas. A third girl comes running from behind, out of breath, with an umbrella. These are just three of her bullies, but they're some of her worst. "Whatcha got there?" says the girl.

"Some . . . stupid diorama." Anna pretends not to care for it, but in truth she cares quite deeply about the work she put into her miniature reenactment of the battle of Fort Sumter. Anna notices another girl walking their way towards school, but she stops and watches the circle around Anna.

"Dio-*rama*. Wow. Did you make your little model for your gifted history class?"

"More like retarded," says the girl with the umbrella. It's Annalise, their leader. She has a sharp, paper-thin nose and pointy ears. Anna has always thought she looks like a mean elf.

She spins the umbrella at Anna, and Anna gasps and turns to protect the shoebox from the water flying off its top.

"Oh, so it's not so stupid to you, is it?"

"I need it to pass."

"What happens if you fail?"

Anna is quiet. The truth is that she could lose her scholarship, but that's exactly what these kids want. Anna is poor and unversed in the same interests that her classmates have. She's different, and to children, different isn't fascinating; it's something to be rooted out. An abscess to be removed.

Her bullies don't wait for a response. Kyle, Annalise's brother, snatches the shoebox while his tongue hangs from his mouth in an idiot's grin.

"Hey!" Anna tries to catch him, but he's far too fast. He disappears into the woods.

She goes stomping in after him, but by the time she's caught up to him, he's walking past her with a giant smile, rubbing his hands together as if to clean them. "Too late, Bleeder."

He shoulder-checks her and she doesn't even respond. She's scanning the woods for the diorama. Anna thinks it can be salvaged for at least a grade if she can find it, but her heart quickly sinks.

She can see a small stream through the thicket. It's running quickly from the recent rain. Anna searches its banks for as long as she can, but it's hopeless.

She stays in the woods awhile and cries. Long enough for her bullies to have gone into school.

When she emerges, she's soaked, and the girl who had watched was now standing where her bullies had been. Anna freezes like frightened prey. Then the girl waves, and Anna frowns.

There's a shoebox diorama at her feet. For a second she thinks it is hers, but then she recognizes this waving girl. She's in all the same gifted classes as she is. She has bright-red cheeks that always look flushed and thick brown braids.

Her name is Sylvie.

Anna walks the rest of the way to the sidewalk but doesn't slow for conversation.

"I'm sorry."

"It's fine," Anna says dully, not wanting to be pitied. She keeps walking towards the school.

"I meant, I'm sorry I didn't do anything to stop them."

Anna stops. For a second, she's hopeful she has a witness, but her bullies act like angels around the teachers of the Covenant of Christ. A witness in middle school isn't much leverage, even if Sylvie is a trusted source.

"It's fine. They'd just bully you, too."

Sylvie slings her backpack off one shoulder and unzips a pocket. She pulls out some wet wipes.

Anna is watching her the entire time with a furrowed brow. She's even more confused when Sylvie reaches up and starts wiping her face.

It's not until she sees the wet wipes come away red that she realizes her nose has been bleeding. She was too wet with rain to tell.

Anna is surprised when she starts to cry. At first, she thinks it is because she'd lost her project, but the more Sylvie wipes her face, the more she realizes it's because she hasn't been touched, not lovingly, for as long as she can ever remember.

She steadies her face so it's just tears. No ugly scrunching or sniffling. She doesn't want Sylvie to notice.

But she does.

"Hey, it's okay. Things will get better. My mom says middle school was the worst time of her life."

Anna just nods. Sylvie is significantly shorter than Anna, and she's reaching high above her head in order to get the blood. "Can you look down?"

Anna looks down, and then to her absolute shock, Sylvie quickly hops onto her tiptoes and kisses her on the nose. Then she collects all the bloodied tissues and puts them in her backpack.

"You don't have to . . ." But Anna's confusion returns as Sylvie is suddenly holding her own diorama out to her.

"Here. Take it."

"I can't."

"Please, there's no way anybody would find out. We all have the same topic, and my writing is printed. There's no handwriting."

"What about your grade?"

"It's okay. I'll be okay. Mrs. Riley has it out for you. I don't think you'd just get a pass this one time."

To Anna, it feels incredible to have another student say that about Mrs. Riley. Her teacher is almost just as bad as a bully. She'd pull Anna to the front of the class to show her uniform off as an example of how not to wear it. She'd chide her mockingly for mispronouncing things, and she has never, ever, given Anna an "A"—although she gets them in every other class.

Mrs. Riley seems to be just as upset as her bullies by Anna's poverty.

"*Please,*" begs Sylvie, extending the shoebox towards her. It's how she annunciates the word that makes Anna suddenly understand.

Sylvie wants this. She needs it. This is what makes her happy.

Anna takes the box slowly. "Thank you." And then, Sylvie beams a smile so bright that it burns itself into Anna's mind, forever.

Now, that smile is poisoned.

Antisocial

Anna stares up at her apartment and stalls for another couple minutes before she goes in. She doesn't want to appear on the scene all teary-eyed.

She stands from the grass, wipes herself off, and starts towards the front door. The whole building smells like a construction site—sawdust and paint and plaster dust.

It's another con of living here, but it was better than the stink of the halls in some of the places she lived in right out of high school.

She heads up the stairwell to the third floor. The bass thumps in the stairwell, and there's a burst of laughter.

She waits outside the door for several seconds before opening it. There's a haze in the air and the skunky smell of weed smoke. Her shoulders sink and she sighs. Then immediately, her face is flush with the chest of a man in his early thirties. He's handsome, or it just might be his full dark beard.

She knows from the smell of his cologne before she even looks up to his face that it's Jake, her boyfriend.

"I texted twice. I even called." He doesn't say it angrily, just like it's a matter of fact.

Anna realizes that in the last nine hours, since she'd first caught wind of the body on Church Street, she hasn't thought of Jake once. Her eyes seemed to tunnel-vision past his texts whenever she opened her phone.

Maybe it's a sign she should end things. They've only been dating a month, and she's only known him for two. Best to rip the Band-Aid off early.

"I'm sorry. Have you seen the news? They have us running around for every hurricane-related thing they can think of. It's non-stop."

"So non-stop you couldn't send a text?"

Anna feels worse about it than she lets on. She just lifts her arms and lets them flop against her thighs.

Jake looks her over. Anna knows he's begun to understand that this relationship isn't going anywhere serious. This moment feels like the nail in the coffin.

"Come on," Jake sighs, moving out of Anna's way and extends an arm to the living room. "At least have a drink."

Anna slips her shoes off and walks deeper into her apartment. She's made it a cozy place, with rugs over the hardwood. Matching thrifted furniture and plenty of houseplants.

Right now, however, the place is strewn with empty beer cans and the smoke is so thick that near the ceiling bands of it hang like cirrus clouds. She had said no smoking, and now she wants to scream. When she had agreed to let Jake have a party at her place, she thought she'd be here to control things, and now she just wants to go to bed.

But Jake's friends are skeptical enough of her as it is. When she enters the living room, she gives them a shy wave, and they wave back. A drink is put into her hand, but Anna doesn't take a sip. She's busy trying not to combust.

Jake runs with a rowdy crowd. They're older and have jobs, but when it comes to the weekends, they like to let lose. They're cooks and welders. Tattoo artists and bartenders. Anna likes them because she likes to escape from her life too, but right now the scene is too much. There's about twenty people crammed into her small apartment.

Someone has forgotten to take off their shoes, and there is dirt on the rug that trails into the kitchen. Again, Anna takes a deep breath.

Don't be a bitch. Don't be a bitch. Don't be a bitch. What's done is done. She takes a gentle sip of her drink, trying to get into the swing of things. If she can't go to sleep, she might as well forget the day.

Forget Sylvie's smile.

Sitting in her favorite recliner is a very tall man wearing all black.

She doesn't recognize him like she does Jake's other friends. His legs, even though he's sitting, seem to stretch unsettlingly high like a spider. He has thin matted hair, and his face is pocked with scars. He appears high because all he is doing is staring off across the living room into space.

In the next five minutes, Anna has already finished her drink. One of Jake's friends is wearing a goofy baby-face mask. It has creepy eyes and big bucked teeth. The mask is supposed to be funny, but it's downright disturbing. He's dancing to the music, grooving by himself, and soon, the baby-faced dancer makes his way around to Anna. She's sitting on the arm of the couch. He's dancing in front of her while she stares at him plainly.

"Why are you a baby?"

He just keeps dancing with no response. He reaches for her hand, and Anna sees Jake near the kitchen, not so slyly keeping an eye on them both.

The man in the mask holds her hand and is trying to take her towards the little open space where he'd been dancing, but Anna's not going to budge. She speaks loudly over the music. "Seriously. Do you go to all parties like this?"

Mr. Baby Mask shrugs.

"Why can't you talk?"

He points at the mask.

"Because you're a baby?"

He nods, and Anna tilts her head back. "Gotcha. You're a little young for me. Sorry."

He shrugs and dances while walking away.

Anna is more agitated than before. This is her own home, and after a long day, she shouldn't feel uncomfortable in it. She walks towards a large window in the living room that looks out to the field.

Inside, on the window's ledge, in the planter of her biggest and healthiest philodendron, is a mash of gray ash and the burned butts of a couple joints. The calm voice in Anna's head quiets.

She sees red.

"Are you kidding me?" she says softly to herself. "Are you *kidding* me!?" Anna then thunders. She walks over to the Bluetooth speaker and thumbs it off.

"Which one of you *idiots* ashed in my plant?"

"Anna . . ." Jake walks towards her with an expression that suggests she's being ridiculous. Overreacting. But that's far from it.

She swats his arm away. "Which one of you?"

"I mean . . . we kinda all did," says a thin girl with a spider web tattoo covering her arm. Jake's friends all nod to one another.

"Instead of a plate, or a cup, or an empty beer can, you ash in a plant?"

Nobody responds.

"You know what? Get out."

Most of Jake's friends look to him, and Anna fumes. "This isn't even his apartment! It's mine. Now all of you out! Get the hell out!"

Everyone is slow to move, and a few try to get in a last word.

"Buzzkill."

"Damn Jake, you really got a keeper."

"Just get out." Anna points to the door. It's not long before they've all filed out. Jake is the last one. He stands in the doorway with his hands in his pockets.

"I don't know what to say."

"Sorry would be nice," says Anna.

"You agreed to let me have a party here!"

"Sorry for assuming people in their thirties wouldn't trash my place."

"It's not even that bad!"

"Just leave, Jake."

"Oh, I was planning on it." He follows his friends down the stairs, and Anna shuts the door behind him.

She leans against it and then slides to the floor so she's sitting. She stays there for a while, until the sound of their laughter has faded. They're probably headed to some bar, all of them ready to convince Jake how much of a bitch she is.

Suddenly she tilts her head up to the ceiling. There's a thump, followed by another. Then there's the heavy sound of footsteps.

The space above her apartment is vacant. One of Jake's drunk friends must be messing around up there. Or, she figures, maybe two of them.

The sounds cease, and as Anna stands and starts to clean the apartment, she forgets about the footsteps entirely.

Unsightly

There's even more to clean than Anna thought. Somebody spilled seltzer in the kitchen and thought they'd cleaned it up with a pass over with paper towels, but the whole area is sticky.

Not only that, but half a dozen drunk guys had been using her half bath to pee, and some urine had splattered behind the toilet.

Wide awake with rage, she was determined to clean it all.

It's nearly two a.m. when she finishes. She piles the trash bags by the door and goes to the window to look at her philodendron. She gently touches one of its leaves. "You'll be alright, guy."

But then her attention is taken outside. She doesn't know why right away; her subconscious must've seen it first. She scans the field, sees nothing, and is about to head to bed when her heart begins to nervously flutter. On the far side of the field, almost completely in the dark, a man is standing straight and still.

Anna quickly pets the plant again, acting like she doesn't see him, and then goes and turns off all the lights. She goes back to the window, confident now that she that can't be seen.

She was half expecting him to be gone. To be a figure of her imagination from a very long day, but he's there, clear as ever. Anna thinks he looks tall, but from this distance—at least two hundred yards—she can't tell.

She leans on the windowsill and watches. This neighborhood isn't the nicest. Anna gets tweakers and heroin addicts and plenty of drunks. But none of those inebriated are ever able to stand so still.

Tweakers tweak. While they may have their balance about them, they scratch, and twitch and fidget. As for drunks and pill heads, they nod and stumble, playing a constant game of tug of war with gravity.

This person doesn't move an inch. They're as still as a mannequin, and Anna lets out a sigh of relief as she realizes this is what she must be looking at. This was an industrial district now being populated with drunks. People were finding odds and ends in old warehouses they trespassed in. It made sense that one could find a mannequin and think it was funny to leave it in the street.

But then all of Anna's hopes evaporate as the figure suddenly turns on a heel and disappears into the night.

She's almost sick. She can feel her heartbeat in her throat. She's as angry with herself as she was afraid. All she wanted was to sleep, but she just had to walk to the window. Why give this waking day another chance to wreak havoc on her life?

Anna walks slowly to her recliner. She grabs a blanket she'd only just neatly folded off its back and wraps herself in it. Then she goes to her room, grabs a cigarette from her pack, and lights it.

It's the first one she's ever smoked inside this apartment. She'd sworn she wouldn't be like her mom. Wouldn't live in a house that smelled like an ashtray, but right now, she can't help but have one.

She stares at the window and smokes, searching for the man.

There's still no rain. But lightning flashes closer in the distance.

Screams

Hours earlier, Anna had curled up in the recliner, turned the lights back on, and fallen asleep. Now, she wakes in a panic. She thinks for a moment that the sound came from her dream, until it comes again.

Outside, someone screams.

She jumps out of the recliner and looks out the window. A man runs across the empty lot in front of Anna's apartment. His voice is muffled, but still, she can hear him.

"Help me! Oh God! Someone help me!" He keeps looking over his shoulder like he's being chased, though from what Anna can see, there's no one in pursuit.

She hyperventilates and runs her hands through her hair. This could be a trap. The man outside could be screaming for help, trying to lure Anna outside. It feels like it takes her forever to move, and after maybe half a minute of pacing and biting her lip while waiting to see more movement out the window, she runs towards her door.

She puts her tennis shoes on and goes down the stairs two at a time. Her landlord's door opens just as she's sprinting past it.

"Anna, is everything—"

"Call 9-1-1!" Anna shouts in a huff and hurdles out into the night.

She lets the door clap shut behind her and then pauses and listens. There is no sound of pounding footsteps or screams. It sounds like four a.m. in the city—transformer hum, distant siren. As close as it ever gets to silent.

She starts trotting across the empty field where she'd seen the man run. Most of the lot is exposed dirt, no grass. It's all pancaked pilsner cans and stomped cigarette butts, but then she sees a footprint.

Not a shoeprint. A footprint.

Toes, heel. It all shows. The whole outline of a man's bare foot is imprinted in the sandy dirt.

There's some kind of wet glob in the print. Anna bends down and shines her phone screen at it.

It's almost black, but when she sees the red tint, she knows exactly what it is.

Blood.

She stands shock straight and looks in every direction, and her heart stops when she sees the shape of a person, but it's just her landlady, Dalia, waving from the door.

"Everything okay?" the woman shouts.

"Just stay inside."

"Police are coming. Maybe you stay inside, too!"

The idea is tempting. The path of bloody bare footprints does not make for an alluring trail. Still, she forces herself to follow them. "I'll be right there," Anna says and keeps trotting on.

She follows them until the dirt becomes pavement, and here the blood shows more clearly. There are great big streaks of it that have been left from the man's strides, enough for it to shine under the streetlights.

She follows them to a line of warehouses that line the river, where the footprints stop and then continue on the other side of a chain-link fence.

The top of the fence is lined with shiny razor wire, and she can see blood glisten on its barbs. Anna forgets her theory that this could be some kind of trap. This man was running for his life.

She puts her fingers through the chain link and looks around. The other side of the fence is a maze of abandoned semi-trailers and old boats. It was some kind of storage yard, and she's unsure if it's still a business or if all this stuff is just junk.

She keeps walking around the outside of the fence until she reaches the side that faces the river. There's a front gate that's wide open. Tall weeds spurt from fissures in asphalt and sway gently in the wind. The lot certainly seems abandoned. Crickets chirp and rabbits scurry from cover to cover as Anna's steps crunch across the lot.

There's a large sheet metal building in the center with great big garage doors. The one facing her is open, and Anna pauses as something metallic slams within.

She darts behind an old rusted pickup truck and peeks up from behind its bed. In this quiet lot, her breath sounds like thunder out her nostrils. She slows her breathing. Listens.

She creeps out from behind the truck and stays in the shadows as she gets closer to the building. She doesn't have a plan. She doesn't know what she's doing. Anna pulls the knife from her pocket, and its handle quickly grows slick in her sweaty palm.

She thinks she's hidden. If she has one advantage, it's the element of surprise, but suddenly she's blinded.

A pair of LED headlights has turned on at the entrance to the warehouse. She flinches and shields her eyes then goes doubly blind as the high beams turn on and an engine starts to purr.

The car accelerates towards her, Anna spins around, and before she can even take one sprinting step, her toes catch on a rock and she lands hard on her face.

She looks at the headlights approaching. The car is a second away from flattening her. She starts to roll to her right, but she doesn't have to. At the last second, the car swerves in a large arc around her. She thinks she might be able to see the make and model when its tires shower her in a cloud of dirt and dust. By the time it settles, and Anna can see, the car has stopped about fifty yards away.

She pauses and watches its driver's-side window roll down halfway. A black gloved hand appears and gives her a gentle wave. Then the car speeds off.

Believed

She doesn't know exactly what kind of car it was. A black sedan. Maybe German.

Anna doesn't investigate the warehouse herself. Instead, she jogs back around to alert the police. When she gets back to the big field, there's a cop car with its lights on outside her apartment.

"Hey!" Anna starts yelling as she's running. "Hey, they went that way!"

There's only one officer from what she can see, and he's speaking to her landlady. He steps into the street and waits until Anna's close enough to respond to in a regular-toned voice.

"Are you alright?"

"Yes," Anna says, catching her breath. "They went south on Industrial Boulevard."

"Try and breathe for me. Who went south?"

"Someone was being chased here." She points to the field. "A young man, I think. There's blood in his footprints."

"You mind showing me?"

"Yeah."

Anna sees a shadow behind her landlady. It's her husband, Raymond, standing farther back in the doorway. Neither of them seems interested enough to come outside. Then again, maybe they're afraid. Anna shows the cop to the nearest bloodied footprint.

"Here," she says. He shines his light down and squats. She expects him to tilt his chin towards his radio and call for backup, but he doesn't seem all that interested. "Okay, have you seen where these begin?"

"No, I followed them to a warehouse by the waterfront. Right there." She points to the building a couple hundred yards from them. "A car almost ran me over speeding away."

"What kind?"

"Black, sedan. I don't know exactly. It blinded me with its lights."

He nods but seems doubtful of the seriousness of this situation. They walk in the direction the footprints come from to see where they start.

There's less blood the farther they go. It seems like the wounds were made worse the more he ran. But run he did. They follow the bloody steps for two whole blocks and turn down the corner onto Spruill Avenue. There are bars and breweries and taquerias, but they're all shuttered for the night. Some for the storm.

"There it is." The cop shines his flashlight on the sidewalk and the beam multiplies as it catches on a billion bits of broken glass. There's a smashed liquor bottle, and it looks like the runner passed right through it.

"I've seen this twice this year now."

"Seen what?"

"A meth head sprints through glass. Makes one hell of a grisly trail."

"They were screaming for help, looking over their shoulder. I saw them running." Even as Anna says all this, she knows it's no use.

"Did you see someone in pursuit?"

"No."

"Look, thanks for calling this in but this area has had a homeless problem this summer, I'm sure you know. Lots of meth and mental illness. It's typical behavior. Paranoid delusions, hallucinations. Imagine how messed up you have to be to run through glass and not stop."

Anna's not so sure, but all she does is bite her lip. "Can you take samples of the treads of the car? I think they were trespassing and—"

"Like plaster samples?" The cop widens his eyes. He's getting annoyed now. "That's not something that can be done lickety-split. It takes a team. A motive. Tell you what . . . I'll drive around the waterfront and see if I can find this guy. He's going to need an ambulance."

Anna nods. "Thank you."

"Sure thing." They walk back together, and Anna waits outside while the cop drives off.

Her landlords stand in the doorway as if afraid something might get them if they venture a foot out. "Is everything okay, Anna?"

"It's fine. They say it's someone on drugs in need of help."

"Oh," says Dalia. It's clear she wants to hear more.

Anna points her thumb across the field. "I dropped something when I went over there. I'll be in soon. Sorry for the scare."

Anna starts back across the field and to the warehouse. She goes through the gate and looks both ways down the waterfront street. From what she can tell, the cop hasn't even bothered to investigate. His car is nowhere in sight.

Anna pulls out her phone, turns on the flash, and starts taking pictures of the tire tread markings herself.

Overcast

Anna wakes in her bed. It's only been an hour or two since she went to sleep. She heads to the living room and looks out the window. There is nothing out of the ordinary this morning. A woman in a yellow raincoat walks her dog, but the pavement looks dry.

The clouds are darker the farther east she looks, towards the ocean, and Anna figures the cloud cover is here to stay until the hurricane hits.

She stretches and picks her phone up. There's still no evacuation order given by the state. If there was, she'd have gotten an emergency alert notification.

She doesn't even have to go to the local news anymore to get updates on the storm. It's on the front page of every national news site. The headline is not comforting.

HURRICANE CHARLIE GROWS IN STRENGTH, STAYS ON COURSE FOR CHARLESTON LANDFALL.

Two days now until impact. The governor must make a decision soon whether or not to have the city evacuated. He's holding off because the current models give Charlie a forty percent chance of being blown north and missing them almost entirely.

She scrolls to the local news comment section to see that the city still seems skeptical of this storm. Time and time again they've been warned that this *next* storm was the big one. And almost always they've been spared. Whipped up into a worry for nothing.

If the governor evacuates them and the storm whiffs, many South Carolinians in the Lowcountry will not be happy.

It's eight a.m., and Anna's story she'd been assigned about hurricane preppers is already past due. Luckily, it was supposed to only be an online piece, not an article run in the morning paper.

She curses and flings herself to the bedroom and her computer. In forty minutes, she's manufactured a very interesting trip to Lowe's, where the manager and assistant manager were both too busy to be interviewed, and many essentials—batteries, hammers, drills, even axes—were being sold out.

She makes up a few quotes from some real characters she met in the parking lot—preppers and PTA moms buying chainsaws—and sends it to her editor, Bruce.

She wheels back in her swivel chair and chews her thumbnail. Bruce is usually quick to respond, especially in the mornings. Typically, he emails back in a half hour, but today he calls her after five minutes.

"Hey, Bruce."

"You're late. Again."

"Sorry, no excuses. I'm just sorry."

Bruce is quiet for a moment. She can tell he wanted her to give him some bad reason why the article was late so he could tear into her, but she gave him no shot.

"Are you going to get your shit together, Anna? Readership is higher than it's been in years. Even the haters who think this is all overblown are clicking in order to comment on the controversy. We need all hands on deck."

"I'm on deck, Bruce."

"Then why did Justin tell me that you were at the scene of that potential homicide?"

Because that potential homicide might be my best friend. Anna wants to say it, but she can't. It's not her. Such a quote draws sympathy and attention to herself, and she's never been comfortable being pitied.

"I know we have the storm, but this might be something else brewing. You have my word that this will go national. Did you hear about how the body was found?"

"Yeah, the kid filled me in. I get it. I'm seeing some rumblings on the internet, too."

"That's just the tip of it. I found the teenager who broke in. She showed me pictures of the body—"

"I'm going to stop you there, Anna. We're not running any big stories that aren't related to this storm until after it's passed."

"What?" Anna stands up from her chair. "I know it's not good timing, but that doesn't mean this shouldn't be run. This is big."

"I know. I know. But we don't want to look like we're minimizing the threat of this storm by running some other breaking news piece on the front page. There's already enough doubt surrounding its severity as it is. We don't want to play into that."

"So, you just want to sit on this? Let some other paper pick it up? The teenager I found; she's shopping the pictures around already."

"If this storm hits the way the weather service says it will, we're not going to need another story for half a year."

Anna is confused. Bruce is usually fiending to get his hands on every story he can, especially one so local like this: Twisted murder in the French Quarter. But this time he seems determined to bury it.

"So, you want me to give up on it?"

"I shouldn't have to want *you* to do anything. It's not your story. I put Justin on it."

"Alright." Anna relents. "What's my next piece?"

"I'll send you the details in the next hour."

"Okay. Sorry again about being—" But the line is already dead.

Anna kicks her swivel chair so it goes charging across the room. Bruce may want to keep her from this story, but it doesn't make a difference in the world to her.

She pulls out her phone and looks at the picture she took of the riddle on the wall. It's only one of two leads she has, and the other involves somehow getting to the body.

Smart as she is, Anna sucks at riddles. She always reaches conclusions far off the mark but still accurate to the statement. Her brain works differently—for better or worse, she can't tell.

While she might not be able to solve this riddle, she knows exactly who could.

After a quick twenty minutes spent putting herself together, she's marching out the door.

Today, she's doing her own investigating, and she'll happily be fired for it.

Neighbors

When she gets down the second flight of stairs, she gasps as a door is suddenly opened in front of her at the bottom of the landing.

She holds her hand on her heart but then smiles as she sees one of her landlords, Raymond, peek around the door.

"Oh, I didn't mean to scare you. I just heard you coming and wanted to catch you before you left."

Anna waves it off. "Don't worry about it. How are you?"

"Good. I'm good. Quite a spook last night, yeah?"

"Yeah." Anna sighs.

"One of the cons of a neighborhood like this. It's still on the up and up, and you get those . . . undesirables. But anyway!" He smiles and changes the subject. "Fun party?"

"Sure. It wasn't too loud, was it?"

"No, no. Not at all. We've got a floor between us, after all." He smiles, showing a shiny set of veneers that don't look quite right in his mouth. He's about sixty years old, with a small gray mustache, and dark, close-set eyes.

"Is that Anna?" Anna hears a woman's voice shout from deeper in the apartment. Soon, a white-haired woman even tinier than Anna comes shuffling out. It's Dalia. "Oh Anna, good to see you. Was your party fun?"

"Yeah." Anna leans in and they hug. When she pulls back, Raymond puts his arm around Dalia, and the two of them stare at her dotingly from their doorway.

"You said you wanted to catch me?" Anna asks Raymond.

"Oh!" His face lights up. "Yes, yes. Are you going to be evacuating? We're leaving today, regardless. Best to beat the traffic. But don't be afraid . . . Home will still be here when you get back. This building is rock solid." He knocks on the doorframe.

"I've spent thirty years in here. I know she's built well."

Anna frowns. "I thought you guys bought this place last year?"

"Oh, don't you know?" Dalia pats Raymond's chest. "Raymond was a clerk here in this building when it used to be Renner and Johnson Trading Company. They went under twenty years ago, and when we saw the listing, we couldn't pass this place up. Raymond knew it had good bones. And those new zoning laws for housing around here, I mean . . . It all felt like fate."

Anna had thought she would've heard this but, then again, the Shepards weren't one of those talkative old couples. They had always been more interested in asking Anna about her life.

"That's very cool, but I don't know about evacuating. You know this storm has me pretty busy running around town. I'll probably be here until the last second."

"That's right. That must be so nerve-racking, being a journalist during all this. You're on the frontlines. You better be safe," says Dalia.

"Oh, thank you. I'll be alright. I'm not out in the weather. They won't make me go stand out in the wind so people can see what two-hundred-mile-per-hour gusts look like."

"I'd sure hope not. You'd blow away!" Dalia and Raymond laugh, and Anna takes another step towards the building's front door.

"I really have to be going, though. It was good to see you both. Be safe evacuating."

"Sorry to keep you," Raymond says with a smile, showing his shiny veneers again. "Again, you be safe, Anna."

She smiles and heads towards the street, but during her walk out of the building she doesn't hear the Shepards' door shut.

The couple seems a little lonely, and it makes her uncomfortable, but Anna thinks she should be thankful. It would be far more frightening to live in this building alone.

Orangeburg

She gets behind the wheel of her car. It's a 90s Taurus—an ugly, buggy car that belches noxious exhaust, but it runs.

She doesn't drive often. For the hassle of parking and gas prices, she much prefers to be slightly inconvenienced by the bus. But today she has three errands outside of town and no choice.

She gets on the highway and takes it all the way to Orangeburg. Traffic is light. She thought more people might be evacuating with the unchanged hurricane models and it being the weekend, but the lanes are dead. She's able to get there in an hour.

She's read the article about the murder in Orangeburg three times now. Joyce Fox, twenty-one years old, was found in the early morning in a ditch off the side of the road. They have yet to release if there was any sexual trauma, but word has gotten out that she was missing all ten fingers.

It seems so much sloppier than the disappearances of Hannah, Tess, and Sylvie. They were taken without a trace. She wonders if Terry was telling the truth about some kind of connection between this and the body on Church Street. Then again, he is in law enforcement. If there is one, he'd know.

The address in the article of where Joyce went missing takes Anna to a weedy trailer park. She checks her face in the sunshade mirror. Bloodshot eyes. Bags beneath them. She's upset to see that she looks just as bedraggled as she feels.

Her door creaks as she gets out and shuts it. The weather is much nicer inland than it is by the coast, and despite the early hour, Anna quickly starts to sweat as she walks.

It's September, but here it feels like summer's dog days. Cicadas still shriek in the trees, and a distant lawn mower gives the wind the scent of gas and fresh-cut grass.

It's a tranquil morning, and for a moment she forgets she's here because of a murder. She's reminded as she comes upon a house wrapped in crime scene tape. It's where Joyce was killed. Its grass is a gory mess of mud and torn turf from the vehicles of first responders.

Anna looks at the trailer to her right and sees a woman standing near a window. She stares at Anna intently while bringing a steaming mug to her lips. What her expression says is simple: you are being watched.

Anna looks away.

Sometimes as a journalist, she feels like a parasite. She heads into neighborhoods stricken by grief and fear with a notebook, trying to extract these emotions. Always from sobbing parents or near speechless friends.

She tells herself it's to inform the public, but just as often it feels like these articles are another source of entertainment.

It's another murdered woman, and Anna's here to scratch America's itch for the details.

Was she raped?

Did she suffer?

Was she alive when they cut off her fingers?

When Anna drives away from assignments like this, she often can't help but think, *leech*. But this time she's here on her own time. She's the one who wants the answers to these questions.

She keeps walking around the trailer, when two girls on bikes peel out from behind a mobile home and circle Anna on the street. They're young, twelve or so, and giggling among themselves.

"Are you a cop?" one of them shouts.

Anna is slow to respond. She looks the girls over. Anything can remind you of the past, but this feels like too much.

"No," she stutters. "I'm a reporter."

"You're like . . . with the news?"

"Yeah."

One of the girls skids to a crunching stop in the gravel and drops her bike. "Are you here to interview people about the murder?"

"Kinda."

The girl's eyes light up. "Can you do me?! Please?"

"Did you know Joyce Fox?"

"I live like a block that way. Of course I do."

The other girl straddles her bike. When Anna looks at her, she glances away shyly.

"This topic is a little bit adult, girls. I don't think your parents would want me chatting with you about it."

"It's literally all anybody talks about. Besides, I can tell you something the news hasn't been talking about."

Anna hears the hiss of a screen door open. The woman who had been watching her from the window stands out on her porch.

They lock eyes before the woman speaks. "Get out of here."

Anna doesn't respond. Maybe it's because she's not here on account of the paper, but her presence feels extra unethical. She turns to go without a word.

"And you girls, don't follow her."

"You're not my mom."

Anna smiles at that. The girls bike behind her slowly while she walks to her car.

"So, what do you know that the news doesn't?"

"Can you promise me you'll use my name in the story?"

"I can't promise that."

The girl chews her lip, seeming to consider what other leverage she might have. "Fine." She drops her bike and walks to whisper in Anna's ear. "They found a finger."

"One of Joyce's?" Anna says at normal volume.

She leans back, surprised and disappointed that Anna didn't whisper, too. Like she wanted to be in cahoots. "Yeah, I guess. Harry Downs said he saw them find it on the side of the road."

"Harry Downs wouldn't happen to be your age, would he?"

"He's a year older, I think."

Anna nods. "And your parents are okay with you two biking around when something like this just happened?"

The girls look at each other as if there's something they know but don't want to say. "No. They don't care."

The way she says it breaks Anna's heart. She's been that kid. "Be safe. Okay?"

The girl picks up her bike and starts walking the other way. Her friend loops around her. "Yeah, whatever. And it's Mia. If you put that in the news, say Mia Brockovich told you."

"Okay, Mia."

Anna doesn't know what she expected to get by coming here. All this has done is dig up bad memories.

She gets in her car, cranks up the radio, and lights a cigarette. She'll do anything to avoid thinking of the past, but it's almost as if the last day has been designed to make her do so.

Near the crime scene, there are two women standing in the street now. Their arms are crossed, and they glare at Anna.

She accelerates into a U-turn and starts back towards Charleston. Luckily, their unwelcoming stares have saved her from thinking too much about the past.

All she can think is *leech*.

Code-Cracker

That was one of three destinations for the day. Halfway to Charleston, Anna exits onto Southbound I-95.

She's driving to her alma-mater—a small private college about forty-five minutes southwest from the city. It's a Saturday morning, but she knows that won't stop the man she's looking for from being there. He's specific. Detail orientated and, above all, addicted to his work.

She parks in the faculty office lot and heads towards an ugly Soviet-looking building. It's a concrete eyesore—gray, with thin slats for windows.

Across from the parking lot, on the other side of a chain-link fence, excavators sit dormant next to piles of dirt. There's a banner strung across the fence. It reads, "Robinson Study Center. Coming fall 2025."

She stops and takes note. She has heard of the family before from her time at the paper. The Robinsons sponsor 5Ks and back politicians, but seeing the name twice in twenty-four hours feels like an odd coincidence.

When she gets to the double glass doors, she puts her hand on her forehead and peers through the dark glass. She needs a keycard to get in and realizes with it being the weekend, she'll probably have to call. But suddenly, she flinches back. A receptionist Anna recognizes shoves open the door and is already walking back towards her desk without a word.

"Hey, I'm here to see Professor . . ."

Anna is pointing up to indicate the direction his office is in, but the receptionist just nods quickly. "I'll let him know."

She recognizes Anna from her frequent visits and doesn't seem pleased to be working on the weekend. Anna wonders if it has to do with the storm.

"Thanks," Anna says plainly as she walks up the stairs.

She starts walking down the halls of the third floor and is surprised by the activity in the offices. There are students looking through their textbooks while waiting to see their professors.

It's one of the first weekends of the semester, Anna realizes, a time when professors expand office house to help plenty of swamped students. Now, many of them are having to worry about losing their homes to a hurricane, too.

Anna stops outside a mostly closed door. The silver placard reads: Professor James Geller.

Luckily, there's no line of students, but she does hear a muffled conversation from within.

She leans against the wall and waits. After a few seconds, it becomes obvious that he's talking on the phone.

The conversation is a common one right now. She can hear Professor Geller's soft voice. "No, not yet. Lily wants me to come with, but I've got to look after my mother. She's fine but just near impossible to evacuate. I'd have to sedate her." There's a pause. "No, the hotels are already full. You should go west. Take a trip to the Smokeys." Another pause. "Yeah. Yeah you too, Bob. Be safe."

Anna knocks gently after it's been silent for a moment.

"Come in."

A man in his late forties sits behind a cluttered desk. The office is spacious, the desk dark oak. It's piled high with books and folders, and the entire room smells like a paperback.

"Anna. It's been a while," he says and takes a bite of chicken salad from a Pyrex container.

"You knew I'd be back. Happy start to the semester, by the way." Anna sits in a leather chair in front of the desk.

"Happy start indeed," Geller says sarcastically. He's a plump man, shorter, with small round glasses, and a scraggly graying beard covering his face. He wears a wrinkled blue button-down with a pocket protector. His aesthetic is the very stereotype of professor.

"What brings you in? Are you dropping by on your way out of the city?"

"I've got to stick around a while longer yet. Instill a little more fear in the public before I leave. My next piece is supposed to be on the top ten deadliest hurricanes that have hit the Eastern Seaboard."

"Ah, history. Fun."

Anna laughs. Geller takes another bite of his lunch, and then he looks up at Anna and smiles as he chews. To Anna, her senior-year professor of expository writing is the closest thing she's had to a father. When she came to his office hours after class to get help exploring different ideas for a thesis, the two of them hit it off with a shared nerdy love of all things writing.

Nearly every book in his office was a conversation piece. They shared many of the same favorite authors and journalists—Stone, Irving, Elliot.

She found it easier to talk to him than talking to people her own age. But perhaps what she liked most of all was that Geller didn't treat her like an idiot or a conspiracy theorist when she brought up the Flash Girls. He let her talk about Sylvie. Handed her a tissue when she needed it, and listened.

Part of it was because he liked true crime. His eyes would light up madly when discussing serial killers. Anna could tell he even had to hide his excitement from her when she discussed the connections between Hannah, Tess, and Sylvie.

Today, Anna's here for guidance. For an opinion she can trust. "I think I'm done writing about the storm, however."

Geller frowns. "Yeah?"

"It wouldn't be crazy if I quit, right?"

"You could make more at McDonald's. So, don't let the money stop you. If you don't like what you're doing, I say quit."

"Well. I might be onto something bigger."

"And what's that?"

"Yesterday in the early a.m., some kids broke into an abandoned house on Church Street. A mansion, I should say. They found a girl inside, embalmed, marbles for eyes. She was dressed up like a doll. And then there was this." Anna opens her phone and shows him the picture of the riddle on the wall.

Geller's hand crawls over his desk towards Anna's phone. He's itching with excitement. "My wife, Lily, she was talking about some strange mummy being found."

"Yeah, it's going around the internet. But it's true. I was there. I saw pictures of the body."

"Anna." Geller takes his eyes from her phone and to her eyes. He raises his brow in disappointment. He knows about the trespassing charges she's gotten in the past when looking into Sylvie's disappearance.

"It's different this time," says Anna. "I'm onto something."

"They'll stick you with a felony if they keep catching you."

"They won't. Forget it. But you wouldn't believe these pictures."

"I'm not sure I want to see them."

"Don't worry, I don't have them."

"So, what's this?" Geller points to her phone, and she hands it to him.

"A riddle found on the wall above the body."

Geller frowns and holds the phone out at arm's length, as if it's something that can bite him. "The apple of an eye despite that goodbye . . ." he mutters. "The despite could have two meanings here."

"I know. It's not easy."

Geller glances up at Anna. "Is this illegal? Aren't you showing me privileged evidence you obtained trespassing?"

Anna smirks. Geller is a stickler, and Anna's the opposite. But in the time she's known him, she's brought him more to her own side of breaking the rules.

"No one's getting hurt by us seeing this."

"And what do you want me to do with this?"

Anna bets that he knows the answer, but he wants to hear her say it. "I want you to solve it."

Geller literally wiggles in his chair. She watches his breath become uneven with excitement. "I'm busy with the semester starting and the storm coming, but please, send it to me." He hands her the phone back. "I gave all my students extensions. I should have plenty of time."

"Are you evacuating?"

"Lily and my son are. I'm staying with my mother in Park Circle. We should be safe from the surge, but it's the wind that's the worry."

"If this storm is as bad as they say . . ."

"I know, I know." He holds his hands out. "Lily is ready to threaten divorce. I've told her again and again. My mother's place is a brick house. No nearby trees. We'll be able to hold down the fort."

"Those are a lot of people's famous last words."

Geller's expression changes. The smile is gone, and he suddenly looks somewhat afraid. "I know," he sighs. "But my mother's disabled. Hard to move, and she wouldn't forgive me if I tried to evacuate her. She's stubborn, but I can't leave her alone.'"

For a moment, his situation makes Anna almost thankful for how few people she has in her life. But now she's worried about him.

He seems to know what she's thinking. "I'll be fine, Anna. She's got an extra mattress. I've got a way to bolt it down so we can stay under it in case the roof is ripped off. I'm a professor." He taps his temple. "I'll be alright."

Anna wants to make a joke but she's too nervous. She can count with maybe two fingers the important people in her life. Jake still hasn't texted since last night. He is probably waiting for her to make an apology, but that's a standoff he'll never win.

Anna knows the anxiety she feels for Professor Geller should make her happy; it's important to have people you care about. Though all she can think about is what has happened to the rest of the people she's ever gotten close to. She's about to suggest he change his mind, but before she can, there's another knock on the door.

"Be with you in a minute!" hollers Geller. "I'm seeing several students today, Anna. Sorry we can't chat for longer. It was wonderful to see you again."

"That's okay, and ditto." Anna stands to leave. "Oh, and one more thing. The house this body was found in, it was owned by the Robinson family. The same Robinsons who have their name on the new study center, I imagine. Do you know anything about them?"

"They've made large donations lately to a number of schools in the state. Clemson, Furman. It's the same case. A million-dollar-plus endowment."

"Any rumors as to why?"

"The statement the family made to the university here was that the money was to support higher education. Yadda yadda. But I hear they have a son who wants to be a professor himself."

"So, they're trying to buy him a job?"

"Something like that. Keep in mind that these universities might as well be middle schools." He gestures at the walls around him. "Rumor mills. I'm not really tuned in, so if you want the full scoop, I'd ask around."

"Thanks, Geller."

"And don't forget to text me that riddle. I'll get right on it, I promise."

"I won't."

Anna smiles tightly as a goodbye. She shouldn't worry so much. He can take care of himself. But this storm has been a reminder that everyone who's come into her life has gone out.

She walks down the hall while her mind wanders into the past.

March 2011

The last few months have been the best Anna's had in years. She finally has a friend again. As serious and studious as Sylvie is, she's also goofy and witty, and the fact that she's so eager to be friends with Anna makes her feel normal.

Her bullies are still around, but Anna has realized that if she acts stoic and uncaring, she isn't teased as often.

They're looking to get a reaction out of her—fear, anger, disgust—but when Anna meets all their attempts with indifference, they quickly lose interest.

The only person she's still having frequent trouble with is Mrs. Riley.

Sylvie begs Anna to ignore her, the same as she does her bullies, but it's not as easy.

Mrs. Riley has the power to make her life difficult. She gives her bad grades on her homework, denies her extensions if she's sick, and talks to her like she's a child in front of the rest of the class.

Over the months, Anna has been slowly stewing. At first it made her sad. She'd go home and cry into her pillow and avoid her even more temperamental mother. But now, she stares back at Mrs. Riley, enraged.

She doesn't understand. She hasn't done anything wrong. She works hard. Loves to learn. Says please and thank you. How could a grown adult hold such a grudge?

Anna will later understand that Mrs. Riley is little more than a kid herself—twenty-four—and that she never fit in at school when she was young. Being accepted and loved by her students fills the void that mean kids had left years ago. She has her hair bleached blonde and wears bright-red lipstick. Today, she's the mean middle school girl she never could be when she was a kid.

Soon, she'll be a high school teacher, where she'll further fraternize with students who are just like her bullies. For now, Anna bears her brunt. She doesn't understand why she acts like she does; all she knows is that Mrs. Riley is cruel.

Anna only has one more semester—just nine more weeks to be exact—and then she's off to eighth grade, where she hasn't heard any rumors of there being bullying teachers.

She sits in her fourth hour class, Mrs. Riley's Advanced U.S. History, and nibbles on the eraser of her pencil. She's in the middle of a test when she hears her name called from the front.

"Anna," says Mrs. Riley sternly. "Eyes on your own test. First and only warning."

Anna's heart skips a beat and her eyes dart about, confused, before settling back on her test. But she can't focus. She hadn't been looking at anyone else's test. When it comes to the answers, she trusts her own judgement better than her classmates'.

What concerns her is this new tactic by Mrs. Riley. She's never accused her of cheating. Could she really think she was?

Anna keeps her neck craned and her eyes laser-focused on the paper in front of her. She wants to remove all doubt that it's even possible her eyes could wander.

She's tense and terrified, when suddenly things get worse. A big drop of blood falls and splatters on the white paper.

Anna flinches and flings a hand to her nose. Then she shoots her other hand towards the ceiling.

A few students around her put down their pencils and murmur.

Mrs. Riley notices the blood running past Anna's fingers, but she doesn't call on her right away. She narrows her eyes, the cruel gears turning. Eventually, she points towards the door. "Go to the nurse's office."

Anna's chair screeches as she pushes it back, and her loafers clack on the tiled floors. She turns towards the back of the class before she leaves. Sylvie sits with her brow wrinkled in concern.

Anna's been to the nurse's office so often for a nosebleed that they have the process down to a pit stop. The nurse stuffs Anna's offending nostril, and Anna tilts her head back and watches the clock. After ten minutes, the bleeding is usually finished.

It's what she does today, and hardly a word is exchanged between her and the school nurse. When the ten minutes is up, Anna is practically running back to class. If she doesn't have enough time and is forced to make the test up after school hours, it means having to muster a ride from her mother.

When she gets back, there are still a few students working on their tests and twenty minutes left in the period, but her hopes sink. The face of her desk is clear. Her test is gone.

"Excuse me, Mrs. Riley. Can I have my test back?"

Mrs. Riley is already grading some of the test. She looks up, but only momentarily. "You got blood on it, and I don't have extras. I'll have to print another."

The rest of the class is staring at her. Anna glances at them and then walks much closer to Mrs. Riley's desk so she can whisper. "I can't really come in early or stay late. Can I take it in the hall during class tomorrow?"

"And whose fault is that?" Anna recoils as Mrs. Riley doesn't match her whisper. She speaks loud enough for the whole class to hear, and the students snicker. "Other students don't get special exemptions. Why should you?"

Anna doesn't say anything. She walks back to her desk, avoiding eye contact with Sylvie, and plops down.

When the last few students hand their tests in, the period becomes a study hour until the end, but most the students are chatting. Anna just sits at her desk and stares ahead at the whiteboard.

She gets her notebooks stacked and ready to go. When the bell rings, she stands quickly and starts speed walking out, but right as she's about the leave, Mrs. Riley speaks again. "Anna, I'll need to talk to you for a minute."

Anna is mortified. She can't go sit back down. She's forced to stand off to the side by the whiteboard while the rest of the students file out, but today Anna doesn't shy away from their eyes. As they grin and giggle, she stares at them with a plain expression of hate.

Some students don't notice. Others stop smiling and look away. What Anna doesn't know is that this stare she's throwing back at them will soon become legend.

Sylvie is the last in line to leave. She lingers for a second and whispers to Anna, "I'll be outside."

Anna doesn't respond, and she doesn't even look at Sylvie. She's sick of being pitied by her best friend.

The door clicks shut slowly.

"You won't be making your test up, Anna. It's going to be an F."

"*What?*" Anna can't believe it. She was expecting to be chastised, not crushed. "That test is a fifth of the grade. I won't pass without it. Mrs. Riley."

"Lower your voice."

Anna listens and pleads, "Mrs. Riley, please."

"You don't think I know what you're doing? Faking a nosebleed to get out of a test is intense, Anna, but intense is just like you."

Faked? Anna is confused and growing furious. "Mrs. Riley, I can't fake them. It's a medical condition. Genetic. My grandma—"

"You know what I mean, Anna. You picked your nose, scratched it on purpose. The second I caught you looking at other students' tests, you started to bleed all over yours. I'm not buying it."

"But I know all the answers. I don't *want* to get out of the test." Anna gestures towards the stack of stapled papers. "Here, let me take it now, right in front of you."

"No need. You've had plenty of time to see the correct answers by glancing around the class."

Anna is muttering to herself. She's in disbelief. This could mean the end of her scholarship. She'll be back in public school, where her bullies are even worse. Sometimes physical. And her mom . . .

"Mrs. Riley, you can't do this."

"I'm your teacher. I can do whatever—"

"No!" Anna shouts so loud Mrs. Riley flinches and then begins to smile. It's as if this is the outburst she was waiting for.

She opens a drawer in her desk, pulls out a purple stack of little sheets, and starts writing on one.

Anna's heart races. "What're you doing?"

"Detention won't help your case, but you don't give me much choice."

Anna can almost feel the hot slap burn on her cheek from where her mother will strike her. Anna is smart—gifted, even. Homework comes easier to her, but that doesn't mean she hasn't worked hard.

She's spent summer evenings inside studying, blown off all her interests and hobbies and books in order to be a better student.

In order to succeed.

Now she's seeing it slip away, and all at the hands of a spiteful bitch. Anna scowls. From the tenseness and the stress, she feels her nose begin to bleed again. It tickles as a drop runs over her lips, but she doesn't wipe it away. She lets the blood run and drip onto the floor.

Mrs. Riley looks up from her detention slip suddenly, and her lips coil in disgust. She rips the detention sheet off the stack and extends her arm out to Anna. "You're going to clean that before you leave. Act like trash in this classroom, and it'll be your last day of school."

That's it. The fizz of the fuse grows silent when it first disappears into the dynamite, but then Anna blows. She exhales heavily out of her nose so more blood leaks to the floor and over her face. Then she grabs Mrs. Riley's hair and gets in her face.

She could easily push Anna away—she's sixty pounds heavier—but she's shocked by the gore. She puts her hands in front of her face helplessly.

"Ahhh!" she screams. "Stop! Stop!"

But it's too late. Anna is blind with rage. She wants to make someone feel the same way her mother makes her feel. She pulls Mrs. Riley's hair towards the floor, and instead of fighting back, Mrs. Riley yields in the same direction to ease the pain. She shouts out, and the door bursts open.

Anna doesn't even turn to look. She hears Sylvie begin to yell, "Anna, what are you doing?!"

She ignores her and looks back to Mrs. Riley. Anna is lucid enough to know it's over. She's attacked a teacher. Instead of stopping at rock bottom, she digs. It's like she's watching her actions from above as she begins beating Mrs. Riley with one open hand. She takes tips from her mother and puts some of her hips into the strikes.

Mrs. Riley begins to scream and falls to the floor. Anna lets go of her hair, straddles her chest, and blows her nose as hard as she can onto her teacher's face.

It's a bright-red shower of blood.

Sylvie is suddenly pulling on her shoulders and screaming. Anna pushes her off, hard. "What did you do, Anna?" Sylvie is scream crying. Anna suddenly notices the doorway is filled with students. Their eyes are wide, the blood is drained from their faces in horror.

"What did you do!?"

Anna can feel her face wet with blood. Her hair is frizzled and a mess. She must look like a monster.

Mrs. Riley just whimpers on the floor, in shock from the blood. But it's too easy for her. She'll go home and shower it off. Anna will be dealing with the fallout of this for maybe the rest of her life.

She pictures how her mom will treat her when she's home on suspension.

Expulsion.

Mrs. Riley can't get off so easy. She hears heavy footsteps in the hallway. An adult is on their way, but before she can be stopped, she wants to give Mrs. Riley something permanent.

She snatches a stapler off the teacher's desk, cracks it so the handle is separated from the base, and presses the staple part against Mrs. Riley's forehead.

Then she brings down her open palm like a hammer. There's a click, and Mrs. Riley thrashes and screams. A staple shines in her forehead.

Someone throws Anna off her. She lies belly down on the floor like a wild animal and stares at Sylvie.

When she's hauled away by her collar, the two girls are still making eye contact.

It's the last time they'll see each other for four years.

X

Anna's back behind the wheel of her Taurus. It's her third and final stop for the day.

Before she heads back home, she takes a series of turns that take her past dingy rows of homes. Finally, at the end of the road, there is a trailer park surrounded by woods. A dilapidated sign reads: Oak Grove.

When she steps out of the car, two dogs tied to a pole in front of a trailer announce they are displeased with her presence. They yank their chains taut, and while their tails wag, their ears are pinned back. When the bigger of the two barks, great globs of saliva fly from its mouth.

Anna locks her car and walks to where there's a wide trail leading into the forest.

She takes it for a while, walking past old televisions and discarded couches. Eventually, she gets to where the pickups can't pull in, and the trash consists of beer cans and plastic bags.

It's a five-minute walk to where the foot trail ends and a service road begins. It runs along a set of train tracks and is owned by the rail company. Technically, she's trespassing, but there's no one around to care.

She walks along it for another few minutes and takes a right down another trail into the woods. From here, she can see a small concrete building through the trees. She walks towards it and into a clearing with a blackened fire pit at its center.

There are boulders and stumps for seating, and the area is grassless from the thousands of footsteps that have trampled this ground over the years.

She steps towards the structure. It's covered in bubbled graffiti letters and initialized hearts. At the base of its south wall sits a large pile of broken glass. It is a tradition for the teens of this nearby trailer park to smash their empty beer bottles here.

All the local kids called this spot The Station.

Whether that is because it's by the train track or that the concrete structure used to be a pump station, Anna doesn't know.

She steps into the concrete structure. It's dark inside—the only light comes from the open space where the door used to be. Otherwise, there are no windows. Anna runs her hand on the cool wall and pauses. The traditional graffiti that used to litter this place is gone. The walls have been repainted.

She fumbles in her pocket for her phone and brings it up with the flashlight on.

A painting covers one of the three solid walls, and it's not from a spray can. The paint drips and runs like it's been heavily brushed on.

Anna freezes. The painting is a silhouette of a woman with long hair. There's not much detail, but the way she's positioned is strange—she holds one arm up, almost like she's waving.

Anna is about to brush it off as the work of some more artistic kids, but then she notices a red halo around the woman's head and, at her feet, a red X.

Anna looks down. Just inside the doorway of the little concrete structure, a red X is painted on the floor.

It can't be a coincidence . . . This is the exact place where Hannah Greenwood, the first Flash Girl, had said someone took her picture from the woods.

Not only that, but Anna thinks it's the same red paint that the riddle was written in at the mansion on Church Street.

A train horn sounds, and Anna jumps and flings herself around. She touches the knife in her pocket while scanning the area. She hears the bells of the nearby train crossing and then the rumbling of the engines. She steps outside. The clouds have parted, and she feels the sun on her face.

She doesn't have to go back inside and look at the painting on the wall again to understand it.

It makes perfect sense.

The woman isn't waving; she's fending off a flash.

Unexpected Guest

Anna's opening the door to her car when she hears the sound of a distant voice.

It's a familiar voice, but out of place.

She looks towards its source, and thirty yards away on the porch of a trailer is Justin.

Anna can see the face of the woman he's talking to. She looks confused, and she quickly shakes her head and shuts the door. Justin walks on the gravel road, and Anna walks quickly to meet him.

She expects anger. Justin certainly knows by now that she was lying about Bruce assigning her to the homicide on Church Street. His eyes widen when he sees her, but he doesn't look angry.

"Oh, hey," Justin looks around like there might be somebody else he doesn't expect to see here. "So, you're still trying to steal my story?"

"What are you doing here?" Anna asks, but she knows he must be going back through the missing girls and found out Hannah Greenwood grew up in this trailer park.

"I caught wind of a little rumor."

"What's that?"

"That you were the foremost expert on the Flash Girls. That you even gave them their name."

"Who told you that?"

"A crime podcaster emailed me after I posted my article on the Church Street corpse last night. He said he had you on the air a couple of years ago. I listened to your episode."

Anna cringes. That was back when she was trying to bring national awareness to the cases. She thought that if she could get enough people to look into it, she could pressure law enforcement to open more thorough investigations into Tess's, Hannah's and Sylvie's disappearances.

She had no such luck. The connections were all conjecture.

"I get why you showed up to Church Street. You could've just told me you knew Sylvie Platt." Anna doesn't respond. Sylvie Platt was a famous name in Charleston. Whether or not she was a victim of a serial killer or just a vanished girl, is another debate. "Do you think that body is her?" asks Justin.

"I don't know," Anna lies—she's almost positive it is. "We'll find out when the DNA results come back in a few days."

"With the storm, it might be longer than that."

"It might be. I've been waiting years to see the end of these cases. I can wait a little longer."

Justin walks a little closer to Anna with his hands in his pockets. He chews his lip like he's preparing something he doesn't know how to say. "This story is going to be huge. If it weren't for this stupid storm, we'd be front page."

If it weren't for this stupid storm, Anna thinks, *someone more senior than you would've been given the story.*

"Do you want to maybe . . . work together on this?"

"On the story?"

"Yeah."

"Bruce wouldn't allow it. I'm in the doghouse."

"Does he know you and Sylvie Platt were friends?"

"God, no. And don't tell him. He hates conflicts of interest."

"He's never listened to that podcast?"

"Bruce is a print journalist purist. You won't catch him keeping up with the Kardashians."

"What?"

Anna sighs. "He reads the paper. Like a physical paper. That's the only way he consumes media."

"No wonder our paper loses money." Justin kicks at some gravel. "We've got dinosaurs at the wheel."

"Welcome to the world."

"But really, will you? I'll credit you, or we can take this story somewhere else. This is big league shit. Have you heard about how that body was found? I have a source in the police department that confirmed it. Embalmed. Marble eyes. When's the last time a missing girl turned up taxidermied?"

Anna tenses at the memory of the photos of the body, and Justin seems to read her expression.

"Shit, I'm sorry. I didn't mean to talk about her like that."

"It's okay. I'm not offended."

"But what do you say? I've been waiting to ditch this paper since I started here. We ignore the storm. It's journalism, but guess what? Every reporter in a four-state radius is writing shit about that hurricane."

Anna looks away. She's more than unsure. Justin is a rich kid who can afford to ditch the paper. Anna doesn't have the luxury to be jobless for very long at all.

"Anna . . ." Justin waits until she looks back to him to keep speaking. "This is an *opportunity*. Everyone else is distracted. Let's do our research, see if we can put an actual link between these missing girls, and when the country loses interest about our hurricane recovery the way they always do, we have a heavyweight story ready to go. And it's *ours*. We sell it to the highest bidder."

Anna looks Justin over. He's young, ambitious, and he has no clue what he's getting himself into.

This killer is out there, and Anna doesn't think she'll have any trouble finding him on her own. But she's experiencing a new feeling: she's being believed.

For years, she felt like she was wearing a tinfoil hat. Finally, others are beginning to realize something sick has happened to these girls. It lifts her spirits in a strange way.

"Maybe . . ."

"It could be good to have another set of eyes . . . Someone to go over things with. I'm going to be working on this regardless. I'm assigned to it. I know you're going to be working on it anyway, too. Why not join forces?"

"Okay," Anna says. "But I know more about this case than anyone. When it comes to leads, and judgement, I call the shots."

Justin looks away, and Anna thinks he's smirking. Perhaps it's because he's getting a much better side of the deal. He needs her, but Anna doesn't need him.

"Deal."

They shake hands, and Anna starts to walk quickly back towards her car. "Follow me."

Justin is slow to follow and trots to keep up. "Where are you going?"

Anna walks past the trail that leads to the old pumphouse and opens the door to her car.

She's going to show Justin something she's never shown anyone, because now, perhaps she won't look as insane.

Locked Away

Justin follows Anna twenty minutes back to her house. When they both park and get out of their cars, Justin turns in a quick circle to have another look at his surroundings.

"I didn't know there was housing here."

He doesn't say it like it's a slight at Anna's poverty. He's seems actually thrown off by the fact that they're only a stone's throw from the industrial action on the Cooper River.

"They shove housing in wherever they can now. Just watch. They'll be renting out studio apartments in shipping containers for one thousand dollars a month soon enough."

"Hmm. Sounds low."

Anna smiles a little. "It's this one." She nods towards her building. She sees a curtain flap back into place in the Shepards' apartment. Raymond, or Dalia—or both of them—had been watching her.

Anna can see that their car is still out front. They still haven't evacuated. As far as nosy neighbors go, they're not bad. She can't blame them for being interested. They knew that she had a boyfriend, and here she is, bringing a new guy into her apartment. But Justin could be her cousin for all they know.

Anna keeps quiet as she heads up the stairs. It's only once she's inside her unit that she talks again. "You can leave your shoes on."

Justin doesn't respond right away. He's looking around, clearly surprised by how nice her apartment is on the inside.

Anna follows his gaze. With its restored wood floors, high ceiling, and brick walls, it is a beautiful place. "I know it's nice. I'll be priced out of here as soon as they finish renovating the building."

"Huh?"

"I got a deal because of the construction. They're still turning the rest of the building into units."

"Oh. That sucks."

"Tell me about it," Anna says, but she doesn't mean it. She doesn't want anything tying her to Charleston. As soon as this case is solved, she's canceling her lease and driving west.

"So, what have you got to show me?" asks Justin.

Anna gestures for him to follow her and walks through the kitchen. At the end of it is a narrow hallway that leads to a door of the same tight width. There's a lock on this door.

She opens it and steps in, quickly pulling a string switch that dangles comically low so that Anna can reach it. The room is cast in orange light, revealing a tight, cluttered space. There are two desks, each strewn with papers, and pictures hang on the walls.

Pictures of intersections and alleys—parks and swampy wetlands.

"This is everything," says Anna. "Everything I know about Hannah Greenwood, Tess Gibson, and Sylvie Platt is in this room. Everything up until yesterday afternoon."

Justin is somewhat dumbfounded. His mouth hangs open slightly as he thumbs through a few papers on one of the desks.

"I didn't know there was so much."

Anna just stares at him. She doesn't know how much she should say. Whether she should tell him that these cases are the reason she's a journalist. The reason she still lives in Charleston.

It's the reason she gets out of bed every single morning.

"You're obsessed," says Justin.

"Do you have a best friend?"

"Not really. I have friends, but they don't even know about each other."

"What about a sibling?"

"I've got a little brother."

"What if he went missing and nobody in the entire world would listen to what you had to say?"

"Anna, your case . . . Everything you said on the podcast was conjecture. I was doing some research last night, and do you know you're the only one who said that Sylvie mentioned she had her photograph taken before the stalking began? She didn't tell her parents or any other friends. Don't you think she would? If some creep took a flash photo when she was walking home in the dark, why would she tell only you that?"

Anna crosses her arms. Her tone is defensive. Angry. "What are you trying to say? I was her best friend. It makes sense that if somebody was going to know the full story, it'd be me."

"Right. Right. It's just . . . Forget it." Justin sighs and looks around. "As someone who barely knows about these cases, where do I start?"

Anna picks up a blue leatherbound journal and opens it to the first page. It reads:

Property of Hannah Greenwood

"Start at the beginning."

Hannah

July 6th, 2018

Fucking nightmare last night.

I was at The Station with just Dolly and Frank. No fire or nothing. We didn't really know why we were even there. Wednesday night, and we're the only of our friends who don't work evenings or early in the morning.

Loser squad.

But Frank had some Oxy. He could've told me sooner, because I'd drunk a little already. I always black out super quick when I mix the two, but I could care less. I'm not passing up free Oxy. We all popped a couple, and then things felt less awkward, more fun. For how long I don't know.

I blacked out. (Surprise.) But I'm pretty sure we had a good time. Frank had a speaker he boosted, and when you only have each other, three can be a party.

The fun ended when at some point, I passed out. I woke up and it was dark. Like twice as dark as it was when we were partying. The moon was out early but now that bitch was GONE.

I was freezing and soaked in the grass. It rained when I'd been out, and I didn't even wake up. How's that for messed up?

But when I woke up, I didn't get up right away. I rolled onto my back and fought the urge to throw up.

I had NO idea where I was. I was still flying. I heard nothing but all these bugs, and when I did stand up, I realized I was still at The Station. I could see the outline of the little building in the dark, and in classic Hannah fashion my phone was dead.

And to top it all off, Dolly and Frank were gone.

There was no sign or sound of anyone. I was so light-headed I had to try not to fall over.

I called out for my friends and the SECOND I made some noise something cracked in the woods. I wanted to shit myself. It took a minute for me to even move. I went towards the fire pit calling for Dolly and Frank. But there was no one.

Finally, I figured out it was some prank, or the two of them were hooking up in The Station building getting too hot and heavy to hear me. I walked over quickly, not even caring if I caught them naked.

I peeked my head inside and said their names. But again . . . Nothing. They ditched me.

I started to get a little mad but not for long.

There was more noise from the woods. Like walking or footsteps. I called their names again and the sound stopped. I went through all the basic shit they say in horror movies. "Not funny guys! Seriously!"

Then I was blind. I tried to cover my face but there was a flash as bright as a nuclear bomb coming out of the dark.

There's a click that comes with it. A Ka-Click. Like it was an actual camera. This wasn't some silent iPhone pic.

When the flash was gone, it was quiet again. But I didn't waste time. I booked it.

I knew how to get back home without taking the trail. It's just a good way to tear all your clothes and scratch your face.

Thankfully I didn't veer in a circle or any of that lost-person shit. I made it home and slammed my door. I woke Mom and she was all pissed, yelling at me, but I was still high and when my head hit the pillow I was out.

It wasn't until I woke up that I had some déjà vu. The flash from the woods. That's just like one of Dolly's stories.

Identical. At least, I think. I can't remember last week. To remember things from years ago now? Pfft.

I talked to her and Frank today and they said I wandered off at some point. They were messed up too and thought I walked home. But no, I fell into the grass.

They walked right by ME.

I'm not even mad. I've got to be more careful. But all I can think about is that flash.

I mean what the fuck. Was it a rail worker who's documenting that we're trespassing? A cop?

I'm lost. Dolly and Frank don't know shit about it. She thinks I'm making things up based on shit I've read before. They said we were alone all night.

I'm not going back there when we don't have a group. It's probably no big deal. But I can't stop thinking about it. It's like that flash is burned into my vision. I wasn't imagining things. It was real.

What kind of a creep does that?

Credibility

Anna reads over Justin's shoulder. She pretty much has the thing memorized. When he finishes the entry, he leans back and looks at her.

"Where'd you even get this?"

"The police took it into evidence initially. But when a body never turned up, they dropped it back off to her mom."

"Did you steal it?"

"No," Anna says quickly. "Her mom gave it to me. I told her I was a journalist. That I might be able to get some national attention on her daughter's disappearance. She didn't care. She didn't want to look at it ever again."

Justin flips through the pages. "Why are the passages I'm reading highlighted?"

"They're the ones that mention something is wrong. Unless you want to read about more of her drunken shenanigans."

"There aren't highlighted pages before it ends."

"Two weeks," says Anna.

"What?"

"From when she saw someone take her photo to when she went missing. It was two weeks."

"I can see why the police think her disappearance isn't that strange. Taking Oxy and passing out in the grass . . . She's lucky *that* didn't kill her."

"Do you think it's bullshit?"

"Huh?"

Anna points at the journal. "That entry, do you think she was so high she hallucinated?"

"I don't know. She could've dreamed it. A high teenaged girl waking up after blacking out isn't the best source. Have you ever interviewed Dolly and Frank?"

"Dead ends."

"You mean deadbeats?"

"Yeah."

"What about her mentioning the flash is like something from one of Dolly's stories? What the hell did she mean by that?"

Anna needs to decide how much she wants to keep Justin in the dark. It's her case, and she doesn't trust he won't try to take it for himself. "No idea," she lies.

"This isn't very convincing that something happened to Hannah that wasn't done by herself."

"Well, read the next entry. I think you might change your mind."

Anna reaches towards the journal and turns the page.

Hannah

July 10th, 2018

I can't take this sober. I've been cutting back on drugs. I swear I have. I'm writing it here as an oath to myself.

I cut back.

I've been taking less.

I've only been getting fucked up with friends and not alone in this trailer.

It's a big step.

But I can't take this sober. I've pushed my bed across the room. I can't sleep right next to the window anymore. Last night, I woke up to the glass shuddering in what I thought was the wind. But Mom has got that annoying little wind vane on top of the trailer that whines with the tiniest breeze and IT was silent.

Someone was trying to open my window. I was too much of a coward to look. I had a panic attack in the corner. I know I'm a coward for that.

No one believes me about the flash. Even Dolly and Frank joke that I was on another planet.

But they can't deny these. They're here in the dirt.

A photograph interrupts the journal page. It's on printed paper. There's a set of footsteps spaced evenly apart in the dirt. The size is large—men's 12 or even bigger. They aren't sneaker prints. There are no treads or patterns. The dirt inside the imprints is smooth, as if they were from dress shoes, and the wide heel further suggests this.

Mom laughs it off as a Peeping Tom. She said I should go

over and talk to Jeffrey Lemay's mom. He's been caught looking into girls' windows before, but Jeffrey is out of town. If Mom cared enough to leave the house, she'd notice he's not sitting in his lawn chair filling his Folgers can with cigarette butts. Jeffrey's not here and besides, he's a small guy with small feet. These prints are massive.

There's another thing weird about them. There aren't any footsteps apart from these two. It's like someone came up to my window and stared at it all night. They didn't fidget or anything.

I want to board up the window but Mom's acting like this shit trailer is a palace. She said she's heard me using a drill like I was trying to be sneaky but when she came into my room I wasn't there. She says she knows I climbed out the window and ran for it.

I told her she's crazy, which hasn't helped things between us. She says she kept hearing it and kept going in my room, but I was never there.

I think she's using again. But then again, she said she smelled saw dust in my room, and I think I do, too. I don't know. All I know is that she's hearing things. I can't sleep. So yeah. I'm getting high alone again.

July 13th

Window is boarded. I spent my last forty bucks on lumber and Mom's pissed demanding my next paycheck for damages but whatever.

Maybe I can sleep.

Last night I got back from work to find this journal on my bed. I don't think I'm losing it. I don't want to make a fuss about this. But when I'm done writing, I put this journal in my nightstand EVERY SINGLE NIGHT.

I never leave it out. I know I've been tired and forgetful. Dolly came over trying to calm me down and get me to come hang out, but she doesn't understand. Somebody was in here.

I know because I can smell them. It smells like someone else in here. BO and kitchen grease. It's so strong it's like they never left.

I had my mom come in and smell, but she said I was on the fast track to being a tweaker and slammed the door.

But I'm not. I'm sober right now, and I smell sawdust again, too. My room smells DIFFERENT.

If I could afford a security camera, I'd put it up on the trailer next door so it had a view of my window. I don't know what to do. Somebody is watching me.

I never cried wolf before, so why is no one believing me now?

July 17th

I. Am. Always. High. Goodbye.

Between the Lines

It's the last entry. Justin looks up from the journal, and Anna can tell he's disappointed. "As far as firsthand accounts go, this isn't very reliable."

"Read the last line again."

Justin looks back to the page and quickly scans it. "What about it?"

"Look at the letters, like the A for instance, and then look at how she wrote them in the other entries."

Justin understands what she's trying to say and starts checking the journal. After a minute, he leans back with a little frown. "The last entry, it's not her handwriting."

"Right, and it's obvious."

"What did the police have to say about that?"

"What do you think? They never even brought in a specialist. When I called in after I went through this journal myself and found it, the detective on the case said they were aware of the handwriting difference but attributed it to drugs."

"Is that not possible?" asks Justin.

"I don't know."

Justin is quiet. "And Hannah, you said on that podcast that she disappeared from her room?"

"Yeah, her mom went to wake her up, but her door was locked. When she didn't answer, she kicked it in, thinking Hannah had overdosed, but the room was empty. No signs of a struggle or anything."

"What about this Jeffrey guy? Did he actually have an alibi?"

"Yeah. He was staying out of town with his dad. It was confirmed by his dad and friends but never an independent witness."

"What about for Sylvie Platt or Tess Gibson? Does he have alibis for them, too?"

"Yeah, an even better one. He's been in prison the past five years. Drug charges."

"Did you ever visit to interview him about their disappearances?"

"Why would I?"

Justin shrugs. "I don't know. Maybe he knows something or someone."

"I doubt it. He's an idiot bum. He got intent to sell charges for fentanyl. He'll be away awhile."

"Okay, fair enough. So, this looks like Hannah took off. Paranoid delusions and all that. I'm not going to lie—from the police's perspective, even with this journal, it seems pretty simple. The only real evidence is the footprints. But . . ." Justin frowns and flips back through the pages. He looks bothered. "Did you ever inspect her room after she went missing?"

"Of course. I looked around."

"What about the floor?"

"What do you mean?"

"Is the trailer still there?"

"Yeah. I saw it today."

"Come on." Justin walks past her into the narrow hall.

Anna stays in the little room and gestures towards the desk. "Don't you want to know about Tess, too? Don't you want to get the full picture?"

"You've already got the full picture. It's not going anywhere. This . . ." Justin shakes his head and smiles. Anna can tell he thinks he has something. "Just trust me. This is a new lead."

Square

Justin insists they take his car. Maybe he doesn't want to be seen in a 90s Ford Taurus, or maybe he doesn't like the idea of being a passenger while a woman drives. Either way, they pull off from the curb in his shiny little Audi A3.

He tells Anna his theory, and while it might be better for the case if he's right, she hopes he's not. She's spent so much time going over the journal that she could recite it in her sleep. To think she missed something that this kid was able to catch on his very first read-through makes her itch.

Riddles and reading between the lines aren't her strong suit. Anna excels with physics, formulas. Problems where the answers are concrete, and you reach them by following a set of rules.

In twenty minutes, they're back at the trailer park. There are two families loading their trucks getting ready to evacuate, but other than that, it just looks like another Saturday.

It's noon now, and a few kids are chasing each other around. Two teens smoke cigarettes at a park bench. They watch Justin's Audi pull up with intensity, and when Anna gets out of the car, she avoids their eyes.

"So, you know which one Hannah lived in?"

"Yeah."

"Does her mom still live here?"

"No, she died."

"Oh."

Anna leads the way to a gray trailer. There's a car on the concrete pad, but it's jacked up and missing a wheel. It's possible nobody is home.

She walks up the steps and knocks on the door while Justin stays several feet back. When there's no response, Anna turns to Justin and shrugs. "They might've evacuated."

"Knock again."

Anna is annoyed but listens. She knocks again but makes sure it's gentle and in a rhythm. A heavy-handed knock in a trailer park like this means trouble—cops, debt collectors, angry exes.

The blinds move to the side, and a woman's skeptical eye looks over them both. She cracks the door an inch so the brass chain that locks it is still slacked. The woman's lank gray hair is wet, and she glares at them both. "What do you want?"

"I'm sorry to bother you, ma'am, but we're with *The Charleston Journal*. We're here about a girl who used to live here, Hannah Greenwood."

"Greenwoods don't live here no more."

She starts to close the door, and Anna puts her palm against it. "I know that. We'd just like to see your spare bedroom. Not the master. We think she might've left something there."

"You think I'm just going to let a couple of strangers barge into my house? Get a warrant."

"We're not law enforcement."

"I don't care what you are. Get lost."

She shuts the door and Anna turns to Justin. He's walking up the stairs. He pounds on the door and then unravels a one-hundred-dollar bill. He presses it against the glass window on the door. "Ma'am, we can make it worthwhile."

There's a pause while the chain lock is undone, and then the door opens again. The woman takes the bill and pockets it like it was her money to begin with.

"Five minutes. I won't be leaving you alone, and don't *touch* anything."

She holds the door open, but before they step in, Justin turns to Anna and gives her a smirk.

She doesn't have a hundred dollars to spare on a whim like that. She's irritated but smiles back anyway.

Inside, the trailer is more like a cave. There are thick curtains on the windows, and even though it's noon, the blue light of the TV shines against the walls as if it were night.

"Spare bedroom is here. I just use it as a closet now." She opens the door, and Justin and Anna feel defeated. The floor is littered with overflowing boxes.

"Can we move some of these?" Justin asks.

"Hell no, you can't."

Justin sighs and is quick on the draw. "Another hundred if we can touch shit."

"Deal." The woman snatches the bill, and Anna and Justin start moving the boxes onto the bed and into the hallway to clear the floor. The woman doesn't help. She just watches with a squint and lights a cigarette.

Once the floor is cleared, Justin gets down on all fours and inspects the carpet. Anna stays standing, and the woman blows a column of smoke past her head. "What are ya'll looking for?"

Neither says anything. Justin puts his eye as close to the carpet as he can. "Anna, get down here."

She kneels. The carpet is brown shag. It's thick and its thousands of little furs stick up half an inch.

"Look where my hand is. Do you see this?"

Anna bends in close. Justin has parted the strands of the carpet like hair on a head. There is something wrong with the fiber. The square of carpet looks like it had once been cut.

"Look." Justin shuffles on his knees. "I bet this is a square. I bet this whole section of carpet was cut in a square and stapled back to the subfloor. Yep!" Justin parts another section of carpet. Anna is less enthused. Meanwhile, he's ecstatic. "It's the same cut. Help me pull this up."

"Hey! I don't care about your two hundred bucks. You're not messing up the carpet."

Justin pauses for a second. He leans back so he's sitting on his knees. "Would you take a check?"

The woman grumbles and then nods. He takes two fistfuls of the carpet and begins to pull, but Justin is wiry. He's not made of muscles. The carpet doesn't budge. "Help me out here, Anna?"

She grabs on to the carpet, too, and both of them pull. There's a tearing noise and a square section three feet by three feet peels away. Justin sets the carpet to the side, and both of them stare.

Now, with the subfloor exposed, it's obvious that Justin's theory was right. In the wood, there's the square outline of where a saw had cut.

He'd inferred from Hannah's mention of the smell of sawdust, and her mom's complaints of noise, that whoever was watching her at night had snuck under the trailer and cut right through it into Hannah's room.

Justin presses on one corner of the wood subfloor. The lip of it pops up enough for him to get his fingers underneath, and he removes the piece of wood and sets it on the carpet.

Justin can't stop smiling, and Anna feels a little stupid. She realizes that perhaps he was right when he was first selling her on teaming up. Already, another set of eyes has proved invaluable.

She's grown too accustomed to these cases and the facts. She knows every little detail, and her eyes glaze over seeing the same patterns over and over again.

"Anybody got a flashlight?" asks Justin, but it's a rhetorical boast; he's already pulling out his phone.

The woman who owns the trailer doesn't say anything. She looks confused and maybe hopeful that this damage means she'll get a bigger check out of Justin.

Anna leans towards the hole in the floor, and Justin shines his flashlight. Both of them flinch back in fear, and Justin drops his phone. "Fuck!" Justin scrambles backwards, and Anna stays still on her knees.

"What!? What is it?!" says the old woman.

The fear on Justin's face morphs to glee. Anna looks away from him. She's fighting off shock from what she's seen.

His phone has fallen face up, and she can see clearly into the space beneath the trailer.

A mummified face stares back at her. This one is cruder and more wrinkled than the body found on Church Street. Her mouth isn't pinned in a smile, but her eye sockets are empty. There are no marble eyes like the last one.

There's just two black holes, staring into Anna's soul.

She almost wants to pinch herself, but this nightmare is real.

"I think . . ." Justin crawls back towards the opening and looks down with a smile. "We just found our first Flash Girl."

Panic

Anna doesn't even realize she's leaving until she's walking out the trailer's door. She's been after this moment for years, yet it's light-years from what she pictured.

Hannah, here all along?

The fact that Justin figured this out so seamlessly is almost just as bad as those empty eye sockets; Anna had thought she was good at this.

She's hyperventilating when she hears her name called and footsteps pounding behind her.

"Anna!" Justin catches up to her and taps her on the elbow, but she's hesitant to even turn around; she doesn't want to see his shit-eating smile.

"Anna, I'm sorry."

She looks over her shoulder. Justin is far from smiling. His face finally looks disturbed, like the reality of what he's found is settling in. "That lady already called the cops."

"You don't want to look at the body first?"

"What? It's a crime scene. I don't want to touch anything else."

Anna realizes that she shouldn't have taken off. Her first reaction was flight, the same as it always is. She should've kept calm and climbed down into that hole. For all she knows, the body was left with a clue like the last one. Anxiety burns in her stomach.

She can run back in. There is still time before the police arrive, but the trailer owner is now on her porch, and she's on the phone hollering to someone hysterically about the dead body.

Those who were packing their cars begin to take notice and walk over. It's too late now, and Anna lowers her head and starts walking out of the trailer park.

"Where are you going?" asks Justin.

"Taking a walk."

"We've got to wait to talk to the cops."

"*You've* got to wait to talk to the cops."

She turns and hears him sigh and stutter like he's going to say more, but he relents.

Anna can be brave when she has time to make a decision when she's faced with fear, but her immediate instinct has always told her to run. When it's flight or fight, flight wins.

There are no sidewalks outside of the trailer park, and she starts walking on the shoulder of the road.

She has the guts to break into the Church Street Mansion. The guts to go wander in the dark where she might find this Flash Girl Killer. But take away the time to make a decision, and her subconscious is a coward. She kicks at the gravel that litters the side of the road and curses herself.

She turns around towards the park, and the wind blows back her hair. She has to resist the urge to sprint back. She thinks of the riddle on the wall at the last scene and reassures herself that this is not the same.

This body didn't feel like it was supposed to be found. It was tucked away under the carpet and the wood, but it wasn't left to rot.

Like the last one, the time was taken to embalm her. Obviously, it wasn't done as skillfully as the corpse on Church Street. If this is Hannah, and it was his first victim, then it certainly shows that he's had practice.

Soon, a couple police cars race past her with their lights off.

She bites her lip. Two girls found in two days. Neither found by Anna, and she's the person who's trying the hardest to solve this.

She pulls out her phone and reads the riddle again.

There's nothing about embalmed girls.

Nothing about murder.

She thinks perhaps she'll show it to Justin. Perhaps a light bulb will turn on in boy genius's head and he'll see something so obvious that she had missed.

She shouldn't care about who solves this, but she can't shut up her ego.

She walks for a long time, the same thoughts spinning over and over in her head. A half hour later, a car slows as it passes her. Her heart jumps a little in fear. She's alone on this low-trafficked road, and there's not another car in sight. But she relaxes as she sees through the driver's window. It's Terry, the homicide detective.

He looks her over, and for a second she's certain he's going to roll down the window to talk, but instead, he shakes his head at her and hits the gas.

She loops back to the trailer park. Before she reaches the entrance, another car takes her attention as it slows while she walks. She's frightened for a moment and her head snaps up from her feet, but it's Justin. He gestures for her to get in the car, and she does, but something's not right. The blood is drained from his face.

She shuts the door, and he stays stopped.

"I tried calling you."

"Sorry." It's all Anna says. Justin is quiet and takes a moment to put the car back in Drive.

"I, uh . . . I talked to the cops."

"Yeah?"

"I mentioned that the body was embalmed like the one on Church Street." Justin is talking slow, like there's something bugging him that he doesn't know how to say.

"And?" Anna says, annoyed.

"And they said this girl wasn't embalmed."

Anna frowns. "So, what? She was mummified somehow?"

"No." Justin chuckles, but it's not because something is funny. Anna can tell he's a little bit terrified. "According to the detective who touched the body, this girl has only been dead for a couple of days."

Anna leans back in her seat and stares out the windshield. With the find of the second body, she thought this was getting easy. Now, she's certain this is going to be anything but simple.

Politics

"You can't tell me, for one second, that the police don't think these girls were murdered. Or that these two bodies are unrelated," says Anna.

"Want to hear a secret?"

Anna is tired of feeling like she's the odd one out. "What?"

"The police are asking this to be kept out of the press."

"Like that's going to work."

Justin shrugs his head to one shoulder, as if he knows something she doesn't. "This body will be kept off the front page, and it'll only be a small mention on the website."

"Are you kidding? Have you talked to Bruce? Does he know about this?"

"Yeah. He's the one who told me. The city is having enough trouble getting people to take this storm seriously as it is. Apparently, it's our civic duty to keep this storm dominating the headlines. He doesn't want any competing pieces."

Anna shuts up. She realizes that when she got drinks with Terry, he didn't actually think that the corpse on Church Street wasn't a homicide. He wasn't an idiot.

"Why do the police want this story buried, too? Do they have a civic duty to not take people's attention from the storm? Two women were murdered. One of them apparently two days ago! Is that not something that should be front page?"

Justin holds out a hand. Anna realizes she's taking her anger out on him, but she still doesn't relax. "I don't know. But I imagine it's a problem for them if people don't evacuate."

"That'll be a problem for the National Guard."

"What's it matter anyway? We're making progress. We'll have a serious story when this hurricane passes."

Anna leans back in the passenger seat with a huff. Justin is right. What bothers her is that if these bodies are Hannah and Sylvie, then they're being ignored in death just as they were when they were missing. The public at large has never entertained the idea that these disappearances were connected, and now the police and the press won't let them.

For a moment, it dawns on her that this timing is intentional, but then they turn onto Cypress Street. It's a quiet block just behind the trailer park. You can see the trailers through the trees.

"Justin, where are you going?"

"Sorry, is this the wrong way?"

"Yeah. Turn around."

He pulls into a U-turn while Anna is transported into the past, back to the beginning.

August 2013

It's been two years since Anna was expelled from the Covenant of Christ, and she's almost thirteen. The school didn't want any charges pressed. They wanted the incident to be forgotten as quickly as possible.

Anna was ordered to see a psychiatrist for several months, but when her mom forgot to take her to the first appointment, and then every subsequent appointment afterwards, no one ever checked in.

That was that.

She spent the previous years in public school. She kept her head down, didn't get bullied, and had actually made friends when her mom suddenly moved them into another school district for a house with cheaper rent. Now, her school experience this semester is again a question mark.

It's August, and the breeze that blows is not off the cool Atlantic. It's been traversing the continent, and Charleston is its last sweltering stop before the relief of the sea.

Anna has spent most of the summer by herself, reading next to the A/C window unit in their new living room. This house is somehow smaller than their last one, and the whole thing tilts. If Anna drops a marble, it will roll until it meets a wall, but she's been able to make a game of it.

She sets up a cup sideways, so its bottom is on the kitchen wall and its mouth faces the living room. Then, she tries to roll marbles into it.

She's doing this one afternoon while her mom is passed out, when there's a knock on the door.

Anna lets go of a marble and then looks towards the door while it clacks against the wall, missing its mark. There's giggling outside, and she stands quickly and walks to the screen door. When she opens it, there are a couple of girls her own age standing on the stairs.

One of them has a small gap in her two front teeth and is standing a stair higher than the other. She looks to be the apparent leader of the two. It's her who speaks.

"Hey!"

"Hey," says Anna guardedly.

"Is your mom home?"

Anna looks over her shoulder. "She's sleeping."

"So . . . Weird question." The girl on the top stair turns to the other, and they laugh. "But do you have any cigarettes?"

"Cigarettes?"

"Your mom, I mean. We've seen her smoking. Do you think you could take some for us? We'd pay you."

Anna just stares at them. She's heard of girls who are just going into high school who drink alcohol and smoke cigarettes, but she's never met any. "Maybe."

"We have five bucks," says the second girl.

The leader turns to her and slaps her shoulder. Whether it is because she doesn't want her to talk or doesn't want Anna to know how much they're willing to pay, Anna can't say.

"I'll go check." She heads back inside while the girls stay on the stairs. She can easily get them the cigarettes. Her mom loses entire packs all the time when she's drunk. It's a common occurrence.

It doesn't take Anna much time to decide. She's eager to gain someone's approval. She goes into her mom's room. The curtains aren't drawn. The room is hot and well lit, but her mom snores lightly in a sunbeam. Anna checks the nightstand but finds the pack in the pocket of her mom's pants that she left strewn on the floor.

She walks back to the front door and holds the pack out with an outstretched arm.

"Here."

The girl with the gap tooth takes it quickly and opens it. Her eyelids peel back. "Holy shit, you're kidding? A whole fucking pack, are you serious?"

Anna just nods.

"Menthols, too." She gives the pack to her friend, who stuffs the contraband in a small backpack.

The leader of the two suddenly looks guilty. "Look, we don't actually have any money. We were just going to run away."

Anna doesn't know how to respond, and she stays silent.

"But . . . you could come hang out with us if you like. Do you smoke?"

Anna looks at their bikes and then shakes her head. "I don't have a bike."

"I'll stand. You take the seat. Come on."

"One—One sec." Anna stutters from excitement. She's been living here three months, and this is the most interaction she's had with another kid her age. She puts on her shoes and jumps down the steps, and soon the three of them are riding into the heat shimmer that lingers above the blacktop.

The girls don't ask Anna many questions while they ride. They go off the trail and head into the woods. Then they dismount their bikes and don't use the kickstands, letting them fall at their feet.

"It's been . . . too long." The girl with the gap tooth pulls out a giant box of matches and strikes one after her friend hands her a cigarette. "You sure you don't want one?"

"If my mom smells it on me, she might think . . ."

"Oh, smart. Yeah. None for you."

Anna notices the girls don't smoke cigarettes the same way her mother does. They only take the smoke into their mouths, and it's still thick when they slowly blow it out.

The two of them talk about boys and other girls from the neighborhood who Anna doesn't know. Young as she is, she's smart enough to understand that these girls are bad company. The peer pressuring type they warned her about in health class. But she doesn't care. They are nice, if not a bit unruly, and Anna would do anything to have friends again.

They extinguish their cigarettes in the tall grass, and the more talkative of the two suddenly turns to Anna. "Your boobs are big, by the way. How old are you?"

"Thirteen."

"Oh, we thought you were a year older."

"Really?"

"We've heard boys talk about you. Or about your . . ." She nods towards her chest. "Tatas."

"Oh." The thought that Anna's been talked about by people she doesn't know excites her. For years she's felt invisible. For the first time, she thinks that maybe early puberty wasn't the curse she thought it was.

"That's cool." She tries to say as casually as she can, but the two girls laugh.

"What's your name?"

Anna starts to speak but again she's interrupted by the leader. "How tall are you? Five feet?"

"Something like that."

"Do you know who Dolly Parton is?"

"Sure."

"That's who you remind me of. A young her. Have you seen a picture?"

"No."

"She was like . . . all boobs." The two girls laugh again, and although it's not funny to her, Anna does, too.

"My name's Anna, by the way."

"I'm Hannah," says the gap-toothed girl. "And this is Tess." She points to her friend with a thumb. "Anna's a bit too close to my name. They're like the same."

Anna doesn't know what to say to that and shrugs.

"Why don't you wear any makeup?"

"My mom doesn't give me money."

"Ours don't either." They laugh again, but this time Anna doesn't. She wonders if these two chipper girls are beaten by their mothers, too.

"Tess and I are great friends because we don't have dads. I mean, obviously we do somewhere. But they're deadbeats. We haven't seen a man around your house. Do you have one?"

Anna feels a weight lift from her shoulders. Her mom's house is just through a patch of trees from the trailer park these girls are living in. Here, her weirdness is normal. "No."

"It sucks sometimes. One less wallet to steal from." Hannah and Tess laugh, but there's pain behind their smiles.

"Anyway, come on." Hannah stands and picks up her bike. "Let's get you some makeup. The Walgreens on Melon is super easy to steal from."

Anna is slow to rise. She feels elation building in her stomach. These girls aren't just hanging out with her as a thank-you for the cigarettes. They want to be friends.

Hannah pedals in a circle around Anna. "Are you coming, Dolly?"

Anna stands with a smile, and Hannah slows while she hops onto the bike seat.

When they get out of the woods and back to the streets, the hot wind whips around her head, and the hairs on her arms stand on end from happiness.

She sees her future unfurl. Summer nights and laughter. Nights where she will live her own stories, ones that don't come from a book written by an adult.

God, she thinks, trying not to cry, *is it good to have friends.*

String

Justin and Anna are nearly back to her apartment when they both get a text.

It's from Bruce; he started a group chat with every one of the paper's reporters who are still in the city. The mayor is having a press conference where he's breaking from the governor and pleading for earlier evacuation.

It's Democrat mayor vs. Republican governor, and Bruce wants all hands on deck for the partisan battle.

"Should we just go together?" Justin asks.

Anna doesn't respond for a moment. She's decided to put aside her ego. She wants to show Justin more about these cases. It doesn't matter if the answers were in front of her the entire time; she needs them. Still, she can't decide when to tell him how she knows Hannah and Tess.

The last time she revealed that she knew all three Flash Girls, it didn't go well.

Justin speaks before Anna can again.

"I think you should go, if you're worried about a paycheck. Bruce only gave you a research piece for your next article. He knows you're not out and about in the field. He'll be expecting you there."

And then, as if he had heard, Anna gets a separate text directly from Bruce.

Expecting you at this PC. No excuses.

"Yeah," says Anna. "Fine. Let's go."

Justin takes his next right without a word and starts towards downtown Charleston. The press conference is at a historic hotel right by the tip of the city that meets the bay. Anna knows the game.

The location was picked so the mayor can say something along the lines of, *"By this time 48 hours from now, this event room could be under twenty feet of water."*

"We've got an hour. Want to grab a bite?"

"Half the restaurants are already closed for the storm."

"Yeah, and the other half are owned by restaurateurs who don't want to close for a day. Come hell or hurricane. Come on, there's a new diner on King I want to try."

"Okay."

Twenty minutes later, she's sitting in front of a BLT with chips. She's not hungry in the slightest, but she's running off only a couple hours of sleep, and the least Anna can do for herself is eat a little. She starts with the pickle spear, and after it's gone, she has somewhat of an appetite.

"What can you tell me about Tess Gibson?" Justin says with his mouth completely full. The fact that he talks with his mouth full is less surprising to Anna than if he didn't; Justin is just that kind of guy. Baggy jeans. Stained running shoes. She pictures the fights his mom has had with him to kick the habit, but it never took. "She grew up in that same trailer park as Hannah, didn't she?"

"She moved away her junior year of high school. Her stepdad found some better job in Columbia. Not like he ever spent the money on her, though."

"But wasn't she last seen in Charleston?"

"She came back often. Her mom was nice. She let Tess take the car when she got her license."

Justin nods and takes another bite of sandwich. "And where do you think she is? Any guesses?"

"None."

"She didn't have a journal?"

"No."

"But she was heard complaining to friends about having her picture taken one night and then being stalked just like Hannah?"

"Yeah. Just like Hannah."

Justin chews his sandwich and considers this. Anna knows he wants a puzzle to piece together, but it's not as simple with Tess. She didn't leave hints like Hannah's journal, but if there's a clue waiting to be found, Anna knows it'll be at the place where she was photographed.

She's itching to ditch Justin so she can go.

He has a big splotch of mayo on his upper lip, and Anna wants to say something, but at the same time he *has* to know it's there. It'd be impossible not to feel it. Is he really that oblivious? Or is he pretending to be dumber than he is?

"You have some . . ." Anna says, pointing to the same place on her lip.

"Oh." He wipes his mouth on his wrist like a kid. "Thanks. By the way . . . I'm sorry you had to see what you saw. I want to clarify that I'm not some creep. I hope you don't think my reaction to finding that body was . . . inappropriate."

"You're good, Justin. Don't worry about it. It's exciting, morbid as it may be."

"Cool. It's just like . . . Never in my wildest dreams. You know? A dead body. A dead body for homicide cases that are shaping up to be serial. I used to dream of Davos. Economic journalism. How do I go back to that from this high?"

"You don't. What you did is practically unheard of in journalism. Joggers and hunters find dead bodies, not reporters. I think what you want is investigative journalism. Finding the missing pieces is what gave you your thrills. At least, I hope, anyway."

"Don't worry. I don't get off on dead bodies. Did you see how far I scrambled when I first saw that corpse?"

Anna tries to smile just to be friendly, but she can't. For the first time since she saw it, she's trying to picture that corpse's face, trying to picture whether that wrinkled mask could possibly be Hannah. But it couldn't be because Hannah vanished close to five years ago now. How could she only be dead for a couple days?

Justin has mentioned how kidnapped girls have turned up after five, ten, fifteen years. It's happened plenty of times in America. Maybe Anna doesn't want to think that throughout all these years, Hannah has been alive. She could've been saved until just days ago.

Justin wipes his mouth with his napkin. "I'm just thinking of what other pieces we're missing. Besides Tess, obviously. Something has to connect all these girls . . ."

Anna breaks eye contact and looks towards the wall. Justin keeps looking at her. Whether he's hopeful she has an answer or is reading her troubled expression, Anna can't tell.

Suddenly, her attention is taken towards the kitchen. The cooks are all clamoring about something. Two of them walk out into the dining area, paying no attention to the patrons. They walk towards the bar, where there's a television playing the weather channel.

"Hey, Todd," says one of the cooks to the bartender. "Can you turn it to CNN? We want to see if they're showing this shit."

Justin has heard them, too, and now looks over his shoulder. Most of the restaurant has stopped to watch. This is it, Anna thinks. Their story about these girls is going to be national.

Then the channel changes, and she frowns. No, this is something else. Anna's glad for the distraction. She didn't want to answer Justin's question.

It's always been hard to explain that the only thing connecting three possible murders is her.

Sunk

The scene on the TV behind the bar turns into a vertical shot. The news is showing a video shot on someone's phone. Anna notices that they now have a countdown clock for Charlie's landfall. It reads: "35:32:21."

The seconds tick down continuously. Thirty-five hours, Anna thinks, and this city changes forever.

"Wait, wait, wait!" the cook shouts. "This is it. Don't change it! Turn it up!"

The bartender holds up the remote, and while he turns up the volume, people set down their forks and drinks and stare. The only sound in the restaurant is coming from the television.

There's a woman's voice playing over the clip. "We're just getting word that this video comes to us from the brother of a French sailor and was taken about six hundred miles off the coast of the Bahamas."

Her voice fades and a video plays. Men are yelling in a different language. They wear yellow rain gear, waders and jackets. Some are wearing what looks like extra-thick wetsuits that Anna soon understands are some kind of survival gear.

The footage is taken from the bridge of a ship. There's the wheel, navigational instruments, and then a big line of windows that are getting rained on so heavily, it's hard to see out of them.

A few people go back to eating their food, but Anna and Justin keep watching. The person filming the video approaches the line of windows and points the camera out.

A woman a table over gasps, and Anna feels her insides knot. All eyes dart back to the screen.

Out the ship's windows, not far in the distance, is what Anna first thinks is a cliff. Then she sees it move closer and realizes what she's looking at is a fifty-foot wave.

There's panic in the sailors' voices, but the camera stays fixed on the wave as the ship begins to ride up it. The screen goes black for a moment, and then there's a blur of movement and muffled shouting. Whoever is filming is being tossed around. In several seconds they stand again and the shot steadies.

They survived the impact. Anna feels some relief, but then the camera pans back out the windows.

There's another wave just like it, and behind that, another.

"That can't be real," says a younger woman. She looks around at the others in the restaurant for reassurance. "I mean, that's Photoshop. CGI. Right?"

Nobody responds to her. Justin laughs a little, and the overlayed voice returns as the video on screen pauses and goes dark. "This was from the deck of the *Maverick*, a seven-hundred-foot bulk carrier. It, along with another ship of its class, the *Carme*, deviated from course, hoping to miss Hurricane Charlie. When it was obvious they were going to face the brunt of the storm, the two ships rendezvoused in case of emergency.

"This video was sent via satellite, along with a farewell message to his family. Jean Lambert, the man filming, and third officer onboard wrote, 'This is what they make us sail through. We are only in the eye and have already taken on too much water. I love you all beyond words.'"

"Jesus," says Justin, taking a sip of his water.

"The *Maverick* and the *Carme* sent out distress signals roughly six hours ago, but both are currently lost to satellite and radar. It's assumed both ships, with a total of forty-six crew aboard, have been lost at sea. They are likely the first victims of this devastating hurricane and are likely not to be its last. We'll be back with more updates on historic Hurricane Charlie after this."

The screen goes to commercial. It's some cleaning ad, and everyone in the restaurant is still so transfixed on the television that they watch a golden retriever shake mud off in a white kitchen with just as much intensity as the storm footage.

An older man in a flannel shirt stands and tosses a couple twenties on the table. He puts on his hat and is quickly out the door.

A few people watch him, and then everyone slowly comes to life. The restaurant fills with voices as people begin to panic. They all want to pay and leave. Many of those left in the city were denialists. It seems like the swirling white graphic of a hurricane with "Category 5" next to it wasn't enough to worry them, but the video of the waves sure did.

"Waves are always worse out at sea," Anna hears someone say. "I don't think they'll look like that coming off the harbor." But the voice is filled with doubt.

Evacuation order or not, Charleston is finally ready to panic.

Hooky

Anna and Justin arrive at the hotel where the mayor is set to speak. His timing couldn't be better. He no longer has to predict the damage Charlie will cause; he can point to what it's done already to two ocean-faring ships.

Soon the two of them are at the back of an event room with a coffee-stained carpet and stains of the same color spreading on the ceiling. The Hotel Calhoun was picked for its location, not its character.

Justin says something about networking and disappears to go chit-chat. The mayor is late, and there's time to kill. Anna pretends to look at her phone. Really, she's thinking about Hannah and Tess. The feeling of making a mistake has only grown in the last two hours. She should've checked Hannah's body. Gotten down in that pit herself before the police, who want to put these cases on hold, could get there.

Suddenly, she perks her head up. It's as if she can tell she's being watched. Anna sees Bruce across the room. He's a thin man. Tall, with a long forehead and prominent cheekbones. He has a schoolmaster look to him—always serious.

He's looking at her, but not at her face. Her chest pulls male gazes like gravity, but while it's fine to glance, staring is another story. She gives him a little wave, thinking he'll be embarrassed to be caught staring, but instead, he looks her in the eye with the same plain expression and raises his eyebrows in acknowledgement.

He doesn't come over to say hi, and it doesn't look like he's going to.

For a moment, Anna is disappointed. This whole thing feels like a waste of time. She despises covering political events. She's thought about making bingo charts before for speeches like this, and each square would be a stereotypical platitude.

Anna became a journalist because she wanted to get paid while trying to solve these cases. But she probably would've had more free time to focus on Hannah, Tess, and Sylvie if she'd worked at a coffee shop.

The room begins to get crowded. She sees Justin approach Bruce, and the two begin talking. They speak close in what looks like whispers, but then there's another flow of people into the room, and she loses sight of them.

She realizes she doesn't need to stay. The event room is large, and it looks like it'll meet its three-hundred-person capacity. Anna doesn't want to stick around for the theatrics.

She has much better uses of her time.

At 5'1", she doesn't have to duck in order to not be seen by Bruce or Justin as she walks past the other reporters and into the hotel lobby.

She has to get to the place where Tess says she was photographed before it's underwater.

Flash

Anna takes the bus back to her apartment. It's late afternoon by the time she's there. She doesn't go inside. Instead, she takes her car keys from her pocket and gets behind the wheel.

She starts the car but doesn't pull off from the curb right away. She stares at the first-floor windows of her landlords' apartment. Their Volvo station wagon is still outside. It seems like by now they probably should've evacuated. Especially if they've been watching the news.

She wonders if they're alright, but it's only for a moment before she's driving down the street.

The rain comes down hard and suddenly. She sets her wipers at full blast and ignores a call from Justin.

That takes her mind to Jake for a moment. He still hasn't called, and at this point, she assumes he never will. He probably won't even send a "be safe" text for the hurricane. He's an asshole, she realizes. Thirty-four years old, but forever twenty-four at heart.

The rain stops as suddenly as it started. She looks up and sees a dark cloud move west of her, swift and low, strafing the city.

She looks at her watch. Still plenty more than a day before landfall. Plenty of time for the forecasts to be wrong. For the storm's strength to shrink.

The roads are slick, but she steps on the gas. The countdown clock on the news is having its desired effect, and Anna begins to think that maybe this entire puzzle is on the same timer.

The killer is leaving his clues, and if Anna doesn't find them in time, they'll vanish along with the city.

She crosses the Stono Bridge into the southeastern part of the city. In another five minutes she gets to a small park that runs along the river. She parks and looks out the window at the clouds. None appear ready to burst, but she takes her umbrella regardless.

The park is based around a boat launch, but there's not a soul around. The wind ripples the river, and little waves lap the shore. There's a light spray coming from the clouds, but not enough to soak her.

Anna keeps her umbrella closed as she walks towards a dock that runs adjacent to the concrete boat ramp. She walks out on the splintered wood, but nothing catches her eye.

This is where Tess was photographed. It was just after sunset. She was smoking a cigarette and looking at the dark water when she heard footsteps on the shore behind her.

Then, a blinding flash.

There is nothing spray-painted on the dock like there was at the concrete structure at The Station. No red X like last time. Anna sighs and stares out at the water. Perhaps she's wrong.

Perhaps there is no grand puzzle. She didn't interrogate anyone at the trailer park. She hates being recognized. It was possible that the painting was all done by teenagers. They surely know of the legends of the Flash Girls.

There is a long list of people Anna never wants to talk to again—exes, bad friends, creeps—and most of them are in that trailer park. Maybe that is why she ran when she saw the body; she couldn't stick around to face the crowd.

Anna turns from the river and looks at the park. It's possible there is something on the swing set or on one of the oaks, but it feels unlikely. The mark for where Hannah went missing was precise. It was exactly where her photograph was taken. There was no reason Tess wouldn't be the same if this was some sort of sick game.

Anna starts walking back down the dock. Her gaze is still at her feet when she freezes.

She'd missed it the first time. It's barely noticeable, but a slight X has been carved into the dock.

She squats immediately and runs her thumb over it. The pulp of wood that has been exposed looks fresh. There are other carvings and initials on the dock, but the wood exposed is grayed, faded.

Here on the X, it's fresh.

X marks the spot, but for what? Suddenly, Anna spies something through the dock slats. It's a plastic bag. The boards are close together—most people's fingers probably couldn't fit through, but Anna's can.

She has to extend them as far as she can, and little by little, she gets a better grip on the plastic until she has enough in her fingertips to pull the bag through the slat. It was taped to the underside of the dock, and while it tears a little, it's otherwise intact.

Inside is a folded piece of paper, but the material is thicker than loose-leaf. When her fingers move to open the bag, she realizes exactly what it is—a photograph.

Although Tess and Hannah both mentioned having their photographs taken, the pictures themselves have never surfaced. The picture must be of Tess, Anna thinks. The photograph taken of Hannah must've been back at The Station by the X. She probably missed it.

Anna's fingers shake as she opens the bag and plucks it out. She unfolds it slowly.

For several seconds, she stares, confused.

The photo wasn't taken on the dock. There's a brick wall in the background. It's a street in Charleston, and the face of the girl in the center of the flash is scribbled out with a sharpie.

But even so, Anna knows exactly who it is.

Her.

She was a Flash Girl, too. The only one who survived.

She's been hoping to find this picture for years, and now that she holds it in her hand, she can't quite believe it. She keeps looking at the picture while it's lightly sprinkled with rain.

Her fingers feel something on the back. She frowns and turns the photo over. Attached to the back is another picture. It's much smaller. This picture is a Polaroid selfie of Anna and Sylvie pushed cheek to cheek. Written on the little white shelf of space below it is a single line in scribbled handwriting. It reads:

Missing something?

Anna repeats the line to herself, trying to make sense of it, and then suddenly, she's running.

Paranoia

When she gets back to her apartment, it's only five p.m., yet from the thick cloud cover it looks like it's hours later. She slams the brakes and parks crooked outside the front door. She fumbles with the keys, and before she even realizes what she's doing, she's charging up the stairs.

She opens her apartment, and only when she's greeted by its silence does she remember she's in danger. She digs for her folding knife and flicks its blade open. Then she slips off her shoes so her footsteps are quieter.

Her heart throbs so much it angers her; she can't hear as well while it pounds in her eardrums.

She starts in her bedroom, swinging open closet doors and jumping back ready to stab. But there's no one and the room looks as she left it.

She checks the bathroom and even the kitchen cabinets large enough for a person. Only when she's sure the apartment is empty does she venture towards her office.

She can't remember if she locked the narrow door but assumes that she didn't. Justin was in a rush to leave with his lightbulb idea, and she didn't spend time messing with the key.

She stands in the narrow hall and stares at the door. The knife is sweaty in her hand, and she readjusts her grip.

The floor in the little old file room is creaky. The slightest shift of her weight can make it creak loudly.

She waits a minute, and when she hears nothing, Anna begins walking towards the door. She twists the handle so it isn't latched in the wall and then takes a step back. She holds the knife back, ready to plunge, plants one foot on the floor, and then boots the door open.

It bangs against the wall, but what she's forgotten is that the old file room is windowless. The light from the hall does little, and the doorway now opens to a black abyss. Anything could be inside.

She takes a quick step forward and pulls the string bulb on. The little room is thankfully and obviously empty.

She sighs and looks over her shoulder, and then she steps into the room. Anna begins going through a little photo album filled with Polaroids she'd taken when she was a teen.

Sure enough, there's an empty slot right where the selfie with Sylvie has always been.

Somebody has been here. Her mind jumps to Justin, but when he was here, he was seldom out of her sight. They never went through these albums together. No, it couldn't have been him.

She thinks back to the party. Maybe somebody got in then, but she didn't keep a spare key for this room. Jake sure as hell doesn't know how to get in. She told him this room was just a locked linen closet anyway. And he isn't the kind of guy to be interested in what's behind a locked door.

The thought hasn't quite sunk in that whoever killed Hannah, Tess, and Sylvie has been in her apartment.

Is it possible? Or Is this some other sort of trick?

Anna has been distancing herself from the idea that these clues have all been laid out for her to find, but she's never really believed that.

She's known from the beginning that this maze is meant for her. For the Flash Girl who got away.

She's been avoiding it, brushing it off, but to figure this out she needs to make sense of that riddle. She pulls out her phone and walks back into her living room where it's light. Again, she reads.

The apple of an eye despite that goodbye
See all I say true, I promise not to lie
I am had by all, but not by some
Called a name but not my one
I am a beginning. You, with just a little skinning
The apple of my eye, and it is there where one can find me
What am I?

She had sent it to Professor Geller a few hours ago, and she's anxious to know if he's made any progress. Anna sits in her recliner and texts him, asking what he thinks.

It's at least ten minutes before he gets back to her.

Honestly haven't had the chance to look yet. I'll get back to you tonight.

Suddenly she's sorry she texted him. She's sorry she showed him the riddle in the first place. Geller knows where she lives. He is the only person she knows with a truck, and he'd helped her move in.

Every face she's seen in the past few weeks starts racing through her head. Jake, Justin, Geller. The tall man at the party.

This killer had to be closer to home than she realized, but she's always sensed in her stomach that it was a person from her past. A face she hasn't seen for years.

She realizes she's being ridiculous, but she can't bring herself to trust anyone. There's a little table across the room with liquor bottles on it. She stands and picks up a fifth of vodka. She drinks straight from the bottle, just one pull, and then she sets it down and falls back in the chair. The burn of the shot shuts everything up.

She breathes, keeping her eyes open and alert.

The file room is locked again. The front door is locked. There's no evidence anybody has been in her apartment other than the missing picture. And she can't say how long that photo has been gone for. It could be years.

The effects of only two hours of sleep are taking their toll. Her eyes are heavy, the liquor hot and calming in her stomach. Outside, the light-sensing streetlights are already on from the darkness of the storm clouds.

It's hard for her to keep her eyes open. It takes effort to get out of her recliner, but she does and goes to her bedroom where she can sleep behind another locked door.

She lies down to nap for just a little bit. She thinks of setting an alarm in case she oversleeps, but before she can think twice to do so, her head is on the pillow and the thought is gone.

She's already falling asleep.

* * *

It's an hour later when she wakes, and the room is dark. There's the sound of wind and rain against the glass, but her eyes are narrowed in confusion because that is not what woke her. She moves so her feet are on the floor and sits on the bed.

There's a clattering noise coming from above her. She stands quickly and steps out into the living room.

She pauses after flipping on a light switch and listens. Several seconds pass with no noise other than the weather. She sighs in relief, but before she can even exhale fully, there's a sound like something has been dropped onto the floor above her.

Hey eyes dance on the ceiling as it dribbles and rolls. Then she hears it bounce against a wall and go still.

Anna knows exactly what the sound is; she's heard it a thousand times, but not since she was fourteen.

It's the sound of a marble rolling across a floor. She stands, and as she does, the sound comes again.

Visitor

There isn't a single other room in this building that's supposed to be occupied. Even the Shepards had said they were going to probably evacuate today.

There should be nobody else here at all.

Anna ponders all this with her knife in her fist. There had apparently been a squatter problem when the property was first purchased, but that was years ago. She considers running to her car and squealing away from the curb.

Anna is terrified. As much as she's fantasized about finding this killer, the thought that she has a chance to confront him now feels very different from her daydreams. She doesn't want to rush upstairs with the knife, and even with time to think, her fight-or-flight instinct is yelling for her to run.

She doesn't give time for the fear to take hold. She walks quickly towards the front door, laces up a pair of her boots, and locks her door behind her as she steps into the hall.

She curses her mistakes already. She should've shut the door silently. Now, whoever is upstairs knows she's left. Knows she might be on her way to find him. She takes her time walking up the stairwell.

In all the time she's lived here, she's only been to the fourth and final floor once. It was still all original then—ancient wood floors, dusty brick walls, and exposed pine pillars that leaked creosote.

She gets to the third floor, and by then she realizes her second mistake—she forgot to take an actual flashlight. All she has is her phone. She thinks about going back, but it's only for a moment. She goes up the last flight of stairs. The doorframe to the fourth floor is doorless, probably for easier construction access. Just like her little file room, the rectangle of darkness in front of her looms like a bad omen.

To go in would be madness. It's the moment in the horror movie where the audience screams at the screen, but Anna isn't in this for justice or curiosity. She's filled with hate, and now she doesn't hesitate to step into the black.

The fourth floor is completely different from when she last saw it. It was once an open space, but drywall had been hung to make rooms and a hall. She peeks her head into the first room. It's the beginnings of an apartment unit. There are unplugged floodlights and construction equipment lying about on top of a painter's tarp.

None of the frames have doors, and it gives the rooms the appearance of a maze. She goes back into the hall and walks slowly. The floor doesn't creak beneath her feet, but regardless, her position is given away from the flashlight.

She glances into the other drywalled rooms as she passes them but can't bring herself to go in. She doesn't like going through doorways. There could be someone waiting for her on either side of the wall.

When she gets to the end of the hallway, another one begins to her left. It leads to a wall with a sheet of plastic hung over it. She approaches and sees something shine under the fogged sheet.

With the same hand that holds the knife, Anna grabs a fistful of the plastic and pulls it from the wall. It's hung with painter's tape and falls easily to the floor.

Behind it is a door. The shine she had seen was its brass hardware—the handle and hinges. But this door is not new like everything else on this floor. This area hasn't been touched.

It's original.

She thinks about where the room behind this door is in correlation to her apartment below. She isn't certain that the area is directly above her apartment, but it has to be close.

She grasps the handle and turns, but anticlimactically, it's locked. She frowns, and then without even thinking about it, she throws her shoulder against the door. The impact hurts so bad, she gasps in pain. A little shower of dust rains from the ceiling while she rubs her shoulder.

The door is an ancient rectangle of hard wood, and the frame it sits in is sturdy as well—it's not budging.

For a moment, she's happy to have an excuse not to pursue this any further. Her adrenaline is fading, and the reality of what she's doing is beginning to dawn.

Then, there's another sound from behind the door. It's the same as before—something hard has been dropped on the wood floor. It bounces and rolls.

Anna sets her ear gently against the door, but what she hears is a slight roar of wind. There's a window open. She sets her fingers in front of the keyhole and can feel cool air pouring out.

She feels a bit crazy. It could just be the wind knocking something over. Now that she's heard it again, she's not even sure the sound is a marble.

She's being ridiculous. Trying to tie every little coincidence together.

Anna pushes off the door and heads back down the stairs. When she gets to her apartment, she has the key ready in her fist.

She throws open the door and locks it in the same second it slams behind her.

She keeps her boots on and walks into the living room. Her nostrils start to flare as she sniffs the air. She thinks the room smells different, like someone else. Maybe she's been spooked by Hannah's journal. Crazy or not, thinks Anna, she can't stay here.

She grabs a roll of Scotch tape from the kitchen, packs a small bag, and goes back into the hall. Before she goes any farther, she takes a piece of tape and squats low. She attaches it to the frame of the door and then takes several pictures on her phone so she can remember exactly how it looks.

If someone else has a key and uses her door, she'll know now.

There are no toiletries in the bag she's packed. It's all black clothes and a few tools. She's not going to a hotel or crashing on a couch; she has another break-in to commit.

Stainless Steel

She had Googled the address yesterday afternoon and written it in her notes. It's not very far away, but even at almost eight p.m., traffic is heavy.

People are fleeing the city. The video taken onboard the *Maverick* has made the rounds. It's all that's being shared on social media, and by now practically everybody in Charleston has seen the size of the waves that are making their way across the Atlantic.

Anna makes the mistake of getting on the interstate and is quickly in standstill traffic. She flinches as her phone vibrates. It's Justin, and she ends the call without even letting it ring out. At eight p.m. on the dot, she turns on the radio to hear the hourly updates.

The news makes her more anxious, but she listens to the reporter speak. "There's been only a few reported cases, but there's looting taking place in North Charleston and Charleston. Right now it's isolated, but the fear is that it will spread. Traffic is making it difficult for law enforcement to quickly respond, and according to a source in the police department, they're getting so many 9-1-1 calls that they're transferring many less urgent calls to operators at nearby departments."

Anna can see just what the news is talking about. There's an ambulance in the left lane with its lights whirling, but it's moving at the same slow speed as the traffic.

"The governor still has not ordered a mandatory evacuation for any county on the coast in the direct path of Hurricane Charlie. Today, he chose instead to declare a state of emergency and wait until tomorrow's forecast before deciding if evacuations are necessary. Charleston's mayor said today that the governor's inaction was 'partisan punishment' aimed at the city and urged residents to move inland as soon as possible.

"This storm has sparked debate about whether it's time to adjust the Saffir-Simpson Hurricane Wind Scale. Many climate scientists are saying it doesn't go *high* enough to properly categorize a storm as powerful as Charlie. With sustained wind speeds currently clocked at over one hundred and eighty miles per hour, Charlie should be ranked as a category six hurricane. The storm is projected to be the strongest hurricane to make landfall in the United States in nearly one hundred years. On the phone we have—"

Anna turns off the radio.

It seems like the fear has finally worked. The city has gotten the memo. This storm isn't going to weaken or change course drastically enough to not be devastating. Now everyone is moving inland at once.

Anna gets off at the next exit and takes side streets the rest of the way. She gets to a slightly industrial area and knows she's close. There are hotels—all empty—and then warehouses with their vast parking lots vacant.

She takes a right and pulls up to a one-story building. The parking lot isn't completely empty. There's a van there, but that doesn't mean there's anybody here.

She has to be careful to stay off any security cameras. She doesn't scope out the building. She'll have to do that on foot. For now, she parks next to a dumpster two businesses over. If the police show up and her car is right out front, she'll be toast.

She puts on a black sweatshirt and slips on a face mask, but as she walks towards her target building, she realizes she could be wearing a neon vest and still nobody would spot her. There's no one around for a quarter mile.

She gets to the front door of the building and reads the words above it:

Charleston County Coroner's Office

She's already on camera. She ducks around and starts walking the sides of the building. All the windows are at ground level. It won't be difficult to break in. She shines her flashlight inside to see if there are any burglary sensors on the glass, but there don't appear to be any. This is looking far easier than she imagined. She doesn't even have to climb anything.

She chooses a back window and grabs a large stone that sits in the mulch landscaping. Then she smashes the glass.

It's louder than she thought it would be, but with the wind and the nearby interstate, she figures she's safe.

She uses the rock to knock the glass that's still hanging in the frame so she won't cut herself climbing in. She can't leave blood or fingerprints. Even with the hurricane, this crime will probably be investigated, and it's definitely a felony.

When the glass is gone, she puts her palms on the frame and pulls herself in. Her boots crunch the glass under her feet.

No alarm blares.

She's in an office and opens the door to the hall, stepping into it. She flinches when the lights suddenly turn on. She's about to bolt when she realizes they're motion activated. Still, it makes her nervous.

If there are motion sensors for the lights, are there others that could detect her after-hours presence?

It's too late to have second thoughts. The police are distracted enough. If there is ever a time to do this, it's tonight.

She needs to find the morgue. All the doors she passes are offices. She makes it to the front, where there's another camera. This one has a little red light inside its black dome. *Do they all have that?* Anna wonders. *Or is that red light indicating some kind of silent alarm?*

Her heart thumps and she picks up her pace. Offices, conference room, kitchenette.

What she can't find is where the bodies would be kept. She starts to feel like an idiot. Maybe this is just the coroner's office, and not the morgue itself. That must be somewhere else. She opens a fire door with a big bar as a handle and smiles when she sees stairs.

Of course, the morgue would be somewhere cooler. She trots down the epoxied steps and opens another door. There's a small room with a desk, and beyond that another door with big windows on either side of it. On the other side of those windows shines the stainless steel inside of the morgue.

The lights have been left on here. She goes to the door and says a prayer before turning the handle.

It's unlocked and she's in.

What surprises her first is the sound. It's coming from the wall, with its square doors where the cadavers are kept. It's the hum of a refrigerator. She walks to the wall and puts her hand on the stainless steel. It's cold to the touch. The whole wall is refrigerated. It makes sense. The bodies have to be kept cold. Still, it's surprising. The room itself is probably cold enough to deter any decomposition. Anna shivers under her sweatshirt.

Out in the open, there are two corpses on their cooling boards hidden under white sheets. Anna has been rushing, but now she slows. She lifts the corner of the closest sheet, revealing the hairy ankle of a man. She sets it back down gently and walks to where the other body lies.

This close, she can tell just by looking that it's a woman. There's a Post-it-note on a steel tray of scalpels, saws, and other autopsy equipment. It reads:

Forensics is coming by for a full day with her. Do not touch.

She has to resist the urge to turn and run. It's the body that was found on Church Street. Anna has no desire to see that smile again, especially in the flesh.

She grabs the sheet and rips it away quickly.

The corpse is horribly pale beneath the fluorescent light. Anna looks at her for a moment. The body hasn't been touched at all since the pictures were taken. The marble eyes are still there. Even the pins remain, holding her cheeks up in a sick smile.

Anna gently rotates the girl's left foot. There, just below the ball of her ankle, is a little crescent moon tattooed on her skin.

It's Sylvie, but suddenly the constant doubts slip into her head. The tattoo is far brighter than she remembers it. Anna chews her lip. She composes herself, silences her doubts with logic. The tattoo's altered shade is probably just because it's juxtaposed with her paper-pale skin.

She looks back to the face and sees the little red letters that she had seen in the picture that the girl in the park, Dylan, had shown her.

It's obvious there's something under the makeup that powders her face. CPD Homicide hasn't bothered to take a look yet. Terry and forensics apparently had better things to do this weekend than get a start on this case.

Anna needs something to wipe the foundation off the body's face. She looks around for some kind of cloth or paper towel and sees a roll by the sink. She takes a step over, when suddenly, she hears a door shut and a radio squawk.

Her heart jumps and her eyes go wide.

Cops.

Anna panics. She rotates in a full circle looking for an exit, but the room only has the one.

She turns to the cadaver wall and, without thinking, begins to unlatch every single door. There's only nine, and she's quickly done. While unlatched, the doors stay closed. Anna bends down to the lower right square in the wall of nine and pulls the handle.

She scuttles inside and hears voices in the room outside the morgue. She still has to close the cadaver door from the inside, and there's not exactly a handle for the dead. She pushes her fingers on the corner of the inside and pulls it towards her.

Just as the door to the morgue opens and the cops' voices become clear, the little door shuts.

Oxygen

With Anna's head towards the door, she can hear them quite clearly.

"Someone took this sheet off," says a man's voice. "They were in here."

"How long ago did the alarm go off?" There's another voice.

Two cops, she figures. One squad car.

"Twenty minutes."

"They could be gone."

There's a pause. "Whoa, whoa, whoa."

Anna's heart stops, and she cringes. They've seen the unlatched doors.

"Look at this girl's eyes! They weren't fucking kidding, were they?"

"Wow."

"What's on her face?"

"Don't touch anything. Come on."

She hears them go quiet as a dispatcher speaks over a radio. The voice is scratchy, and it seems like the cops can't quite tell what's being said either.

"Did she say arson?"

"Let's make this quick."

She can tell they're walking around the room, and then she hears the question she fears most. "Don't you think these are supposed to be latched?"

They come so close she can hear their boots on the floor. There's the sudden noise of one of the doors being opened. They shut it quickly and then open the door directly above her.

"Whoa!" an officer says. "This one stinks." He slams it. A voice comes over one of their radios again. All Anna can make out is "all units."

"What do you think?" asks one cop to another.

"Let's just check these, give the offices another quick sweep, and get out of here."

Anna begins scooting towards the back of the drawer she's in. It's much deeper than she thought, at least seven feet.

She listens as more of the cadaver doors are opened and shut as they're searched. Then it's her turn.

The cop opens it, but she's in the bottom drawer and it's apparent he's tall. He shines the flashlight in halfway for what may be half a second and then slams the door again.

Anna's elated. That's it.

They're done.

She begins to hear clicking sounds, but Anna's too stupefied by not being found to even think of it. In fact, she has to try not to laugh.

She's able to make out the sound of the door to the morgue shutting behind the officers. She waits another minute and crawls to the front. She pushes against the door, but it doesn't give. She frowns and pushes again, and then as swift as a bolt of lightning, she realizes the clicking sound was all the latches being flipped.

She's been locked in. In a space this small, it's not the cold that will kill her; it'll be the lack of oxygen.

She panics and pounds on the door. She'd rather be a felon than dead. "Hey!" Anna yells. "I'm in here!"

But there's no response.

The police are already gone.

Blackout

She checks her phone immediately. By some miracle, she has a single bar. If she calls 9-1-1, Anna thinks she'll probably end up on an episode of *World's Dumbest Criminals.*

Instead, now that she's had time to calm down, she looks at her contacts.

Her first try is Jake, and despite her circumstances, she's still a little shocked when the call goes straight to a robotic voice.

"We're sorry, the number you have dialed is currently unavailable."

He blocked her number.

She curses and keeps scrolling. She can't remember the last time she looked through her contacts, and the short list depresses her.

She watches her phone battery tick down. It won't last as long in the cold. Justin might come to her aid, but the thought unsettles her. She already feels junior to him because of how swiftly he put together Hannah at the trailer park. He'll probably think this was some desperate move by her to try to get ahead in the case after she ditched him at the mayor's speech.

From the moment she opened her phone, she knew who she was going to call. She says a little prayer and calls Professor Geller. The call doesn't connect right away, and her stomach sinks. If she doesn't have service, she's dead. Finally, it starts to ring.

And ring.

His voicemail must've been one more ring away when finally, he picks up.

"Anna, I'm sorry, but I still haven't got to the riddle. I'm with my mom and—"

"That's not why I'm calling. Can you hear me?"

"Yes, I can hear you."

"Listen . . ." She takes a deep breath before speaking. "I'm in the basement of the Charleston County Coroner's Office. It's off Bridge View drive. You can Google it. I broke in, and I'm locked in one of the cadaver thingies in the wall. There's a window already broken on the side of the building."

"Okay, okay, okay. Is this a joke?"

"No. I don't know how long I have, but if I don't get out of here, I'll asphyxiate."

"You need to call 9-1-1. I can call them for you."

"No!" Anna says in a panic. She wants to cry. "Please, please don't call the police. I'd be in a lot of trouble. I know I'm asking a lot. I know this isn't very cool of me to spring this on you. But can you please, please do this for me?"

"You want me to come get you out?"

"Please."

"Wouldn't I get in a lot of trouble, then?"

Anna is slow to answer while she thinks. "Well . . . the police have been here already. It's why I hid, but they're gone. I promise they are. There's too much going on in the city for them to spare a squad car to stake out here. Just don't park right out front."

There's a long pause on the other line and for a moment she thinks she lost the call.

"And there's no way out?"

"None. I'm locked in."

She hears him mutter.

"Okay, Anna. I'll be there as soon as I can."

"Thank you," Anna closes her eyes and whispers. "Oh, and Professor . . ."

"Yes?"

"Make sure you wear a mask."

He sighs. "Just sit tight."

When the call ends, Anna thinks about going online to try to calculate how long her oxygen will last, but she can't bring herself to search it. The answer might make her hyperventilate.

She sticks her phone in the waistband of her pants to try to keep it warm to preserve the battery and curls into a ball. She lets her cheek rest against the cold steel. This wouldn't be the worst way to die. Anna knows she'd probably pass out before she even realizes she's running out of air.

Hannah's body has to be in this wall with her. She pictures her body above her, laid out peacefully on the cooling board. Gone for years but supposedly only dead for days. She pictures where Hannah had been for all that time.

She's heard stories in the national news about girls who are found chained up in basements or storage containers who have been there for years.

Sometimes it's decades.

To think Hannah was somewhere behind every memory Anna has had for the last four years. When Anna was living, laughing, or just watching TV, Hannah had always been somewhere.

Tortured. Screaming. Raped.

Anna begins to cry, but she doesn't wipe the tears away. She lets them fall, and when she doesn't feel them on her cheeks, she remembers she's still wearing a mask. She pulls it down to her chin and cries harder, wondering what she did to deserve this.

What did she do to be chased by a monster that came from her own imagination?

October 2012

From working after school and through the summer at a sandwich shop, Anna has enough money for a computer.

It's a two-hundred-dollar Lenovo that's been refurbished. Some of the keys stick, and the screen doesn't get very bright, but it gets internet and more importantly, she can write on it.

That's what she's doing this hot afternoon when there's a pounding on the screen door.

Anna is in the middle of a paragraph. She whispers to herself to not let the knocking distract her from finishing her lines.

"Anna!" someone yells from out front. She can hear footsteps on the grass, and then there's another knock. This time on her window.

"Anna! I can see you."

She turns from her computer to see Hannah standing outside her dirty window. Tess is a few steps behind her.

She stops typing and goes and opens her window.

"Hey."

"Are you avoiding us? I texted you like four times."

Anna shakes her head quickly. "No, sorry. I've just been busy."

"Look, we love you. I'm sure you want to be real rich and fancy one day, but nobody I like does homework on a Saturday."

"It's not homework— "

Hannah ignores her and grabs on to the window frame. "We're coming in." She scrabbles up the side of the house, and Anna helps pull her in. Then she does the same for Tess, who's even less graceful of a climber.

The two girls sit on Anna's bed, and Hannah slings her backpack off and starts digging through it. "Check out what I got." She pulls out a plastic pint of schnapps and wiggles it.

"My cousin is staying with us, and he leaves this shit around. Want some?"

Anna looks over her shoulder to her laptop and then at the bottle. She takes it without a word, spins off the cap, and takes a mouthful. It's syrupy and peachy but still bites. She exhales through her open mouth and hands it to Hannah. Then she sits across from them in the chair she'd been writing in.

"We see your mom isn't home. Care if we hang out here for a while?"

"No that's cool. Just dip out the window if she gets back."

"So." Tess leans forward and sets her palms on her knees. "We have something to discuss."

Hannah gets animated as if suddenly remembering something. "Yes!" She tosses the pint on the bed. "Anna, were you ever going to tell us?"

"Tell you what?"

"About Frank?"

Anna shakes her head. "We're just friends."

"Uh-huh," Hannah says incredulously. "How big is his dick?"

Anna blushes and starts to laugh. She flexes her bottom lip into her top one and tilts her head to one shoulder—an expression that suggests it's impressive.

Hannah bursts from the bed and slaps her shoulder. "How could you not tell us!"

Anna flinches. For a moment she thinks Hannah is mad until she sees the smirk beneath her excitement.

"I don't—"

"I thought you'd die a prude. That you'd wait for marriage. Blessed be!" Hannah extends her arms towards the ceiling. "My girl is a slut!"

Anna is shaking her head. She looks at Tess, who does the same with a smile. Hannah, meanwhile, is humming some kind of hymn while doing a little dance.

"Dolly could *run* this trailer park with those cannon balls!"

"You can't be that drunk." Anna gestures to the schnapps. "You hardly put a dent in that."

Hannah wraps an arm around Anna's shoulders. "Can't a girl be high on life? Can't a girl just be *happy* for you? Celebration time. Shots!"

Tess is leaning back on the bed on her elbows. She picks up the bottle and hands it to Hannah. "You first."

They all take turns drinking and then are quiet for a minute while they scrunch their faces and bite their tongues to keep the nasty liquor down.

"How about you invite him out tonight? We could all go to The Station and drink there."

"So you can harass him with questions?"

"No. I promise I'll be chill. I'll act like everything is normal. I just want to see you with him. Holding hands and kissing and shit. You're so cute, Anna. I want to see that."

"You creep," says Tess. "You probably want to watch them bang."

Hannah quiets. She doesn't find the joke funny, but she's not mad. Anna thinks it's because Hannah genuinely likes to see her happy.

"I'll text him."

Hannah taps Anna's ankle with her foot. "What're you doing right now? Want to come sunbathing with us in the meantime?"

"I don't know."

"Come on. You never come."

Anna's uncomfortable being naked around them, but plays it off like she's afraid she'll burn easy.

"Come be trailer trash with us. What doesn't sound awesome about lying on the roof of a mobile home and smoking cigarettes nude?"

Anna points over her shoulder. "I've got to finish up some work."

Hannah frowns and walks behind Anna to look at her computer. "What the hell kind of homework is this?"

"Uh . . ." Anna stutters. "It's not."

"Not homework?"

"Yeah."

"Eight thousand, three hundred and forty-seven words?" Hannah reads from the screen and raises her brow. "And it's not homework?"

Anna has kept her hobbies and her friends separate. Hannah and Tess don't read books or watch the kind of nerdy TV that she does. "Um, I write fiction. It's for this online forum."

"What?" Suddenly Hannah's eyes go wide. "Oh my God, are you one of those smut writers?"

"No, no. I don't write smut. It's true crime." Anna turns to the computer and goes to her blog page that has all the parts she's published. "Serial killers and stuff. I have this character, Grace. She's a private detective. She solves crimes. I have more than six hundred followers."

"Get out of here. You've been living a double life and not telling us? Wait, do you get paid for this?"

"No. Not at all. But my readers, they really like this story. That's kind of like its own payment."

"You dork. Why didn't you tell us?"

"Because you'd call me a dork."

"Yeah, but only lovingly. Wow." Hannah takes over the track pad and starts scrolling through the stories herself. "You're going to get out of here."

"What?" says Anna.

Hannah looks her in the eye. "When I'm chasing my kids around this trailer park, you'll be in Bangkok or something. I don't know. You're going places."

"Bangkok?"

"Yeah. I don't know. China is big right now. Important shit will be happening there."

"Bangkok is in Thailand."

"See! Exactly! You're getting out of here. I mean, seriously, who knows that kind of shit?"

Hannah looks at Tess for reassurance, and she shrugs. "You can bang this cock."

"Exactly!" Hannah looks back to the screen, "Exactly. Let's see. Part twelve." She clicks on the link.

"Oh," Anna says, tapping her shoulder. "You can read?"

"Shut up." Hannah squints while she scrolls. "So, what's this story about?"

"It's about Grace, really. The cases change every few parts or so, but her character is consistent."

"What's the first case?"

"A serial killer is loose, and he's killing girls."

"Well, duh."

Anna bites her lip. She sucks at synopses. When it comes to summing up a story, it's not one of her strong suits.

"Well, nobody knows how he's killing them. The girls go missing first, and none of them has ever been found. So, it's up to Grace to do the work of the police, essentially. She was hired by one of the families."

"So what's the motive? What happens to the girls?"

Anna takes over the computer and scrolls to a passage that she highlights. "They all have the same story they tell before they go missing. They're walking home alone, when suddenly, there's a flash. Somebody is taking their picture. In the days afterwards, they see a man, always at a distance, following them."

"Gross. Why's he do that?"

"Do what?"

"Take their pictures?"

"Oh. I guess as a memento. Or because it scares them. And that's what he likes."

"You've got a sick mind, Dolly Klein. How's your story end?"

"I don't know," says Anna, staring at the screen. "I haven't finished it yet."

Rage

Anna's face is wet with tears. Her fingers have gone numb from the cold. As she relaxes, she begins to feel like this would be a fitting death. She could just fall asleep forever in this morgue, right next to her friends.

But then she pictures the mortician opening up the cadaver door to find her dead inside. The convenience of her corpse already being laid out on a cooling board makes her laugh.

"Oh, that's an easy one," he'd say. *"Why can't everyone do that?"*

She's crying while she laughs aloud. Maybe her body is beginning to feel the effects from the lack of oxygen.

She pictures what Hannah would say to her. She wouldn't want her to die; she'd want her to fight until the very end. But what is there to do? She's drifting off, and not even conscious enough to realize it, when suddenly, there's noise outside.

She perks up. Stars scatter across her vision. She starts banging on the door madly. "Hello? I'm in here!"

There are footsteps, and then blinding light as the little square door opens.

"Jesus." Geller bends down and offers his hand.

She takes it and pulls her mask back over her face. Anna stumbles a little while she stands.

"Should I even ask?" he mumbles under his own mask. "You're freezing."

"I'm okay." She's staring at the floor fighting a headrush as she says it. "Thank you. Thank you so much."

"Come on." He ushers her forward. "We need to go."

"Wait, wait. I'm not dying." Her blood begins to level. Her vision clears.

Geller looks her in the eye. "Anna, you don't need a hospital?"

"No." She leans forward and whispers, "And don't use my name."

His eyes light up in fear and he looks at the cameras in the ceiling. "Are these closed circuit?"

"They must be. If someone was watching, then the police would've known where I hid."

"How long were you in that thing?"

"I don't know. Forty minutes?"

"Well, come on now. We still need to get going."

"You saved my life. I'm grateful. Please, please don't think I'm not. But there's something here . . ." Anna trails off, looking at Sylvie's corpse. She's suddenly very light-headed again. "Something here I still have to do."

Geller looks at her like she's insane. She begins to realize that this looks like she needs serious psychiatric help. She has to explain. She speaks quietly in case the cameras can pick up audio. "That girl, the one they found yesterday . . . It's my friend. The one I told you about that went missing years ago."

Geller looks confused, but he's a smart man and puts it together quickly. He turns over his shoulder to the body with the sheet removed. The police who searched the morgue didn't even bother to cover her back up.

"And this is her?"

"That's her."

"Your best friend. The missing girl. Sylvie Platt?"

Anna just nods. She looks into Geller's eyes. How did he remember her name? She last mentioned Sylvie to him years ago. Did he have an interest in the case? Her stomach clenches. Her eyes narrow. A mantra replays in her mind: *Trust no one.* She takes a step from him and pats the knife in her pocket. It feels like a new low. She's ready to stab the last person she cares about. This case has turned her into a wild animal.

"Why didn't you tell me this when I saw you this morning?"

"I didn't know for sure. I didn't know it was her until about forty minutes ago."

"Okay." Geller breathes a big sigh in relief, as if he has realized Anna is not in the middle of a mental breakdown. "Okay. I'm not so sure about your means, but you found out it's her. So now . . ." He gestures to the door with both hands. "Can I persuade you to go?"

"That's not all," Anna says, walking towards Sylvie's body. Her heart rate quickens. So far, this has been the hardest clue to find. She figures it was supposed to be this way. What's written on her skin is meant for Anna to see.

It's the next piece in the puzzle. A map. A riddle.

An answer.

Anna stops next to the corpse, and Geller stays put where he's been standing. "I don't want to look at that."

"You don't have to." Anna steps to the sink for the roll of paper towels. She wets some and comes back over.

"What are you doing?" Geller holds out his hands. "That body is still evidence."

"Evidence I have to see."

Anna is revealing a side of herself she's otherwise kept secret.

"I came because you were in distress. But you're acting like a criminal."

"You can leave."

She turns and starts rubbing Sylvie's cheek with the paper towel, but she doesn't hear him go. She has to scrub hard to get off the foundation.

"What is that?" Geller's curiosity has won, and he suddenly stands close over her shoulder.

"I don't . . ." says Anna. The letters turn to words. The same word. Repeated over and over and over again, dozens of times. It's on her cheeks and her chin. Anna stops wiping it away. It reads: *Cheese.*

"Cheese?" says Anna. "Cheese?" she repeats looking at the word that's scrawled across Sylvie's face. She brings her gaze up to Geller's. He touches her shoulder gently.

"Let's go, Anna."

"Cheese?" she says again, wiping the last of the makeup that's on Sylvie's forehead. "What the hell is that supposed to—"

She can see what was under the make up on her forehead now. Her mouth opens in disbelief. One word is written as large as it can be while still fitting on her forehead. It reads: *Say.*

"Say cheese?" Anna whispers, looking down at the corpse's pinned smile.

It isn't a clue, or a puzzle.

It's a taunt.

"That can't be it." She turns Sylvie's body over, looking for more writing, more makeup, but there's nothing.

"Say cheese!?" Anna yells. "Say!" She kicks the metal cart with the autopsy tools, and it goes clanking across the room. "Fucking cheese!?"

Anna flies into a rage. She tosses the paper towels, grabs a metal bowl for evidence parts, and hurls it into the wall.

"Anna," Geller says quietly while she kicks and curses.

"This *sick* fuck! I'll kill him! I'll—" she screams. "Kill him!"

"Hey!" He grips her shoulder, and she freezes. "We need to go."

She exhales through her mouth, out of breath. She's still so enraged that she almost hits his hand off her arm, but suddenly she begins to feel embarrassed.

Geller's eyes are fearful. She sees him for what he is—a dorky academic, miles out of his element. She knows he's never seen this side of her. He didn't even know it existed.

"I'm sorry."

"Come on." He walks to the door.

"Wait," she says, still angry. She takes a deep breath and says it softer. "Wait."

She walks to the refrigerated wall and starts opening the square doors. When she sees a female's foot in one of the top left drawers, she pulls out the cooling board. Even though the corpse is refrigerated, it still kind of smells.

On it is the body they found in the trailer park. She studies it while avoiding looking at her empty eye sockets.

Hannah didn't have any tattoos. Anna tries to remember her moles, her scars, but nothing jumps out at her. Suddenly, she feels stupid. She lifts the body's top lip to reveal a slight gap between her two front teeth.

No doubt it's Hannah.

"This is another . . ." She's about to tell him something she hadn't told anybody, that the first Flash Girl, Hannah Greenwood, was also her friend. But the sound of a closing door interrupts her.

Geller had left.

It's not until now that her actions become apparent to her. She just used one of the last people on earth who gives a shit about her as an accessory in a felony. She's let this case consume her. Still, she doesn't chase after him.

She checks Hannah's back first in case there's anything written there, and then she gently pushes the body back into its drawer.

Then she goes to the table that Sylvie is laid out on. It's on wheels, and she disengages the wheel locks with her feet. Then she wheels it towards the cadaver wall, opens the door next to where Hannah is, and pulls out the cooling board so that it hangs out like a long metal tongue.

If the storm hits like they say it will, Anna thinks the basement of the morgue will flood. The bodies shouldn't even be here.

Sylvie's corpse is stiff and light, and Anna moves her so she's on the tray. She plucks both pins from her cheeks, then she pushes the tray into the wall and latches the door.

She inspects the pins in her palm, hoping they might be some kind of clue, but there's nothing interesting about them. She tosses them onto the table where Sylvie had been placed and leaves the morgue.

Cool Down

When she crosses the parking lot away from the coroner's building, a dark figure approaches her from a line of bushes. She panics for a moment before realizing it's Geller.

He rubs the back of his neck anxiously. "I'm sorry. I didn't mean to wuss out. It's just . . . if they find out it was you in there, they're going to check your phone records. They're going to check all the cameras on the freeways and the businesses on the way here. They're going to know it was me who helped you out. Right?"

There's a nervousness in his voice, and it doesn't fill Anna with dread so much as guilt. "If this storm hits half as strong as they say it will, this building will be gone by Monday. The basement will flood. It will be fine."

He nods and crumples his mask in his fist. "I have a family," he chuckles. "I mean, what on earth was I thinking?"

"You saved me from a jail cell. Hell, I'm so stubborn I probably would've died before calling the police. Geller, you saved my *life*."

"Okay," he says, as if knowing she's just trying to make him feel better.

He had taken Anna's advice and not parked directly outside the front entrance. His truck is a lot over. They walk there together, and when they're several hundred feet from the coroner's office, Anna stops and sits on the curb of the parking lot.

It's lightly raining, little more than a mist. There's honking from the highway and sirens wailing all through the city. Anna is tired from her anger. She sits so her knees are up close to her chest and leans her head against them.

She can see that Geller doesn't stop walking. He goes all the way to his truck and opens his bed cover. He reaches over the tailgate for something and then starts back towards her.

He extends his arm out, and Anna slowly looks up from her feet.

It's dark in the parking lot. She can't exactly tell what it is. It crinkles and shines.

"Take it."

Anna reaches out and takes it gently. When it's close enough so that she can see it, she looks at Geller. "Cheetos?"

"You should eat something. I don't know."

Anna starts to laugh. "You keep a snack-sized bag of Cheetos in your truck bed?"

"There's not just Cheetos. It's one of those variety packs. Sometimes, the kid gets hungry on the road. And my wife. They're for emergencies."

"You didn't have to get so defensive. I just think it's funny." Anna pulls the bag open and eats a few.

They're both silent for a moment while they listen to the city panic around them.

"A secret, by the way," says Geller suddenly.

"What?"

"Your riddle. I read it again driving over here. I think the answer to some of it is a secret."

"How so?"

He repeats some of the lines. "'I am had by all, but not by some. Called a name, but not my one,'" he sighs. "That first bit, I think it's trying to say while everybody has secrets, everybody's are different. Like some people's lies are less severe. And the 'Called a name, but not my one' part . . . Think about it. Secrets are called secrets. They aren't actually given the name of what that secret is about."

Anna looks into the distance while she considers it. "Could be."

"Anyway, that's what I got thus far. You should give it some thought."

"I will."

"But . . . I feel like it fits. It reads like someone's secrets are following them. Do you think it was left for the law enforcement detectives trying to solve the case?"

She thinks of bumbling Terry and shakes her head. "No."

Anna is about to say it was meant for her but lets her mouth hang open. The answer of secret makes perfect sense. The facts she's tried to keep in the dark are finally catching up with her.

Arrival

Geller offered her a ride, but Anna declined. After she finished the bag of Cheetos, they went separate ways.

Now as she drives home, she's fretting about how much evidence she left behind.

She left no prints. Had her hair and her face covered. And she'd been with Hannah's body earlier, so if any of her DNA is found in that morgue room, any good lawyer could easily argue that it was transferred to Hannah when still at the trailer park and then fell off in the morgue.

She's thinking too much of it. The county coroner's building is an unsheltered structure with a clear wind path leading to its front door. It would be leveled come Monday.

The future doesn't exactly matter much to Anna anyway.

It's all coming to a head.

When she gets back to her apartment, her mood immediately worsens. She had forgotten why she'd left in such a rush in the first place. Forgotten about the noises upstairs.

She stares at the building as she turns off the ignition, pulls out her knife, and flicks the blade open. She runs her thumb against the steel as she thinks.

It's times like this that Anna wishes she had a gun. The only reason she doesn't is because when she's fantasized about finding this killer, she's pictured plunging a knife into his guts.

A gun would be far too quick.

Impersonal.

Pulling the trigger harder makes no difference. Anna wants to stab and twist, but now that she's closer to that dream than ever, she realizes a gun would increase her odds of winning. Then again, she always pictured putting the puzzle together on her own. Finding where he lived. Slipping through a window and waiting in the dark.

She didn't think she would be the one to be hunted.

Anna opens the door and slams it shut. The entire apartment building is black. She didn't leave a light on, and neither did the Shepards, but still, the stairwell light should be on.

She turns on all the light switches in the entry hall and doesn't waste time heading to the third floor. When she's at her door, she looks both ways before bending to inspect the tape. She takes her phone out at the same time and compares the pictures she took.

The tape is in the exact same place. Unless it was replaced down to the millimeter, the door hasn't been opened.

She enters her apartment and locks the door behind her. Even with the tape in place, she still searches every room and closet. She feels like a little girl as she bends to look under her bed, but it's worth the peace of mind.

The windows are all locked as they were when she left, and being on the third floor, someone would need a comically long ladder to reach them.

Despite the hour, she puts on a pot of coffee, changes into comfier clothes, and heads into the little office.

Tonight, she is going over everything.

She knows whoever is behind these murders has read the stories she posted when she was a teenager, but when Hannah first went missing with the same surrounding circumstances, Anna panicked.

She deleted every part. Every document. She even deleted her account off the website she wrote on.

There's not a night she doesn't grit her teeth about it. It was tens of thousands of words. There are entire parts she's certain she doesn't remember. The answers could've been written in her own story, and she's never been able to go back to check.

It's left her little to give to the police.

There was no evidence any of the three Flash Girls had ever actually had their pictures taken. Anna had tried explaining everything to the police just once after Tess vanished too; she was taken into custody on suspicion of drug use. Her story sounded like pure lunacy.

When she got the chance to make her case on the podcast, she toned it back. She didn't mention that she knew the missing girls other than Sylvie. She presented nothing but the facts, but that got her nowhere.

There were three missing girls, and while people knew Tess and Hannah were friends, there was no link to Sylvie other than Anna. Telling the full truth makes her sound insane, or worse, she's suspected of being behind the disappearances herself.

People knew about Sylvie Platt. But the problem with her case is that she had never told anyone that someone had taken her picture before she went missing, because no one ever did. The fact Anna says so is just another one of her lies.

She leans back and sighs. The key to solving this lies in her past. A past that she's been trying to forget, but to figure this out she must dwell on every little detail she can remember.

Anna thinks back to before anyone went missing. Before the drugs and the depression and the paranoia. There was one day in particular that put her on this path. That maybe if it hadn't happened, none of this would've either.

April 2015

Anna is almost fifteen and seriously grounded for the first time in her life.

She had pushed the envelope and stolen a bottle of vodka out of the freezer. She had hoped her mom would think she misplaced it or never had it to begin with, but she was more diligent when it came to keeping track of her booze than she was her cigarettes.

At this age, Anna will have a drink or two. Enough to liven herself up and rid her of social anxiety, but not enough to be sloppy or sick. It was a waste to even try to take a whole bottle.

Lesson learned.

Her mom won't leave Anna alone in the house, and today, she has some errands downtown. She takes Anna with her, and when her mom parks in a small parking lot next to one of the tallest apartment buildings, she tells Anna to wait in the car.

Anna doesn't know what she's doing—buying drugs or seeing a boyfriend. It doesn't matter to her. When her mom disappears inside, Anna gets out of the car and starts walking.

Her mom will yell and scream if she's not there when she gets back, but Anna isn't bothered by it anymore. The freedom is worth the abuse.

It's a Thursday afternoon after school, and she wants to explore the city. She ends up on King Street, and to escape the heat, she ducks into every interesting shop she spots.

She's watched closely by the clerks. Since she's been hanging out with Hannah and Tess, she's started dressing more alternatively. Her jeans are ripped, and her shirts don't reach down to her pants, so a sliver of her stomach always shows.

Anna just smiles as she's watched. She'll steal from Walgreens or Walmart. Corporate conglomerates who can get screwed for all she cares, but she won't shoplift from a ma-and-pop shop.

She looks at touristy T-shirts and thousand-dollar cowgirl boots. Eventually, she wanders into an art gallery.

It's cooler in here than in many of the tourist shops and twice as quiet. There are no bells on the door or radio playing. The sound from outside evaporates into silence as the door shuts behind her.

She slows her pace and gazes at the paintings. There are seascapes and palm trees and self-portraits. When the entrance hall opens to a square room, she sees there's a couple dozen people there. There are some tourists, but another large group stands by a set of paintings. There must be some kind of exhibit.

She starts to circle the room. What fascinates her just as much as the paintings are their prices.

She hasn't seen any for less than five hundred dollars, and most are in the thousands. She's thinking about what it's like to have that kind of money to spent on art, when she suddenly stops walking. She's seen something. Not on the walls, but in the crowd.

There's a girl her age, standing as stoically as the adults around her. They're all listening to a woman speak while she gestures at paintings.

It takes Anna a minute to put it together, but when she sees the girl's flushed cheeks, her heart erupts.

It's Sylvie.

She must've sensed she was being looked at, because she turns to look at Anna.

Anna can't whip her head away fast enough. She's sure Sylvie thinks she's a freak. She probably tells the story about the kid she was starting to be friends with who suddenly stapled their teacher's face. Anna turns so quickly she bumps into somebody.

"Sorry," she says without looking and makes towards the front door. She speeds up her pace on the sidewalk, but she can hardly get a few steps away when the door barges open again.

"Anna!"

Anna cringes, and she holds her hands out, ready to try to explain herself—she was just a kid, her mom hit her—when Sylvie rushes in to her and gives her a hug. Anna doesn't hug back.

Her arms hang at her sides. "Hey."

"I never thought I'd see you again." Sylvie is much taller than the last time she saw her, and she almost has to look down at Anna while she talks to her. "I tried to find you. I called the number in the school directory. Your mom said you weren't there. She said you were sent to boarding school."

Anna is speechless. She wants to be angry with her mom for lying, but she's too relieved with Sylvie's reaction.

"You don't care about what happened?"

"With Mrs. Riley?"

"Yeah . . ."

"My dad always says poke a dog enough and it bites. I was worried about you. You're a good person."

When Sylvie says that, Anna's shoulders sink. It's something she has never been quite sure of. But if someone like Sylvie thinks she's a good person, maybe she is.

"I need your number," says Sylvie.

Anna is a little perplexed by how quickly she was able to get outside. "Did . . . did you run after me?"

"No. I sprinted."

Sylvie hands Anna her phone, and she puts her info into her contacts. Anna's still typing when she feels her own phone vibrate in her pocket. She knows it's her mom. She's probably furious that Anna's not back at the car and there'll be hell to pay.

Sylvie points towards the art gallery. "You should have dinner with us sometime. My parents would love to have you over. I live just a few blocks from here."

Anna looks around, uncertain. She knows Sylvie's rich; she was gifted, yet not on a penny of scholarship at the Covenant of Christ. Anna's not sure she has nice enough clothes to wear to a dinner in this neighborhood.

"This area is kind of far away from me."

"I could pick you up with my mom! We can work it out. Don't worry about that."

Anna's eyes widen. The last thing she wants Sylvie to see is the shack she lives in with a tarp covering half the roof.

"I can get a ride, too. That's okay." She quickly changes the subject.

"My mom's calling. I should probably go," says Anna. "But text me?"

Sylvie suddenly hugs her again. "I'll text you tonight. Uh." Sylvie stomps her foot and shakes her head. Her face brightens with her beaming smile. "Anna Klein. It's so good to see you again."

When Anna's walking back, she's on cloud nine. She thinks no matter how angry her mom is, this feeling won't fade.

Little does she know how her mother is done with the physical abuse. Anna has grown too big to be so easily beaten by an aging drunk. Today, her mom's abuse begins to get creative.

When Anna gets in sight of her mother, she begins to scream. There are pedestrians on the sidewalk who stop and stare, and Anna reddens.

"You little shit! Sneaking off without the decency to even be here when I get back. Get in the car! I shoulda let you take the bus. Maybe you would've met a man who would make you his problem."

Anna's in too good of a mood to quip back. "Sorry" is all she says while fastening her seat belt.

Her mom smells boozier than before. Anna curses quietly to herself. She should get out. Take the bus. Call her mom's plates in as a suspected DUI. But she doesn't; she's afraid. Until she's eighteen, she's worried she'll end up in a foster home if she tattles on her mother.

"Sorry. Yeah, sure. I bet you're sorry about stealing my booze, too. Sorry you got caught, that's all. Do you have any idea . . . I mean *any* idea whatsoever how hard I have to work to keep a roof over your head?"

Anna smirks. She just can't help it. Anna's mom doesn't work for a living. She collects checks.

"Yeah, Mom. You really put your back into it."

Her mom slams on the brakes, and Anna nearly hits her head on the dash before her seatbelt locks. "I could have given you up for adoption. I could have *aborted* you. I had money back then, you know. Before you needed books and food and a house with an extra bedroom."

Anna thinks that's a lie. Her mom was broke before she had her.

She'd been kicked out of her parents' house and living with older boyfriends she'd cycle through.

Anna can only be quiet for so long before she bites back. "Maybe you could still afford those things if you were able to keep my dad around." Anna had heard that her father didn't stick around long after she was born. That her mom would scream at him through the night. She had gone sober during her pregnancy but leaped off the wagon with an Olympian effort the moment she could give Anna formula.

Things might've been better if she had her father in her life, Anna just didn't know. She knew he wasn't reliable. Maybe he wasn't a yeller like her mom, but he was still the kind of guy to ditch his kid completely.

Anna's mom is quiet for a moment. She didn't explode and take the bait. Instead, she's thinking. A sly smile crosses her face. "You know what, Anna? Maybe it's time you met your father."

"What do you mean? I thought you said you didn't even know where he was."

"Oh." Her mom nods and takes a left when she should've gone right. "It's almost seven p.m. on a Thursday. I know *exactly* where your father is."

Anna is suddenly very uncomfortable. She shuts up and crosses her arms. She's always dreamed of meeting her dad. She's pictured him being blown away by the kind of young woman she's become. Someone who is nothing like her mother.

She daydreams about him apologizing for not being there. Explaining that her mom was just too much for him. Sure, he might be a deadbeat in some respects, but she thought maybe he had a heart. Anna does, so she must've gotten it from somewhere.

Now that she sees her mom is eager for her to meet him and prove some kind of point, Anna is not so sure things will go as she imagined.

They get on the highway headed east towards the interstate. Her mom rolls the windows down, turns the radio up, and lights a cigarette. She sings along to Peter Frampton. Her mom is in a fine mood, speeding in the left lane, while Anna's skin begins to itch with anxiety.

It's a half hour later when she takes an exit. They're already past the suburbs. The area they're in is all truck stops and biker bars and billboards against abortion.

She drives for only a few more minutes before pulling into a bar's parking lot. The building is a rectangle of concrete with neon beer signs shining in its dark windows. It's not late, but the parking lot is packed.

"Second shift just got off."

She gestures in the distance, and above the trees, Anna sees the strange metal geometry of a refinery. Waste stacks and five-story cooling towers.

"Come on." Her mom turns the car off and opens her door while Anna sits glued in the passenger seat. "Let's go meet your daddy."

She starts walking without checking to see if her daughter follows. When Anna finally gets out of the car, she trots to catch up.

Inside, it's loud. Rock blares over speakers and pool balls clack and men laugh with their heads tilted towards the ceiling.

"Let's see . . ." Her mom surveys the room. "Let me get a drink first." She already has cash in her palm as she heads to the bar.

Anna stays standing by the door. She wants to leave, and more so, she desperately wants her mother to come back and say that her dad's not here today. When her mom comes back, she doesn't have a glass, and it's not until Anna smells her that she realizes she already had a shot. "He's over there," her mom says, pointing at the pool table. "Stubble beard. Dirty shirt."

Anna sees exactly who she's talking about. A great many of these men are smiling, but this man is not.

She looks for similarities. His hair's the same sandy brown as hers, and he's not very tall. He looks deathly focused as he strokes his pool cue back and forth, and when he takes his shot, he does so with vicious power. The balls crack and run around the table, but none finds a pocket. She watches him curse, and then her mother pats her on the shoulder.

"I'll be outside." Her voice is muffled as she already has a cigarette in her lips. "Don't think you can get away with not talking to him. I'll know."

There's a big beam of natural light as the door opens and shuts behind her. Anna stands for a little longer, but as men begin to notice her and stare, she makes a beeline for the pool table.

When she approaches, the game stops, and so does their chatter. The three men shut up and look her over from head to toe. Two of them grin. The man who is supposedly her father does not.

"You trying to play, sweetheart?" asks one of the grinning men. He wears a flannel shirt that is too small for him. His teeth are yellowed from chewing tobacco, but that doesn't stop him from showing them off in a wide smile.

She glances at him but then takes her gaze back to her father. The idea still doesn't register.

"Oooo," says the other man. "She likes you." He slaps his shoulder.

Anna keeps eye contact with him. First, she wanted to run away, but now she's stuck in place. "My mom, Allison Klein . . . She says you're my dad."

The other men hoot and holler. "You hear that!? You got another baby. My, what's May going to think of that?" The other two men are practically keeled over with laughter, but this man's smile is now twice removed. He glares at Anna and goes back to studying the balls on the table.

"I don't know an Allison Klein."

"She goes by Allie."

"Don't know no Allie, either."

"Look, I don't like my mom. She sent me here to make some kind of a point."

"No, she sent you here looking for some kind of handout. Now scram, because you ain't gettin' shit."

Anna's getting nervous. It's hard for her to talk without crying. "I don't want your money."

"So what? You're here to pull on my heartstrings? It's always money, honey. I'm not dumb."

"No really. I just want to say hi."

"Well then, hi!" He widens his eyes and bends so he's eye to eye. "Bye!" He waves his hand in front of her face.

"You don't want to . . ." Anna's eyes dart around. Men at a few tables around them have begun to watch. She tenses, and tears run down her cheeks. "Talk?"

"Who do you want me to talk to? You? I don't have a daughter."

"Aw come on," says the yellow-toothed man. "If you don't want her, I'll take her. What a man wouldn't do for a daughter like that."

Anna feels his eyes slither over her skin.

They're drawing a crowd now. Anna is crying but trying to keep her face as composed as she can. "Dad," she says, looking into his eyes. "Please?"

He seems to consider her plea for a moment, but then he rolls his eyes and shakes his head. "Get lost, kid."

"Hey!" someone shouts. It's the bartender from across the room. "How old are you?" he says to Anna, but it's rhetorical. There's no way he doesn't know she's underaged. "Get the fuck out." He points towards the door.

The few women in the bar look on with concerned frowns, but none move to console her.

She looks back to the man. To her dad. She can see it now, beneath his sandy scruff. His cheeks are flushed and round like hers. "How could you?"

"Because." He points at Anna and wiggles his finger as he speaks. "For the last time, I don't have no fucking daughter."

One of the men whistles in exclamation. The laughter is gone. The entire bar is silent apart from the rock music.

"Fine. Fuck you, then." Anna turns on her heel, and with her eyes on her feet, she scurries to the door and out into the parking lot.

Her mom hasn't even finished her cigarette, and she smiles when she sees her distraught daughter.

"Is he a good man?"

But Anna doesn't say anything. Not for the rest of the night.

Hours later, Hannah invites her to come out that night. Hannah and Tess typically start acting like it's the weekend on Thursday night. They'll drink and smoke and show up to school hungover on Friday, if they even show up at all.

Anna typically comes out Thursdays, but not for long, and she definitely doesn't partake in Thursday partying. That's only for the weekends.

She meets the girls at The Station. There are a few other kids from the neighborhood there. They're all excited to see her.

"Dolly! We didn't think you'd make it out tonight."

Hannah has a small bag of pills at her feet and a pint of liquor. Anna comes over and sits next to her. They all realize something is up.

"What's wrong?"

"Nothin'," says Anna with a sigh. "Just a long day." She points at the bag of pills. "Can I have one of those?"

Hannah frowns and smiles. "Are you serious?"

"Hundred percent."

"You don't want to take this garbage. You have brain cells to lose."

"Gimme one," Anna says, staring Hannah down.

Hannah looks around at the others. It looks like she's hoping someone else will chime in to reverse peer pressure Anna into not taking drugs, but the circle is silent.

"If you're sure . . ." She takes one out of the bag. "Here. Have half."

But before Hannah can cut it in two, Anna takes it from her. "I'll be fine."

Anna doesn't take the pill right away. The circle comes alive again, talking and joking.

Tess and Hannah are silent.

Anna looks at the pill that's in her fingers as she speaks. "If you could say anything to your dads, what would it be?"

The girls meet Anna's eyes, confused. "Like, my real dad?" asks Tess.

"Yeah. Not your stepdad. Your real dad. The scum bag who left you."

Hannah and Tess look at each other while they think it over. Tess shrugs. "Get fucked, I guess."

"Yeah." Hannah laughs. "Get fucked, loser."

Anna nods. She tosses her head back as she takes the pill and washes it down with a mouthful of vodka. It's the first drug she's ever taken, and while it feels like a mistake, she'd do anything to make herself feel better for a moment.

She leans back on the grass on her elbows and agrees with her friends. "Get fucked."

A half hour later, she's so high she's forgotten the entire encounter with her dad. There are no thoughts running through her head at all.

She'll spend the next few years taking whatever drugs she can to keep it that way.

It wouldn't have changed everything, but if she hadn't been such a druggie, at least Sylvie would still be alive.

Creep

Anna keeps going through the past. Eventually, she lands on her notes on Jeffrey Lemay.

She had interviewed him, so to speak, about Hannah's disappearance. His alibi checked out. Or at least, his dad had vouched for him by saying that he was staying at his house in Savannah, Georgia, for three days. The second day of that visit was when Hannah vanished.

Every girl, woman—hell, grandma in Oak Grove had caught Jeffrey staring at them for a little too long.

No doubt he was a creep. Maybe even capable of murder, but Anna thought for certain he wouldn't be able to get away with it. Nor was he smart enough to hide a body for years, let alone embalm one. He would be caught.

She has a picture of him. He has lank bangs that always look wet. Small beady eyes. He has the look of a dumb killer, but not a mastermind. He would have to be pretending to be an idiot.

Anna tosses the picture down. She's going in circles the way she always has when thinking about this case. Three girls.

Hannah. Tess. Sylvie.

What connects them is Anna, but she thinks maybe she's been looking too deep. Maybe she needs to narrow it down. It's hard to admit, but she knows it's the truth: Sylvie wasn't supposed to die. *She* was.

It's the early morning, and the sunrise is only a couple hours off. She should sleep. Get ready to evacuate tomorrow, but then her eyes prickle at sound coming from outside the heavy wood door. Sound coming from the ceiling.

Music.

She stands. Suddenly, she's awake and she's *pissed*. "This son of a bitch," she mutters.

When she throws open the office door, the music is louder, and louder still in the kitchen. It sounds like it's coming out of the wall.

Here she can recognize the tune. It's punk rock. The Ramones. *I wanna be sedated.*

The lyrics continue, muffled. It sounds like it's coming from right next door. Anna goes towards her front door, but it's quieter there. She puts her ear against it and listens to the hall. Nothing. She walks back into her apartment. Somehow, the sound is finding its way clear into the kitchen.

She goes back and starts opening cabinets. There's no change in volume until she bends over and looks under the sink. With the two cabinet doors open, the sound is a little clearer.

Past the packet of trash bags and bottles of cleaning chemicals, there's a draft. The wood board that lines the back of the cabinet is slightly out of place, and cool air blasts out of the black space behind it, followed by the tune.

Anna touches the wooden panel gently. It's loose and pulls out of place easily. She tosses everything out from under the sink in order to get the board out. When it's gone, the sound comes even louder.

There's no wall behind the panel. Instead, there's a brick space that looks something like a chimney, only wider. It's not until Anna shines her flashlight in and sees a pulley notched in the wall with a rope wrapped through it that she understands what it is.

It's a little elevator. A dumbwaiter.

While the little shaft is big enough for a person to fit in, it's clear it's far too narrow for it to be an actual elevator. Boxes and files must've been sent floor to floor with this when the building was old office space.

Anna climbs so she's most of the way under the sink and sticks her head into the shaft. The music blares above her. She can't see what's at the top, but it seems like it opens into a room. A rope hangs taut in the center of the shaft and connects to some kind of replacement for the dumbwaiter below her.

It's a flat metal tray that doesn't quite fit the square of the shaft perfectly. It dangles slightly in the draft. She pauses as the song is about to end.

The guitar notes rest as the vocals quiet, too. Then, there's complete silence. Anna's breathing shallow, quick breaths.

Suddenly she flinches and hits her head as the same riff starts over again.

"Fuck!" she shouts. She's about to roll out back into the kitchen when she notices something. There are thick knots in the length of rope that connects to the dumbwaiter tray.

She's seen this kind of rope before. It's meant to be climbed.

She scurries out from under the sink. The tape on her door meant nothing. Somebody could access her apartment from this shaft without her ever knowing. She slams the sink cupboards shut, grabs a broom, and sticks its length through the cabinet handles so they can't be opened from the inside.

She's not going to run away. The easy answer is to call the police, but with the chaos going on in the city, there's no guarantee they'd even come.

She doesn't have any ideas. She's not climbing up that rope—that's a trap. She knows exactly where the room at the top of the shaft is in relation to the rest of the building . . . It's what's behind the locked door she found on the fourth floor.

Anna supposes she can try to get through the door there. There's plenty of heavy construction equipment upstairs, but if it's still locked, there's no point. She'd have to break it down, and then there's no surprise, just another trap.

She looks at her feet to the cleaning chemicals she'd taken from under the sink.

Gears turn. An idea forms.

She knows exactly what to do.

Trap

The hard part is figuring out how to get the pulley to work. Anna is able to take it out of the wall and find a lock on it that lets her pull the rope to raise the dumbwaiter. She can now send the little tray up to the fourth floor, where the shaft presumably ends.

The mixture doesn't take as much work. She dons two N-95 masks, uncaps a half gallon of lemon-scented ammonia, and empties the entire thing into a mop bucket.

Then it's time for the bleach.

She doesn't know how long she'll have before the mixture creates the toxic gas she's heard of. It might explode right away, like Mentos and Diet Coke, but she doubts it. The big risk is breathing it in, even with the masks. She'll try to hold her breath as long as she can.

The bleach glugs out of the bottle, and as it splashes with the ammonia, there's no immediate chemical reaction. At least not to the eye.

It doesn't hiss or explode. It's not until half the bottle is gone that she sees the fumes begin to rise. They don't billow out like smoke. They slither around the sides of the bucket. If inhaled, they'll cause pulmonary edema. Those unfortunate enough to take a deep breath will drown as fluid fills their lungs.

She lifts the bucket and sets it under the sink, and then she pushes it to the wall. It's heavier than she thought. She probably didn't have to use as much of the ammonia and bleach as she did.

The fumes are rising faster now, getting nearer to her face. If she gets a little in her eyes, they could burn and go blind. Suddenly she realizes she's not as wise as she thought she was.

What Anna should've done was practice with a bucket of water, but it's too late for that. She crawls in under the sink with the bucket and begins to try and gently set it in the middle of the replacement dumbwaiter tray.

But she can't get the balance right. The tray wants to tilt to one side and have the contents of the bucket splash out. More and more fumes are rising, and Anna is in an enclosed space with them.

"Shit. Shit. Shit. Come on!" Anna curses under the masks. She's not going to be able to get her little bucket bomb to balance. The second she lets go of it, it's going to spill, but she has no choice.

She lets go of it and takes her hands to the pulley as quickly as she can. The bucket tips, spills, and the fumes multiply tenfold. Anna starts yanking on the rope. As the tray rises, most of the liquid is lifted up towards the top floor with it. Some drips down on Anna's hands. It burns like hell, but she keeps pulling as fast as she can.

She grimaces and screams, and then the metal tray crashes into whatever mechanism it was strung to at the top of the shaft.

Even with the music, she can hear the bucket go tumbling off and liquid splash on the floor.

Bullseye.

The surface area of the bleach and ammonia has just exploded in size. Even if only a quarter of the mixture managed to make it to that room and not spill down the shaft, it's enough to fill it with toxic fumes.

Anna crawls back out and throws on the tap. Then she holds her burns under cold water. She tries to listen as best she can to try to hear sounds above the music and the water.

She wants to hear the pound of footsteps. The bang of a door. The shatter of glass as someone dives out a window. But she hears nothing. She turns off the tap and doesn't hesitate as she walks to the front door. It's time for phase two.

She locks her front door behind her and runs up to the fourth floor. She clears corners quickly, with the knife held back at her hip, ready to stab.

She hears the music coming from the end of the hall. She was right—it's coming from the locked room.

In one of the unfinished apartments, there's an industrial fan hooked up to an extension cord. It takes some finessing, but she manages to hold the fan in her right arm like a shield by bracing her hand and elbow through the metal bar on which the fan sits.

Then she puts the flashlight in her mouth and lifts a small sledgehammer off the floor. She's prepared to break the door down, but when she gets in sight of it, she sees there's no need.

The door that had previously been locked is slightly ajar. Fumes seep through the crack slowly and swirl before disappearing. The whole scene looks strangely out of a fairy tale. A chamber of secrets.

Before she enters, she sets the fan down and searches the rest of the unfinished rooms. She doesn't find a man foaming at the mouth and gasping for air like she'd hoped.

She finds nothing.

Anna lifts the fan, straightens the extension cord, and turns it on before bracing it in her arm again. Then, with her two masks and fan, she goes back to the door and shoves it open with her foot. The fan is strong and makes short work of pushing the fumes far from where they can reach her.

The room itself is ancient. It's too small to be made into an apartment. It's a square box without a closet. Its size, cracked brick wall, and sagging ceiling might be why the contractors have left this space alone. It would probably be converted last and only into storage.

But all her eyes can focus on is a tiny twin mattress that sits soiled in the corner. It's sheetless, but a wool blanket stretches its length. Somebody has been sleeping here. She walks in farther.

A window is open, and with the fan, the fumes find it fast. New ones don't replace them from the liquid on the floor. The chemical reaction is already losing strength.

Near the middle of the room is a square hole in the floor where the dumbwaiter opens into. There are four old stumps from where its old support posts used to be. Above her is an eye bolt screwed into the ceiling and another mechanism of pulleys.

Next to the hole is a record player.

Anna lifts the needle, and the rock goes silent. Then she walks to the window. There is no rope leading down, and the three-story fall would certainly break someone's legs, if not their back.

All she feels certain of is that whoever was here had left before she sent up the gas. Unless they had a gas mask.

This isn't the finale. She was led here by the music, and it means there's something here she's supposed to find.

She starts to inspect the room further. She turns over the record and then the record player.

Nothing.

There's not much to find. There are no clothes or furniture to riffle through. Before she turns over the mattress, she strips the blanket off.

She shouts and jumps back. Staring back at her is another face.

It's the baby mask that someone had been wearing at the party. By the man who had wanted to dance with her. Without someone's head in it, it's even more horrifying. The empty eye sockets stretch and the skin wrinkles.

She picks it up gently. Her mouth hangs open under her masks in shock.

Not only had the man who murdered her friends been inside her apartment, he's even offered her his hand to dance.

Countdown

She tries to remember what else she can about the man she had seen wearing the mask, but she'd been sitting. She can't even remember if he'd seemed short or tall. The more she thinks of it, the more she realizes maybe the masked man is a victim. He could've been the one she'd seen running; the owner of those bloody footprints.

If she's supposed to find another clue in this room, she doesn't. There are no riddles or photographs or drawings on the walls.

The room itself, and its access to her apartment, seems likely to be the message: *"I've been watching you."*

Her hair doesn't stand on end in fear. She's only enraged. If she still held that hammer in her hand, she'd send its head flying into these plaster walls. She tosses the mask back onto the bed and storms out of the room.

Anna doesn't even realize that the sun has been rising. When she gets back to her apartment, she stands in the living room. The world outside is gray and wet. She can see a sliver of Cooper River, and the water is beginning to slosh and swell. The wind is here, with the hurricane not far behind it.

Anna feels defeated. In order to win this game, she needs to find a clue on her own. She can't just follow the crumbs this killer leaves all the way into a trap.

It was time to refocus and get the hell out of Charleston. Every hotel room in the state is going to be booked by those evacuating, but Anna doesn't mind driving. She reserves a room in a motel in Chattanooga and goes to check the confirmation email.

That's when knows she's not going anywhere.

There's another confirmation email in her inbox that was sent yesterday. One from the Sweetwater Correctional Institution.

Subject: Visitation Appointment.

Your visitation appointment has been scheduled. Please arrive fifteen minutes early and review our rules and requirements below.

Under that is a list of things not to do during visitation and what can and can't be brought. Then, at the very bottom of the email, is the name of the inmate she has been scheduled to visit.

Jeffrey Lemay.

Anna fumbles with her phone as she races to her contacts. She's calling Justin seconds later. It's early, but he answers, and it doesn't sound like he'd been sleeping.

"Anna?"

"Hey, did you schedule a visitation appointment for us to meet with Jeffrey Lemay today?"

"What? No."

"Oh."

"Why?" Justin asks.

"I uh . . . I just thought I remembered you saying something about it."

"About scheduling a visitation appointment?"

"Yeah. I don't know. Forget it."

"You've been ignoring me for the last twelve hours, Anna. If the police weren't so busy, I'd have called them for a welfare check. Are you okay? Are we still working together on this?"

She ignores both questions. "I just couldn't sit through that stupid press conference."

"What are you doing now?"

"Getting out of town."

Justin doesn't respond right away. "I guess I can't blame you for that. I wrote a draft last night for what we have so far. I think it's best we wait awhile before we publish. Stick to the original plan, wait for this storm to leave the news cycle."

"Right, that all sounds good."

"I'll send it to you after some edits. Add what you want. I wouldn't have been able to—"

"Sounds great, Justin." Anna interrupts. "I'll look it over, but I've got to run."

"Oh . . . Okay."

"Yeah, stay safe," she says and hangs up. She was going to throw together a duffle bag. Now she's putting Sweetwater Correctional Institution into Google Maps.

Someone must've made the appointment with her contact info. If Justin didn't schedule the appointment, then this is another crumb.

She has a strong urge to ignore it. This sick teasing is driving Anna insane, but she doesn't have another lead. And besides, she tells herself, maybe this is it. Maybe this is the reveal. The end she's been waiting for.

She throws together a backpack and keeps her reservation in Chattanooga in case she does end up leaving town. Then she locks up her apartment, for whatever it's worth. When she's outside in front of her car, her stomach sinks.

There's a distant howl of the emergency sirens. She can hear them turn on one by one across the city, until their noise becomes one deafening scream.

She stands on the empty industrial street and listens. The evacuation order must've finally been given by the governor. The trajectory of the storm still hasn't changed.

In fact, this moment probably marks a day until landfall. Anna frowns and looks back up at the dark windows of her apartment building.

Twenty-four hours to landfall.

Twenty-four hours to go.

It's a lyric in the song. The music was just another tease. Something to suggest that the timing of all this madness was intentional.

What Anna can't decide is whether this countdown represents all the time she has left to discover the truth before it vanishes in the surge or something entirely different.

Maybe it doesn't just signify the time until the storm, but the moment this man plans to have the truth come crashing down.

Sweetwater

The visitation appointment is scheduled for the earliest slot—nine a.m.—and the Sweetwater Correctional Institution is more than an hour's drive. According to Google Maps, Anna will not be making it fifteen minutes early.

On her way to the interstate, the emergency sirens still blare. She sees people standing on balconies and in backyards. Most have just woken up. They stand with their staticky hair in their pajamas and look towards the ocean, as if the hurricane is already in sight.

Soon, the interstate will be flooded with the sizeable portion of the populace who was waiting until the last second, sure the hurricane would shift paths in the final days before landfall was projected. Now, they hardly have a choice but to throw together their belongings and run for the hills.

Thankfully, the traffic jams of last night have cleared up by now. Anna figures this is the one lull before the gridlock begins again.

As she leaves the city, she sees several columns of smoke stretch up and fan out from the wind. The looting will only get worse until the storm hits.

Soon she passes rest stops and hotel parking lots overflowing with cars, their roofs bulging with strapped-down belongings. Even this isn't far enough away from the storm to be safe. Wind speeds aren't supposed to subside to under one hundred miles per hour until much farther inland.

Tired as she is, her anxiety keeps her awake, and it flares up as she passes a military convoy heading eastbound.

It's the National Guard.

Dozens of camouflaged trucks rumble by, and suddenly everything becomes a little more real. This hurricane could kill thousands.

When she gets to Sweetwater, she's surprised to see a lack of security. There's no razor wire or guard towers.

There's a single chain-link fence that lines the perimeter and curves at the top like a breaking wave to make it impossible to climb from inside.

It's a minimum-security prison, after all. But still, after seeing it, it's clear that breaking out of here wouldn't be anything like breaking out of Fort Knox.

Anna gets nervous as she realizes she might have to rethink Jeffrey's prison alibi for the disappearances of Sylvie and Tess. Again, she feels like a fool. She'd been so quick to dismiss Jeffrey as a suspect without so much as even checking on what the prison he was in was like. It looks more like a fenced rehab.

She follows the directions towards visitation and heads into the building. It's a one-story concrete structure, ugly and impersonal. The guards inside look bored as she fills out a visitor form, presents ID, and is guided through the metal detector. They're expecting her.

Whoever made this appointment didn't just make it under her email. They left her name and phone number.

Then she's led into a windowless room. There are concrete tables with concrete stools, but the prisoners aren't here yet. There are three women and one man all sitting at different tables. They glance indifferently as Anna enters and then look back to their phones.

She takes a seat at a table as far from the others as she can, but she can't stand to bring her phone out. The news is inescapable anyway. She can hear audio from another woman's phone—voices yell and glass breaks then gunshots ring out. The woman shakes her head and swipes, and Anna knows she must've been watching footage from the looting that's been growing in Charleston.

There has already been a curfew set in place. All outdoor activity by citizens must be related to evacuation. In short, you can't take your dog for a walk. Not like there's much else to do. Since the governor's evacuation order, every single business has closed their doors and boarded up.

Anna is bouncing her foot nervously when there's a buzzer and a door opens. A few prisoners start filing through. They wear ash-colored jumpsuits with black numbers. At the back of the short line is Jeffrey. He smiles when he sees her. It's obvious that this visit is no surprise.

"Ah, Anna Klein." He approaches the table and sits.

She's speechless while looking him over. Though they've hardly talked, she feels a familiarity. Seeing anyone from Oak Grove outside of that trailer park has a strange feel to it. What surprises her more than anything is how young he looks.

When Jeffrey was creeping on her, Hannah, and Tess, he was only in his early twenties, but to a girl of seventeen that gap of four years feels like a gulf. Now, Anna sees they're essentially the same age.

"Expecting me?" she asks.

"Maybe."

Jeffrey parts his lank hair. It's longer now and so greasy it looks damp. Anna feels like she has a rock in her throat. Some obstruction that she has to speak past. "Who made this appointment?"

"I don't know. I'm not going to be able to give you anything like that. Names, descriptions, details. What's good is that you came."

"And why's that?"

"Why's what?"

Anna sighs. Jeffrey might be just as stupid as she remembered him. "Why is it good that I came?"

He eyes her with a hungry expression. Like a man who hasn't seen a woman in years. "I was told to tell you something," he says, like a children's taunt.

Anna doesn't say anything. She waits for him to continue, but he loses his train of thought. "I wish we could smoke in here. Can you imagine? Do you still smoke, Dolly?"

"Not really."

"I bet you still understand. Nothing to do in here all day but watch cable television and play cards. Some guys manage to get them smuggled in and smoke in the bathroom. But for that you need friends. Friends and money."

Anna's nose twitches. Jeffrey smells like cigarettes. Maybe he's toying with her. She feels her rage build but closes her eyes and takes a deep breath. "I'm not giving you a bribe, if that's what you're asking."

"Oh. You don't need to. I'm just making small talk. It's not every day that I get to talk to such a hot little thing."

Some of the other prisoners are glancing away from their private conversations to catch a glimpse of Anna.

She crosses her arms. "This conversation can be over right now . . ." She moves like she's going to stand.

"Okay, okay," Jeffrey says quickly. "Stay. I'll tell you. No guarantees I won't flirt. That's just instinct for me."

She settles back down, and now they have the guards' attention.

"Hannah," he says and then looks off in the distance with a smirk as if picturing her. "If you want to find her, look where she lived. She's still in her trailer. Did you know that?"

"Her body was found there yesterday."

Jeffrey's eyes widen at this. "Huh. Well, that's a shame. She had better legs than you. But . . ." He gestures at her breasts. "You can't have it all, can you? Or, if you did, you wouldn't be slumming it in prison right now with yours truly, Mr. Lemay."

"Did you kill her?"

"Course not. I ain't no murderer."

"Then who told you to tell me that Hannah was still in her trailer?"

He laughs. "Someone who's probably a murderer."

"And you don't care about that? Your conscience doesn't care to turn them in?"

"My what?"

Anna leans back and looks Jeffrey over. There's no intelligent spark in his eye. Her fury is rising. This conversation feels like more than a dead end—it's an insult.

"If I tell the police you have information that makes you an accessory to this homicide, they're going to give you hell."

"Go ahead. Prove I'm working with someone."

"Look. You can't get into this prison without valid ID. Whoever came to see you is going to get caught. And if they called, they have the conversation recorded. You can probably get a reduced sentence if you give them up."

"He didn't say anything about murder on the phone. Just to tell you these things. I don't know nothing except I got a phone call and a carton of cigarettes tossed over the fence. I'm not in no trouble. Quit lying. I can't get more time for telling you things."

Anna leans forward and speaks through gritted teeth. "Then what were you told to tell me?"

Jeffrey moves his face so it's inches away from Anna's, but she doesn't give in and flinch back. "That you killed your best friend," he whispers and licks his lips. Anna can smell his smoke-tainted breath. "That you're a murderer."

"No," says Anna, shaking her head. "That's bullshit."

"Oh, oh, oh. I don't think so. I can see it your eyes. You believe it, too."

Anna stands up. If she weren't in public, she'd scream. She has to keep her mouth shut in order to keep her composure. Every little clue has been nothing but a tease.

"Hannah, too. You know that? You have everyone's blood on your hands."

She starts walking away from the table.

"Come on. Leaving so soon? I mean . . ." He tilts his head and looks at her pelvis. "It's not like I'll mind watching you go."

When she gets to the exit, the guards move to open it for her, but she pauses as Jeffrey yells.

"Oh, and one more thing."

Anna turns back to him.

"Your mom's place. You're supposed to look in your mama's place."

"Her apartment?"

"Yep."

"And who told you to say that?"

Jeffrey pauses. "Nobody. Maybe. Maybe nobody told me to say a thing." He shows her a big grin before she exits the visitation room and the heavy door slams behind her.

Prison Break

Anna is apathetic as she stands in the parking lot. For the first time, she's beginning to think the best thing she can do for herself, the best thing she can do for this case, is to give up on it.

She feels a thousand steps behind.

She's being played with, and the best thing she can do is quit the game. Her exit is the only thing this killer desperately doesn't want.

He needs Anna to keep playing.

The stuff Jeffrey said about Hannah was a surprise. She was supposed to find the body at the trailer park. She wonders if the someone who talked to Jeffrey gave him his lines *before* Hannah's body was found.

It would make sense. Justin just got lucky. If Anna didn't let him read the journal, she never would've gone back there to look on her own. Not without a hint being dangled in her face like Jeffrey had just done. She wonders what's in her mother's apartment. It would make sense if it was Tess, and her stomach churns at the thought.

Before she gets in her car, she walks the perimeter of the prison. Even sixty miles inland, the wind whirls in her ears.

The prison grounds are shaped in a square, and the fence probably runs a tenth of a mile on each of the four sides. Right now, probably because of the hurricane warning, the grounds are empty.

There's a basketball court, picnic tables, and even a little vegetable garden.

It's the epitome of a low-security prison, and here on the north side of the fence, she sees something that looks like an easy exit.

There's a one-story structure about eight feet from the fence. On the side of it is an air-conditioning unit about three feet high. It would be incredibly easy to climb on the AC unit then climb to the roof and, with a running jump, clear the fence.

Getting back in wouldn't be too difficult. You could climb the chain-link fence. The only problem was with the way the top curves down, you wouldn't be able to climb down the other side. You'd have to fall about twelve feet.

Unpleasant, but not undoable.

She realizes she's being ridiculous. No one was breaking out of prison multiple times to commit murders and not getting caught. The idea is preposterous.

It is exactly the kind of reach a bad detective with no more leads of her own makes. Anna heads back to her car and shuts the door.

She has one more lead to check before she leaves the city and quits this game. She has to check her mom's apartment.

They haven't talked in several months, and this storm wasn't a good enough reason for either to initiate conversation. The idea of expressing concern for her mother is appalling to Anna. Doubtless, her mom feels the same.

Her mom doesn't live in the same house she did when Anna was still at home. A few years ago, she moved to an apartment in North Charleston that already had several thousand tenants in the way of cockroaches.

According to the news, it's right in the center of the looting.

"One more lead," Anna says aloud to herself as she gets on the highway eastbound towards Charleston. One more chance to find a way to get a step ahead.

If there's something in her mom's apartment, does that mean she's somehow involved in this? Anna has been suspicious of her mother only once when it came to Hannah's and Tess's disappearances. But maybe it was a moment she shouldn't have so quickly brushed off.

July 2018

Anna sits on the couch eating cereal and watching TV.

It's ten a.m., and already her mother's little house is steaming. Thankfully, she has the place to herself.

Her mom is staying in the city with a friend. Maybe the same one she was seeing when she took Anna and told her to wait in the car, but she doesn't know. She doesn't care.

Anna is sprawled out, picking at strings of fabric that stick out from a cushion, when there's a knock on the door. It's three quick, panicked knocks. Anna stands and peeks through the window. She sees the back of Hannah's head. She's looking over her shoulder.

Anna opens the door. "Hannah?"

She whips her head around to face Anna. "Your mom's not home, is she? Can I come in?"

"Yeah, yeah." Anna stands back and lets her pass and then looks out the door a moment longer to try to see what Hannah had been looking for. There's no movement but the leaves rippling in the wind. It's a beautiful summer day. Anna looks concerned as she shuts the door.

"What's wrong, Hannah? You make it home alright?"

"No. I didn't fucking make it home." She sits on the couch and puts her head in her hands. Anna doesn't sit. She leans against the wall.

"Then where'd you go?"

"I passed out."

"What?"

"In the grass," Hannah gestures out with her arm as if the grass is on the floor in front of her. "At some point I stumbled over. You didn't hear me fall?"

Anna gets a little defensive. She feels guilty that she and Frank left Hannah at The Station, but it wasn't their fault. "It started raining, and we figured you already left. We didn't hear shit. Maybe you didn't fall. Maybe you *lay* down. Do you have any bruises or anything?"

Hannah doesn't say anything. It seems like this is a possibility she hadn't quite considered. "I don't know. Just . . . whatever. That's not really why I'm here."

Anna grins. "You wanna wake and bake?"

"No!" Hannah sticks her arms out at her sides. "I don't want any more fucking drugs, dude."

Anna crosses her arms.

Hannah catches her breath and speaks again. "When I woke up in the grass alone, I was looking for you guys. It was like . . . I don't know. Four in the morning. I was all wet and cold, and then this thing happened."

"What?"

"Somebody took my picture."

Anna doesn't understand what she's trying to say. "Okay?"

"Like, with a flash. Like the same thing that happened to those girls from your stories you posted online."

"Hannah, you were high."

"No. No, it was hours later. Please believe me on this. I wasn't even high anymore. Were you pranking me?"

Anna's trying to be sympathetic, but in reality, she's annoyed. Hannah is acting like a strung-out tweaker right now. A paranoid druggie. Anna wants to think she can do drugs and dodge real life without consequences. If this could happen to Hannah, it could happen to her.

"No one is pranking you. Did you even sleep last night? You should go back home. Try and—"

"Anna, I wasn't high. Someone took my picture with a flash. Middle of the night. Just like you wrote."

Anna goes quiet. "I could check with Tess."

"Tess would never do something like this, and you know it. Just tell me. How do your stories end? What happens to the girls after their pictures are taken?"

"Hannah this is absurd."

"Tell me!"

Anna sighs. "He follows them home. The girls are always super creeped out after having their picture taken in the middle of the night, so naturally they go to where they feel safe. Once he knows where they live . . . he stalks them."

"And then what?"

"Hannah, do you know how ridiculous you sound? This is a story I wrote. Years ago, for that matter. I haven't posted a part in forever."

"He kills them, right?"

"Sure. I guess he kills them. The girls go missing. That's how the stories go. Do you understand how strung out you sound?"

"If you believed me, this wouldn't seem so weird. I'm alone in the dark and then there's a flash. No one is around for like a mile. I was at The Station. You're telling me it wasn't you?"

Anna is beginning to get annoyed. "Why would it be me? How special do you think you are? Like I'm going to wait for your high ass to wake up in the grass just to take your picture."

"I'm just scared," Hannah says, and then to Anna's shock, she starts to cry. Hannah's not a crier. She has her depressions and her problems, but she keeps them to herself. Seeing her this vulnerable makes Anna's heart hurt. But only for a moment. What Anna sees is a mirror of what might happen if she doesn't tone it down—drug addicted and delusional.

"Can I have a hug?" Hannah asks.

Anna walks over to her and wordlessly wraps her arms around her, but her face is stoic, if not angry, while she holds her friend. "You should go home, Hannah. Get some real sleep."

"Okay."

Anna doesn't hold her for very long. She stands and guides Hannah out the front door. "Text me when you feel better," Anna says.

The next few days, Hannah goes out less and less. Supposedly, she's gone sober.

The thought stresses Anna out. To lose her partner in crime means more introspection into her questionable choices.

It's after the Fourth of July, and Anna stands in a big circle of teenagers at The Station. She's already smoked, drank, and is about to take ecstasy when another group arrives.

Among them is Hannah. Anna hasn't seen her since she stopped by, but she's heard the rumors of what she's been saying. Footsteps outside her window. A general feeling of being watched.

Anna knows Hannah's paranoia should invoke pity, but instead, it makes her hate her. She thinks she was weak to let the drugs melt her mind like they had.

Anna nods to Hannah as a greeting, but the two don't talk right away. She watches her friend. There's ample beer and a handle of rum being passed around. Hannah doesn't touch either.

Eventually, they end up standing next to each other. Hannah seems nervous, something she's rarely ever been.

"Dolly, can I ask you something?"

"Yeah."

"Why didn't you ever finish your story? I've been reading them over and over again, and they're really good."

The answer is drugs, defiance. The lifestyle that Anna chooses to ignore the world does not include writing. But she just shrugs. "It was crap. You just think it's good because you're convinced that you're living it."

Hannah leans close and looks Anna dead in the eye. "I am living it." She looks over her shoulder. "I don't know what do. Somebody is watching me."

Anna rolls her eyes, and Hannah puts her hands on her shoulders. "Please! Anna, believe me!"

"Get your hands off of me!" Anna steps back. Most people are watching them now. "You can't handle your shit, that's what's happening."

"Anna, I'm sober!"

"I don't care."

Hannah is in tears, and Anna has to hold back her own in order to look cold. She wants to help Hannah, to hold her, but the drugs in her system have taken over.

They act like a disease, and they will lie and doubt and do whatever it takes to convince Anna to keep getting high.

The rest of the circle is quiet now. They watch Hannah and Anna in silence.

"I think you should get lost," Anna says and nods towards Oak Grove. And that's exactly what she does. Hannah wanders off without a word into the dark.

Besides her mom supposedly hearing her come home, it was the last time Hannah Greenwood was ever seen alive.

There was more than just the sadness in these memories, Anna recalls. There was a moment, a day after Hannah had been gone that sticks in her memory. It was when there were search teams scouring the area around Oak Grove.

Practically everyone turned out to help. The memory that sticks in Anna's mind is when she just got back from her first search.

She's chugging a plastic water bottle and walking back to her house to change clothes. When she passes Hannah's trailer, she sees something she doesn't expect.

On the front steps to the trailer sits Hannah's mom. She's staring dejectedly into space. There's no panic or action in her expression. It was like she had lost something and knew it was gone forever. To her right stands Tess's mom, and to her left stands Anna's own mother.

Their moms weren't friends, although they knew about each other. Seeing them all together like this was strange. There seemed to be something they all knew.

Tess's mom is the first to notice Anna. She smiles tightly, and it looks like she's about to say something to her, when Anna's mom nudges her and hisses something in her ear. The women are quiet as Anna passes.

They ignore her, and Anna thinks it's because they heard it was her who told Hannah to get lost and wander into the dark.

But the more she thinks of it in the present day, the more it feels like these three women knew something the rest of the trailer park didn't. They never asked Anna if anything had been found that afternoon when she got back all sweaty from her search.

Maybe it was because they knew there was nothing to find.

Wrong Way

If their mothers knew more about what was happening than they let on, Anna has a problem.

Hannah's mom had always had health problems and died from a stroke years ago. As for Tess's mom, she vanished not long after Tess did. Their family moved to Columbia soon after Hannah went missing. Then after she lost her daughter, she couldn't stand to stay in the same place. Last she'd heard, Tess's mom had moved to Arizona.

Her own mom might know something, but she always insisted it was Jeffrey Lemay who took Tess and Hannah. She was too drunk to care about anything. Too drunk to be a reliable source.

Now, Anna doesn't have a choice. If her mom is in fact alive and not slaughtered in her apartment, Anna will peer into her liquor-glazed eyes and look for a lie. If she sees one, she'll do whatever it takes to get the truth out of that woman.

Her phone buzzes in the passenger seat. She glances over to read the text. It's from Bruce.

Your article is late again. Expect to hear from HR.

Anna feels a tinge of despair. The text takes her mind to reality. She doesn't have more than six hundred dollars in savings, but those are problems for the future. She'll trade everything—her career, her cash, her life—to find out the truth.

Since her friends went missing, Anna thinks, she hasn't been living anyway. At least she's more sober now. She made that pledge after Sylvie went missing. She has alcohol now and again but hasn't touched hard drugs in years. She thought having a clear head might make a difference in solving these cases.

She doesn't bother to send a response to the text and focuses on the road ahead.

The eastbound lanes to Charleston are practically empty. There's a car maybe every quarter mile. Everyone is headed *away* from the city.

When she gets closer to town, westbound traffic is at a standstill. Everyone has waited too long to leave town, and they are packed like sardines now that the governor has given the evacuation order.

She's trying to keep her eyes from closing, when suddenly she perks up. There's a car in the distance that she's approaching much faster than the others. It takes another second to notice its headlights are facing *towards* her.

Somebody is driving the wrong way.

They're bypassing the traffic by speeding westbound in the eastbound lanes. They're in the left lane, and she pulls into the right and lays on the horn while giving them the finger. They race past without even looking at her.

"Fucking idiots," says Anna aloud as she gets her car back up to speed.

She's hardly driving for another minute when the lanes ahead of her thicken with cars, and they're all coming right towards her.

None of them are driving slowly. They're going the speed limit, only in the wrong direction. She starts towards the shoulder to pull over, but somebody is using that space to drive, too. There isn't a space to get by safely without going into the ditch.

The thought of putting her car in the ditch so these idiots can pass is unthinkable. Anna presses down on the gas. Her old Taurus hums for a long time before she feels it build more speed.

Then she's barreling down the interstate at eighty, right towards the wrong-way drivers. Some honk and flash their lights, as if they have the right of way, and Anna's anger turns to fury.

She doesn't stay in just one lane but swerves across them all so the oncoming cars each fear she's coming towards them.

One car speeds past her and swerves to miss by inches. Anna tugs the wheel towards the cars closer to the ditch. She's playing chicken, and she's not going to lose. She's hoping she can get these idiots to plow into the ditch and get stuck. Anything to minimize the number of morons risking everybody's life to cut traffic.

She's seconds from colliding with the nearest car. She's about to die to make a stubborn point to these idiots, and she doesn't even care.

But Anna underestimates stupid. The cars near the shoulder don't go towards the ditch. Instead, the two vehicles in her path swerve to their right, directly into the other cars.

In an instant, Anna's rage morphs to disbelief. The cars crash into one another and begin spinning across the road. One flips completely, toppling on its roof over and over again. Anna has to swerve and slam on the brakes to avoid a truck careening her way. It clips the very back of her bumper and sends her car into a spin. She holds on to the wheel as hard as she can and expects another impact.

But that was the last of the wrong-way cars. There's a few more in the distance, but upon seeing the crash, they've pulled onto the shoulder.

Anna slowly undoes her seat belt and steps from the car. Outside, people are yelling.

One of the cars that flipped rests on its roof, and a woman has already crawled from the driver's-side window. It's a tricked-out Jeep Wrangler with a *Salt Life* bumper sticker.

"What is wrong with you! You fucking psycho!" A woman in cowgirl boots starts screaming so loud that her voice gets rough and gravelly. Anna looks over her shoulder, but it's obvious the woman is speaking to her. "Robert?!" the woman shouts as she runs around to the other side of the car, shouting. "Robert?! He's bleeding!"

The other wrong-way drivers who had wrecked are leaving their cars and beginning to converge towards Anna. If someone was dumb enough to speed the opposite direction down a freeway, what do they do when they think they've been horribly wronged?

Anna starts walking backwards towards her car.

"Look, did the police *let* you drive west in the eastbound lanes?"

No one responds to this. Obviously, the answer is no. For a moment, Anna thinks she can reason with them. "You're lucky you didn't kill anyone! The hurricane wasn't going to get you in traffic. It's nearly a day away."

A huge man in a filthy flannel shirt has been making his way up from the ditch. He's a freaky combination of tall and fat, and when his feet touch the pavement, he begins to charge her.

Anna is only a few steps from her car door, but in her fright, she drops her keys and wastes a second bending to grab them.

It's all the time he needs.

She pulls open her car door and gets in, but right before the door is closed, his fingers grasp the metal and stop it from closing.

The woman in cowgirl boots is close again, shouting, "Citizen's arrest! Citizen's arrest! Get the psycho bitch!"

The big man throws the door open and grabs Anna's leg to pull her from the car. She can grab onto whatever she wants, but it doesn't matter. He'll get his way. She needs a weapon.

Her knife is in her pocket, but she can't get the angle to get it out. Right as he yanks on her leg, Anna takes the headrest off the driver's seat.

He pulls her out, and she hits the pavement hard on her butt, but before he can get his hands around her, she brings her arm back so one of the rods of the headrest is pointed at his knee, and she swings.

It's a direct hit. His knee buckles under his weight, and the man hits the ground hard with a scream. Anna isn't even thinking, now. She's in a blind rage. She swings and hits him in the other kneecap and then hops over him towards cowgirl boots.

The woman holds her hands out feebly and shrieks, "No! No!" She steps backwards and trips over. Anna stands over her, holding the head rest over her shoulder like a hammer ready to strike.

Suddenly, the rage leaves her. The image of this woman cowering on the ground takes Anna back to seventh grade.

To Mrs. Riley.

Anna walks back to her car quickly. She tosses the headrest in the passenger seat and floors it, heading east.

An exit down, she sees two cop cars at the off ramp putting up metal construction barricades. In front of them, a line of cars honks. This is where the wrong-way drivers got on, and it seems there are ample more drivers vying to do the same.

She wants to be proud of herself for handling those idiots, but she doesn't even know if she did the right thing. Maybe she should've just let them speed on. But then they were a threat to the cars behind her. She's done thinking of ethics. As she gets in sight of the city, the smoke that was rising this morning is thicker. The fires have spread.

If this kind of madness is happening outside of the city, Anna wonders, what is happening inside of it?

Locked

Her mom's apartment is several blocks from the nearest freeway exit, and she wants to spend as little time on the side streets as possible. The looting in some parts is quickly turning into a riot.

It's eleven a.m. when she gets off the freeway, and the street she finds herself driving down is deserted.

The looters understand there is safety in numbers. The police can hardly intervene when there are hundreds of them. Anna is sure there are other isolated incidents of vandalism and plundering, but for the most part, the looters are moving like locusts. For now, she knows from the news that they're several blocks from her at a strip mall.

Anna pulls up in front of her mom's apartment. The building is painted concrete—sky blue—but it hasn't been touched up in some time.

Right now, the place looks like a ghost town. From the sight of the mostly empty parking lot, Anna can tell most the residents have already evacuated. The paint is patchy, and there's a corkboard under the awning by the door covered with glass.

When Anna gets close, she sees that inside is a mugshot of a mustached man and a warning that a known sex offender has moved in. She puts her hand on the door to the building but finds it locked.

Anna could call her mom; she might pick up, but she might've evacuated already, too.

She's just about to start thinking up schemes of how to get inside the building when the front door opens. A Hispanic woman with a box in her arms and a toddler at her waist smiles nervously at her.

"Hi," says Anna as she takes the opportunity to step inside. The door shuts, and the hall is silent.

The building reeks of cat litter, which is better, she supposes, than whatever scent it's probably trying to hide.

She goes up one flight of stairs and down the hall. The lights are dingy; the walls, too, are stained with a dark urine-like substance. Maybe it's decades of smoke that has seeped through the walls.

The whole place feels like she's walking inside a cigarette butt.

She remembers her mom's unit easy enough: 222. Anna knocks on the door and waits. There are no footsteps or shadow cast in the peephole. She knocks again, but this time says, "Mom?"

Still no response. A door does open, but it's not her mother's. Anna turns to see a young woman in her pajamas staring at her from the other side of the hall.

"I haven't seen her in a few days."

"Huh?"

She points at her mom's door. "Allison. She's been out."

"You know her?"

"We talk when we see each other."

"I'm her daughter."

The woman glances her over. "You look like her."

Anna doesn't like to be reminded she's related to her mother at all. She ignores the comment. "Would you happen to have a spare key? Or do you think I could get one from the landlord if they're around?"

The woman laughs. "I don't have a key. And good luck getting ahold of property management. Buncha bastards."

Anna tries her mom's door handle again and puts some weight against it to see how sturdy it is. "Maybe I'll call her." Anna takes out her phone and taps her mother's contact. While it rings, the young woman stays in her doorway, waiting.

Anna's mom doesn't pick up. She sighs and puts her phone away, looking up as her mom's neighbor speaks again.

"You know, I do have a master key of sorts. This is a welfare check, right?"

"Yeah."

The woman nods and then turns over her shoulder. "Ricky!" she shouts. "Need ya out here!"

She doesn't give Anna an explanation while they wait. The woman just smiles at her. A moment later, a large man appears. He, too, is in pajama pants. He has bedhead, and his hair sticks every which way.

"What's up?" he asks.

The young woman, who Anna presumes is his girlfriend, points. "We need a door kicked down."

He looks confused for a moment, but then he doesn't even ask a question. "Okay." He steps into the hall and gestures at the door Anna stands in front of. "This one?"

"Um . . . yeah." Anna's a little shocked. The incoming storm has left everyone with a feeling of lawlessness, but she's happy to take advantage of it.

He positions himself in front of the door and then, in one swift motion, kicks the door just above the handle. The deadbolt cracks right through the old weak wood, and the door buckles open violently.

"There you go." He goes back into his apartment, and Anna watches him, dumbfounded.

"Ricky has some leftover skills from his old days."

"I see."

"I wouldn't worry about the door. This building will be rubble after the storm hits."

"Sure. Thanks for your help."

"Uh-huh." The woman lingers while Anna steps into her mom's apartment. It's clear she wants to stay and snoop.

Inside, the first thing Anna does is test the air. She takes a few strong sniffs in case her mom is somewhere decomposing, but the air, while not fresh, doesn't have a reek to it.

The apartment is oddly clean, and her mom is not a clean person. She leaves dishes in the sink and empty alcohol containers around. But there was none of that now. The sink is clean. The trash is emptied. There are no crumbs on the countertops.

Perhaps she has already evacuated.

Anna heads into the bedroom and then searches the bathroom. Before she looks around more thoroughly, she wants to make sure the apartment is actually empty. Once the curtains are drawn and the closets are checked, Anna looks back out to the hall. The woman has finally gone back into her apartment, and Anna starts to keep an eye out for little details.

She checks her mom's dresser. The drawers seem to be missing some clothes. They're all half full. When Anna can't find a toothbrush or any of her mom's medications, she figures she evacuated.

But where? Her mom can't afford a hotel. She doesn't have any friends or family, at least that Anna knows of. There was the maybe boyfriend she had in the city, but that was years ago. Plus, her mother complained about the pain she'd have after sleeping in a *bed*. There was no way she'd be able to stay in her car for days.

Evacuation is possible. It just doesn't feel likely.

Anna leans forward and chews her thumbnail. The one thing she is thankful for here is that so far, there is no teasing clue. Nothing has been left out for her to find. She stands and goes to the kitchen.

She opens the drawers. They aren't filled with kitchenware, but junk—mail, bills, and other old papers. It was the same way at their house growing up.

Anna takes two drawers out of their sockets and dumps them onto the kitchen table. She's going to go through *everything*.

But before she even gets started, she freezes; face up on the table are two pictures.

Anna picks them each up with a trembling hand. She was presumptuous to think the killer hadn't left a clue for her here.

One photo is of Hannah, and the other is of Tess.

In both pictures, the girls are illuminated in a flash. The pictures are taken close enough to see the fear in their eyes.

She turns the photos over, but there's no Polaroid, no second photo with writing like there was on the picture she'd found of herself.

These are the Flash Girl photographs. Anna now has three. Hannah, Tess, and herself.

She suddenly spreads the papers on the table, desperately looking for a third picture. She's looking for a photo of Sylvie, when she suddenly stops. There wouldn't be one, because the existence of such a picture is her own lie. One she's told so many times, she was beginning to believe it herself.

She has to go back one more time. Back to the day that she herself was supposed to die.

November 2018

Anna has rules. It isn't easy to live a double life as a teenager, but she makes it work. Sylvie never comes to the trailer park, or anywhere near it for that matter. In the years since they started hanging out again, Anna would bus downtown.

And even that is a lie.

She would tell Sylvie that her mom dropped her off a few blocks over since she has a job at an office building on Rutledge. But she doesn't think Sylvie buys it.

Sylvie is a little rich and sheltered, but she isn't an idiot. Still, the façade felt better than ever talking about the truth. "Oh, *my* mom? She's an unemployed drunk who used to beat me. The only reason she doesn't anymore is because I'm big enough to fight back."

Yeah. No, Anna thinks. Better to pretend everything is fine.

Since Hannah went missing months before and Tess moved to Columbia with her mom and stepdad, she'd been hanging out with Sylvie more and more.

Anna didn't know exactly what to think of Hannah's disappearance. While it was similar to her Flash Girls stories, she chalked it up to coincidence. She agreed with what the authorities thought. She'd gotten high. She'd gotten lost, and she'd either hurt herself or run into the wrong person.

Then a month ago, Tess got her license and came to town to visit, and while she was waiting to meet her drug dealer by the river, she had her picture taken from the dark just like Hannah.

She, too, accused Anna of it being some sick prank. Tess was vocal about being stalked. She filed a police report. But at the same time this stalking began, Tess had been getting bruised up by some new boyfriend seven years her senior she'd met in Columbia.

Weeks later, when she vanished, the two different police

departments didn't care to find a connection between her and Hannah's stories. Tess's case was too simple in their eyes—scumbag boyfriend, history of violence.

They kept an eye on him. Served him a warrant to search his apartment, but they never found anything. They probably just thought he got lucky and got away with it.

After Tess disappeared, Anna didn't believe in coincidences. Her story had come to life. She tried to get somebody to listen, but she'd deleted her posts about the Flash Girls. Regardless, every time she spoke, she simply sounded insane.

Anna has thought about running away, and she has. She's seldom sober. Which means she was bound to break her number-one rule—don't be high around Sylvie.

It's a Friday night, and she's bussed to the city to show up on Sylvie's doorstep without so much as a text because her phone is dead. When she's high, she can never keep it charged.

Sylvie's house is grand. It's a two-hundred-year-old colonial with a staircase that sweeps down into a narrow entrance hall. Anna is so high on Xanax, she's a little nauseous, and she holds on to the railing for support. To her horror, it's not Sylvie who answers the door, but her looming tower of a father.

He has a long beak-like nose, which his small glasses hang low on the bridge of.

He looks Anna over, and before speaking to her, he shouts over his shoulder, "Sylvie, your friend is here!"

"Hi, Mr. Platt," Anna says and gulps down her spit. She's afraid she's going to start sweating.

"Hello, Anna."

Sylvie's dad has never been a fan of Anna. He smelled cigarette smoke on her once and has assumed she's vagabond trailer trash ever since. The torn and dark clothes Anna wears certainly don't help either.

Sylvie appears in the doorway, and her dad walks out of sight.

"Anna, what are you doing here?"

She doesn't know exactly what to say, so she just blurts it out. "My friend died."

“Oh.” Sylvie wraps her arms around her, and as she applies pressure, she squeezes a tear or two out of Anna. “Who? How?”

“I’ve told you about Tess.”

Sylvie leans back and widens her eyes. “Tess died?”

Suddenly her name is called from inside. The voice is younger and female. “Sylvie! Where’d you go? It’s your turn!”

Sylvie shouts back while grabbing a jacket off a peg. “I’ll be back in a minute!” She takes Anna’s elbow. “Come on.”

They start walking around the block. Anna is looking over her shoulder every sentence or two. “Tess didn’t die exactly. She’s been missing. Just like Hannah.”

“Are you serious? Why haven’t I heard about this?”

“Tess is in Columbia.”

“Still. They were friends and they both went missing. This should be news.”

“They’re poor, Sylvie. It doesn’t work that way.”

“That shouldn’t matter. My dad, he works with the guy who runs one of the local papers. I could—”

“Nobody cares! Don’t you get that? It’s why I’m here. I’m done. I failed. I think the same person took them, but no one will listen. All they say is that Hannah overdosed in a ditch and that Tess’s boyfriend dumped her in one!”

Sylvie is silent for moment while they walk. “Why do they say that about Tess’s boyfriend?”

“Because he beat her.” Sylvie doesn’t respond to this, and Anna thinks she is probably thinking what everybody else is. “But things aren’t that simple. Remember how I told you I used to write?”

Sylvie nods.

“Their disappearances . . . They’re just like this story I posted years ago. I mean, like, to a T. Someone takes their picture in the dark. They’re stalked. They vanish. It happened to Tess, too. When I saw her after someone took her picture, she was so scared.” Anna starts to choke up, and Sylvie stops walking.

“Hey, Anna. Listen to me. Breathe.”

Anna takes a deep, stuttering breath as she fights back tears.

“This story you wrote, do you still have it?”

Anna shakes her head hard. "I deleted it. All of them. I felt guilty. Like it was my fault I made Hannah paranoid. Then this happens to Tess . . ."

"Why don't we talk about it some more when you're feeling better?"

"I'm never going to feel better."

"What I mean is . . ." Sylvie looks her in the eye. "Anna, you're high."

She's lost for words. Anna didn't even know Sylvie suspected her of ever doing drugs, but the way she said it made it sound like she's always known. "Hardly."

"Come on. I've seen you like this before. Your pupils are huge. Let's go back to my house. You can spend the night."

"You have friends over."

"Only till ten, and then I'll kick them out. Come on, please? I don't want you trying to get home like this."

"Okay," Anna says softly.

Five minutes later, the two of them walk into the living room of Sylvie's house.

There's a large square ottoman in the center of the room with a board game on it. Around it on the carpet, seated on heaps of pillows and blankets, are four girls.

"Anna, this is Emily, Phoebe, Addison, and Brook."

"Hi," the girls all mumble and wave. They're nerdy, like Sylvie. They wear glasses and have their hair in ponytails, and Anna knows they've probably never so much as seen a drug in their lives.

"This is my friend, Anna. She was in the neighborhood and stopped by."

"Do you live around here?" asks one of the girls, as if based on Anna's appearance, she'd be surprised if she did.

"No. I live in a trailer."

"Wait," says another girl, squinting. "I know you. Didn't you go to the Covenant of Christ?"

"Nope."

"Yeah, you did. We were in the same grade. You're that girl that stapled the AP History teacher's face."

"Nah," says Anna, shaking her head. "Wasn't me."

"I'm pretty sure it was."

"So!" Sylvie says loudly and claps her hands together. "We were just playing Pictionary. You want to join?"

"Maybe I'll just watch this round." Anna walks towards the circle and sits in between two of the girls on the floor.

They shift uncomfortably away from her. "You smell like cigarettes," says one of them.

Anna sniffs her own shoulder. "No, that's pot."

The girl wrinkles her nose and scoots a few more inches back. After a few minutes, they all get excited and into the game again, but Anna's had a long day, and as the Xanax fades, she begins to nod off.

Sylvie notices, and Anna's mostly asleep when she feels herself being hefted up under the armpits. "Come on, let's get you to my room."

It's a slow ascent up the stairs, and when they get to Sylvie's bed, Anna falls face-first into it.

She feels her socks being taken off and her head lifted before a pillow is slid underneath it. Then she's out like a light.

Sometime later, she wakes to the sound of footsteps by the bed. She stirs and stretches, and then a lamp turns on. "Hey, I thought I'd let you sleep," says Sylvie. She's setting up a blanket and pillow on the floor next to the bed.

"What time is it?" asks Anna.

"Like . . . ten thirty. Do you want to go back to bed?"

"No. No, I'm up."

"You feeling better?"

"You mean less high?"

"Yeah," Sylvie says quietly.

"Yeah, sure. I'm less high." They're both quiet for a moment. "I don't think your friends like me."

"That's okay."

"Sorry to barge in like a bum."

"I'm here for you, always."

"Always?" Anna says with a slight laugh. She feels like such a mess, she can't imagine someone making such a promise to her.

Sylvie doesn't laugh. She just stares intensely into her eyes. "Always, Anna."

The attention is making her uncomfortable. Anna didn't come here to be a burden. She's suddenly sober, and reality is coming down on her, like a great sheet of steel descending from the sky. If she doesn't get high again, she'll be crushed.

"I really have to pee."

Sylvie laughs and stands from the bed. "Okay. You want any food? I can make you something."

"Maybe. Not quite yet." Anna groans as she gets out of bed and goes into the bathroom.

She locks the door, turns on the fan, but doesn't go towards the toilet. She stands in front of the vanity, looking down to avoid her disheveled reflection.

Then she digs in her pocket. But her fingers find nothing but lint.

She panics and wiggles her hand in deeper. Then she slaps her left side and searches that pocket.

She tosses her phone, lighter, and little wallet on the vanity. Then she sticks her hands in her back pockets.

Nothing.

Her drugs are gone.

"No. No. No." She opens her wallet and searches for the little plastic bag of pills, but it's not in any of the pockets. "No. No. Fuck!"

To Anna, this isn't a matter of want at the moment. Her body *needs* more drugs.

Her skin itches. Her eyeballs bulge as if from pressure. She can finally begin to feel from the weight of the world. The thought of spending the night sober is too much.

The comedown. The minutes feeling like hours as she lies wide awake and sweats. Her next high God knows how far away.

For a stupid second, she thinks she lost them, but then her expression hardens as she looks at the lavender crescents under her eyes in the mirror.

She unlocks the door and flings it open. When she steps back into the bedroom, Sylvie is setting out aspirin and a glass of water on the nightstand. “You can still take the bed. I don’t mind sleeping on the floor.”

Anna is already blind with rage. “You have like a million other bedrooms in this house.”

“Yeah, but . . . I want to sleep next to you.”

Anna just shakes her head. She doesn’t want to be coddled. “Where are they?”

“Anna—”

“Where are they?”

“Where do you think?”

“Please tell me you’re hiding them.”

“I flushed them down the toilet.”

Anna’s eyelids peel back. Without even thinking, she walks so she’s in Sylvie’s face.

“You’re kidding. Sylvie . . .” Anna grabs her by the bicep, hard. “Tell me you’re kidding! You stole from me?”

Sylvie twists her shoulder away. “Anna, stop.”

“Do you have any . . . a*ny* idea how much those cost?! You rich little bitch. You think you’re so good. So helpful. Wow, Sylvie, you saved me!”

Sylvie doesn’t say anything. Anna lets go of her arm and begins to pace the bedroom. She’s already regretting what she said, but it’s like she can’t stop.

The drugs and the rage have taken over, and Anna sits trapped, a spectator from above.

“You don’t help me, okay?! I came here to see you. Not to get your un-asked-for help!”

“Okay,” Sylvie says sadly, her eyes on her feet.

“I mean, what the fuck, Sylvie? You dig in my pocket when I’m asleep like some little thief and think you’re doing the right thing?”

Suddenly the bedroom door opens. It’s Sylvie’s dad. “Is everything alright in here? What’s going on?”

“I was just leaving,” says Anna. She looks at Sylvie one last time, but they don’t make eye contact. Sylvie is still staring at her feet, and Anna watches a tear drop onto one of them before she squeezes past Sylvie’s dad and double-times it down the stairs.

"Anna!" Sylvie suddenly shouts after her. "It's late! We can drive you home!"

But Anna won't hear it. She pauses at the front door and walks instead into the kitchen and plucks a bottle of wine from the counter. Then she's out the front door, walking quickly from the house and into the dark.

When she's far enough away, she breaks the wine bottle's neck off on a stone windowsill and continues down the street. She takes careful glugs of wine, being careful not to cut herself.

She finishes the bottle in twenty minutes, and now she's far from sober. She has to walk slow to not throw up.

She's about to cross Congress Street when her attention is taken to the mouth of a dark alley.

There's a whining sound and then a click.

She pauses, but it all happens so quickly that she can't even register what's happening.

A flash bursts from the alley. She squints, and even though it lasts a fraction of a second, the brightness from the bulb is burned into her cornea. It's a little purple circle racing across her field of vision.

"Hey!" Anna yells, but her voice cracks. She begins to cry from fear.

The alley is a still wall of black, but then she sees movement.

The white palm of a hand waves gently back and forth.

This is her chance. She could charge him. Kill the man who's taken her friends. Or, she thinks, at least attempt to. But the thought doesn't last a moment before Anna starts to run. Flight wins again.

She doesn't know where she's going. She's trying to think a mile a minute, but her booze-soaked brain won't let her.

After stumbling between a jog and a run for ten minutes, she stops, looks behind her, and pants. The street is quiet. Empty. She wasn't running very quickly, drunk and short as she is. But if someone had followed, she thinks she would've been able to hear them.

She has a solution, one that she hasn't thought totally through. If she was being preyed on in exactly the same way as her stories, she has a way to save herself.

Just like in her stories, Hannah had gone home. Tess had gone home, and that's where their fates were sealed. The photographer knew where they lived, and from there, he stalked them. That's the way she wrote it. But is that the way it is?

There's no doubt whoever took Anna's picture knows where she lives. But what if she doesn't adhere to the rules of the story? She thinks. What if, unlike Hannah, and Tess, and all the other Flash Girls in her fiction, she doesn't go home?

It's as if her subconscious was thinking this all along, because she is nearly back at Sylvie's front door.

She never thought it through. If she did, maybe she would've just gone back to her trailer.

Instead, Anna turns the door handle. It's unlocked, probably at Sylvie's request in case she came back. She opens it slowly and steps inside. Then she turns and stares out at the dark street.

She sees no one. There are no cars or pedestrians. Just a soft hum of streetlights, but even so, she knows she's being watched from somewhere in the dark.

She takes another step back and gently closes the door.

Maybe this plan will work, because after all, Anna doesn't live here.

Sylvie does.

Paper Trail

Anna takes her time going through the rest of her mom's papers. It's rare for her to ever recollect that last night with Sylvie.

She didn't think the killer's target would switch to Sylvie like some kind of curse.

She didn't know what she was thinking, but at some level she had to have known. She didn't tell Sylvie about someone taking her picture that night. She apologized and passed out drunk like nothing happened.

It wasn't until she called Anna a few days later that she knew something was wrong.

Sylvie said somebody had broken into their house. That they'd gone through the things in her room specifically but not taken anything.

When Anna tried to warn her, when she panicked trying to tell Sylvie this was what happened to Hannah and Tess, there was silence on the other end of the line, and then Anna heard the hopeless words. "Call me when you're sober."

Delusional druggie. That's what the whole world thought. Even her best friend.

Sylvie didn't have weeks after the photograph like Tess and Hannah. She vanished quick. Three days from when Anna first showed up at her doorstep, she was gone. Presumably kidnapped when she was walking home from work.

Anna keeps leafing through documents on the table. There are user manuals for long-forgotten appliances and power bills dating all the way back to 2006.

Anna takes a third drawer from the cabinet and empties it on the table. It's mostly more paper, but the documents are newer.

There are deposit receipts from her mom's bank. They're all the same amount—fourteen hundred dollars.

But what catches Anna's eye is under the words "deposit type," it says cash. Anna quickly pushes the trash heap of other papers aside to make room on the table and starts laying out the receipts. There are eight of them. Each is dated for the first of the month in the year 2016. Each is for a deposit made in cash.

Her mom claimed she was on disability, but she certainly wasn't getting paid in cash from the government.

She digs into the pile again, looking for anything related to money or welfare. She finds her mom's government assistant forms. She was on Social Security Disability Insurance, but there's a problem.

Anna runs her index finger across the page as she reads and stops it suddenly. Her mom's total monthly payment she received was eight hundred and seventeen dollars.

It wouldn't have been enough to live on. Not with her smoking and drinking. There was more money coming in—$1400 more for at least eight months.

Anna starts going through the documents more carefully. There are no hints in here. Nothing written in ink teasing her.

This feels like maybe she's found something she wasn't supposed to find. Anna picks up an envelope that was returned to sender. Inside is a handwritten note.

To the Assholes at Robinson Assets & Trust,

Hope this letter is finding you well from Vanessa, Ellen, and Allison. That's right, people at trailer parks talk. Did you ever think of that? The three of us have got it figured out. I'm not alone anymore, and we're sure the news would like to know, too.

That said, all this can go away the same way it has. WE JUST WANT OUR MONEY. More of it this time, obviously. A lot more.

If you don't reach out to negotiate this by the 30th of this month, we go public.

You owe us.

It was obviously written by her mother, but the letter isn't dated.

Anna frowns and reads it over again. Someone in the postal service had written *CANNOT BE FOUND* on the envelope and drawn an arrow to the address. It has to be the same Robinsons who own the mansion on Church Street that Sylvie was found in.

Vanessa was Hannah's mom, and Ellen must be Tess's. And the three of them were being paid fourteen hundred dollars in cash each month.

But why?

Anna can deduce that their moms didn't know the others were being paid until not long before the letter was sent. She re-reads the words, *People in trailer parks talk. Did you ever think of that?*

When the money stopped, they found out the others had been getting paid, too. Probably from the stress and lifestyle changes they had to make. It would be easy to tell something was bothering the others. All it took was one of their moms mentioning how they used to be getting more money, and the response was "Me too."

Then the beans were spilled.

But that meant the fourteen hundred dollars in cash they were getting was originally something meant to be kept secret.

Most of the rest of the papers Anna finds are junk, and there are no more drawers to dump on the table.

She's almost through all the contents when she finds a little envelope. It's from WTSP, a local news station. The letter regrets to inform her mother that, even if she did have proof of her accusations, they wouldn't be interested in running the story. What the letter doesn't include is what accusations her mother originally made.

She knows people at WTSP. Maybe they kept the letter in their records, but with the storm coming, it will be impossible to get it quickly.

This stack of papers has only left her with more questions, but finally, Anna knows what direction to start looking in.

Robinson Assets & Trust.

Smoke Signals

Google search results yield nothing. There's no office address or article of any kind mentioning them.

Her mom might've gotten the name wrong. The address wrong. There was no telling with her and her drinking.

Anna searches *Robinson Family Charleston SC*.

There are plenty of relevant results. But when she tries to click a link, the load bar goes halfway and then freezes. She curses and tries another, but she gets the same result.

She tries to refresh and search again, but she's greeted with Google Chrome's digital dinosaur.

No internet.

With all the fires and wind, this was bound to happen, but it feels to Anna like this is the end of the road. She'll have to go inland to get internet. Then the storm will hit, and the timer will expire.

She still has to find Tess's body. She's certain that's another clue. Another piece to the puzzle that will be dangled in front of her before she gets her answers—if she ever does.

She takes the papers that might tell her something, as well as the photographs of Tess and Hannah, and leaves the apartment.

She doesn't know how far she'll have to go in order to get service. As she steps into the parking lot, the emergency sirens begin to blare. Anna checks the time. One o'clock. They're probably going off on the hour.

The anxiety in her gut wants her to leave the city. The palm trees bend west from the wind, as if beckoning her to do what they can't—flee inland. She doesn't have many other options, until her eyes find the smoke that rises into the sky.

She knows one person who might know about the Robinson family, and she thinks she knows exactly where to find them.

Hysteria

Anna grabs a hooded sweatshirt from the back seat and slips it on. She's going into the thick of it, and she doesn't want to look vulnerable. Being 5'1" doesn't work to her advantage very often.

She drives towards the looting and quickly gets in sight of the strip mall. It looks like a battlefield. Smoke, fire, police. The parking lot is filled with people filling the backs of their cars with goods.

Others smash windows for what looks like just the hell of it. There's a smoke shop, liquor store, and a Best Buy, and some big brand outlet stores that are in the final stages of being ransacked.

She parks far from the lot, puts her hood up and starts jogging over. She finds signs of what she's looking for immediately—there's a line of journalists, some with full-size TV cameras on their shoulders, staying close together for safety while they film.

But Justin is not among them.

The police are on the north side of the parking lot. They're lined up in riot gear but not advancing. Perhaps they're waiting for even more backup. The few cops here are outnumbered maybe ten to one.

With little left to steal, some of the looters have turned their attention to the police. There are rock beds ringed around the parking lot, supplying ample ammunition to the looters, who hurl the stones like pitchers and shout insults.

Anna takes in the scene for a moment. There's a haze that rises from a few tear gas canisters, but the wind is too strong for them to have any effect. The fumes are rocketed away.

The fire that guided her here comes from one of the outlet shops. Its sign has melted, and a large contingent of masked men dance and holler in front of the flames. Soon, the whole strip mall will be alight. The locusts will move on.

All most people need to act like animals is a good enough excuse, and this storm has supplied that.

Justin could be here, or reporting at another looting location, or already evacuated. She checks her phone. No service. It's an eerie thing to read while standing in the middle of a city.

"Hey, tits." A boy no older than sixteen struts up to Anna with a couple friends in tow. "You here with your man?"

Anna looks him over. "Are you here with your mom?"

His friends cackle and hang on his shoulders while they laugh. The boy shakes his head and looks like he's going to snap back, but his friends keep walking and their little group moves on.

Anna feels more vulnerable than before. These are men and boys in their most base state. Smoke on the wind. A storm in the distance. The scene screams lawlessness. And whether or not anyone here will face consequences for their actions in this madness is questionable.

Then to Anna's horror, the line of police begins walking not forwards, but backwards. "What? Where are they going?"

Someone from the line of journalists hears her and answers. "There's nothing worth protecting. The storm's going to get it all anyway."

Anna looks back towards the police, when suddenly she sees a man with a GoPro camera on a stick. He's on the other side of the parking lot wearing a gas mask and is hunched halfway over while he films.

He could be anyone, but then Anna notices the man has the same gangly frame as Justin. Anna starts jogging over. She would feel safer in sight of the police anyway.

"Justin!" she shouts when she's close enough. The man turns from his camera shot and strips off his gas mask. It's him.

"*Anna?* What are you doing here?"

"Looking for you."

"So . . . you ditch me and then ignore my calls." He crouches and keeps focusing on his camera shot. Anna notices a bulge on his right hip—a holstered pistol. "If you still want to work together, guess what? Now it's me who's not so sure."

"Hannah was my friend."

"What?"

"Hannah, Tess, Sylvie. Every girl who went missing, they were all my friends."

Justin pauses and stands. "What do you mean? Like you're connected to every murder?"

"Exactly."

"Give me a break."

"I'll tell you everything. See if it makes sense yourself. But I need your help with something."

Justin looks around. "Can you give me a minute? I need to put this somewhere." He gestures to the GoPro.

"Just set it down."

He laughs. "I'm not sure four thousand people want a view of the asphalt."

"What are you talking about?"

"I'm live streaming right now."

"*What?*" Anna takes a step back. "For *The Journal?*"

"Of course not. I went AWOL after Bruce asked me to pick up your slack. You think I was going to evacuate to a Holiday Inn to write about the ten strongest storms to ever make landfall in North America? Bunch of bullshit. I quit. This is for my YouTube channel."

Anna stares into the little black lens. It reminds her exactly of when she posted the stories of the Flash Girls online. Someone, somewhere, was watching her. "Stop filming me."

"Relax."

"Just . . . point it away from me!"

"Here." Justin walks towards a light pole in the parking lot that has a thick concrete cylinder as a base. He props the camera up on it so it faces the police. Then he goes a few feet away to Anna so they're both out of earshot.

"What's your problem?"

"Do you have any idea who could be watching that?"

He sighs. She can tell he wants to call her paranoid, but he doesn't want to risk shutting her up. "So, what's the story?"

She's interrupted frequently by yells and from the crash of rubble as more of the strip mall collapses from the flames, but in not much more than five minutes, she's told Justin an abbreviated version of just about everything. She tells him about breaking into the morgue and the mansion. About the fact that she was photographed too but went to Sylvie's house instead of her own. She ends by mentioning the money her mom was getting and the letter to the Robinsons.

Justin doesn't say anything for a moment. "You sound a bit bonkers, Anna."

"But do you believe me? You can go back to the trailer park. Ask around about me. I lived there." Anna is speaking quickly in desperation. "It's why I took off after Hannah's body was found there. I didn't want to get mobbed, and if—"

Justin holds one hand out. "I believe you. But can I see some evidence for any of this? Do you have pictures of this . . . shaft behind your sink?"

"It was for a dumbwaiter."

"Okay, okay. I still just think it might be good if I could see it. What you're saying is a bit hard to believe. I want to give you the benefit of the doubt."

Anna opens her phone and goes to photos. She goes to the favorites folder and finds a selfie of her, Hannah, and Tess. They're sticking their tongues out and sitting on one of the picnic tables in the trailer park. It might be the last picture of all three of them together.

She turns her phone so Justin can see.

"Shit." The blood leaves his face, and Anna can tell he didn't believe a word she'd said until now.

"The newest lead I have is this letter my mom sent to the Robinsons. I know you grew up in the same neighborhood. Did you know them?"

"No. Their youngest children are ten years older than me. We never overlapped in school or anything. I heard stories though. Mean kids."

"They were bullies?"

"Yeah. Rub-your-face-in-dog-shit kind of kids. But I don't know, that could be shit people made up because they were rich. That can be the case. They're spooky rich. Rumor rich."

"Where are they now?"

"Who, the kids?"

"Yeah."

"Ugh." Justin takes his gas mask off completely and rubs his forehead. "I don't know, Anna. You're stretching my memory for this one. One son went into law enforcement, I'm pretty sure. A daughter moved to New York. Another boy drove his Porsche into an oak tree. I know that for sure. He's dead. Shit. I feel like I'm forgetting one. It's a big family. Not a lot of consequences for not pulling out when you can have a nanny raise the kid, ya know?"

Anna ignores him. "But no one comes to mind immediately? There was no black sheep who tortured small animals or picked on little girls?"

"Black sheep . . ." Justin looks off into the distance. "Not that I'm aware of. I could call my mom. If there was, she'd know. She has her PhD in tea."

"You can try. I don't have any service."

"What do you mean? I've been live streaming."

"You sure you're live?"

Justin starts walking towards his camera, when suddenly, a skinny man in a face mask and hoodie sprints by and grabs it. "Fucking riot, baby!" he shouts and once closer to the flames, he hurls the camera stick into the burning mall.

"Dude! Really?" Justin yells back, but the man doesn't hear. He keeps sprinting around the parking lot.

"Can you believe this?" he asks Anna, but she doesn't say anything.

She's relieved. The thought of being filmed live for any creep to watch from afar was too much. A knot loosens in her stomach.

"Sucks."

"Yeah, it sucks. That's a seven-hundred-dollar set up."

Anna doesn't say anything. She lets Justin fume for a minute.

"Whatever," he spits. "Let's just get out of here. Shall we?"

"Did you drive?"

"Did I take my Audi to the scene of a looting? No. No I did not."

"Alright. Come on, rich boy."

Anna nods in the direction of her car, and they cross the parking lot towards the side streets.

They're quiet while they walk, heads swiveling to see if they're being followed. When the chaos and the clamor of the strip mall loses out to the roar of the wind, Justin talks. He leans close to Anna's ear.

"So, you think your mother and those other women were being paid each month to keep something quiet?"

"You got any other guesses?"

"Yeah. What if they were being paid to do a job?"

"What do you mean?"

"I'm not trying to sound crazy or anything, but just think about it. The way your friends had their pictures taken. Maybe someone wanted to see them. Someone who would be willing to pay a good price based on how pretty they are."

"So what? You think someone was paying our moms to traffic their own daughters?"

"Do you think this would be the first time human trafficking occurred in a trailer park? I mean, sorry, I don't mean to offend. I don't know your mother. Was she the kind of person who would do something like that for cash?"

A particularly strong gust of wind pushes at their backs, and Anna takes the opportunity of the interruption to be silent.

She doesn't want to respond because she knows her mother is exactly the kind of woman who would.

Full Bars

When they get into Anna's car, she starts driving north, inland, while Justin wants her to drive southeast to downtown.

"I'm telling you, there's going to be service in the city. Wait! See!" He turns his phone towards her. "I have a bar!" Justin goes to dial but suddenly brings his phone down from his ear. "Oh, never mind."

"I told you."

"Okay, forget about calling my mom. Is that really the best damn lead we have?"

"You got a better one?"

"The Robinsons have an office. It's on Battery Street."

Anna pulls out the letter her mom had mailed. "Is it 121 North Battery?" she asks Justin.

He frowns. "I don't think so. There is no North Battery Street. The office is at Battery and Limehouse, I think. There's a stencil on the window that says Robinsons A&T." He points at the letter in her hands. "Is that the letter your mom sent?"

"Yeah, to a nonsense address." Anna figures her mom was drunk when she sent it. After all, when was she not? She turns to Justin with a skeptical eye. "Why are you just mentioning this office now?"

"Because I know exactly what you're going to want to do. I'm not as comfortable with the whole burglary thing as you are."

"Oh, you think this is a bad time to break into a business? Because if there was ever a time . . ."

"Just hear me out. I want to look into this mansion on Church Street. Do you think we could get back in?"

"Definitely, but why? I searched the place already." Justin is quiet while he lets Anna figure it out on her own. "Oh, I get it. You think I missed something?"

"Two sets of eyes are better than one. All I'm saying. I think we know more than we did when you first searched the place."

"What more do we know? That Hannah was found under her floor? That—" But Anna shuts up immediately. She remembers something. Something she glossed over the first time. "Floor . . ." she whispers to herself.

"What?"

"The floor in the cellar . . ." She's thinking of the bricks that wobbled under her steps like loose teeth.

Anna suddenly takes a hard left to start heading downtown.

"Yo! Shit!" Justin yells as he's pressed against the passenger-side door. "Care to explain your epiphany?"

"We're going to Church Street."

"What did you realize?"

But Anna keeps her mouth shut and steps on the accelerator. She fears it's her turn to find a body beneath the floor.

"Tess," she says aloud.

Sharpie

There's a National Guard barricade blocking the right side of the street that travels south to downtown. There are two lanes, and about a dozen cars are stopped trying to get through. Cops in blue mingle around with the Guard in their camouflage uniforms.

"Can we even get downtown?" asks Justin.

"They're probably just stopping caravans of looters."

They're both quiet as they creep forward in line. Anna rolls down her window when it's their turn.

A guardsman leans in. "What's your business downtown?"

"Um . . ." Anna stutters. "We need to get my cat."

He purses his lips, as if that's everyone's answer. "Alright." He hands her a black permanent marker. Anna takes it without asking. "I'm going to need you both to write your full name on your non-dominant arm and below it a phone number of next of kin."

"Ah . . ." Anna hesitates with the marker.

"It's to make it easy to identify your bodies if you choose to stay in the surge zone."

"Okay." Anna starts scribbling on her arm. She puts her mom's number. She hands the marker to Justin, and when he's done writing, she hands the marker back.

The guardsman waves them through. "Good luck. Be quick."

Anna starts to drive, but she pauses. In the second line of cars to her right, she sees someone. They're staring right at her. She looks across the passenger seat and makes eye contact with Terry.

His face is wrinkled in confusion. Then he points at her and says something to one of the cops at the checkpoint. Anna doesn't floor it, but she gives the car some gas.

"Is this shit for real? Or just a scare tactic?" Justin says, looking at his arm.

Anna doesn't answer. She's worried about being followed by Terry. What he's doing downtown, she can only guess. But if he's here right before evacuation, he must be investigating something to do with these cases. Something that he fears will be lost in the storm.

She takes a right and then a left and then another right.

"Where the hell are you going?"

"Making sure we're not being followed." She pulls to a curb and stops. "I saw someone at the checkpoint."

"Who?"

"This detective. Do you know Terry Fields?"

"Yeah. He's the lead on this Church Street corpse."

"Well, we go back."

"How so?"

"Like he's caught me poking my head into these cases before."

"Is it a problem?" Justin looks over his shoulder.

"I'm sure he'd like to arrest me for trespassing. Let's just wait a bit before we go any farther. He knows I'm a journalist. He might just think I'm here for the storm."

They stay parked for twenty minutes before continuing to Church Street.

Downtown Charleston is already a ghost town. The brunt of the surge is supposed to hit here, and most families have the means to evacuate comfortably.

Anna sees mostly cops, but they're not patrolling. They're working with other first responders and the National Guard to evacuate the elderly and others who can't travel by themselves. They're putting them into military trucks with canvassed beds and black tires nearly as tall as Anna.

When Anna's back on Church Street in front of the mansion, she looks both ways down the street. There are no cars at all. "He's not here."

"Let's make this quick, then," says Justin, and Anna parks.

It's much windier downtown. She thought the buildings might serve as protection, but Charleston's narrow colonial streets are acting like wind tunnels.

American flags rip and clap on their poles. Shutters fly open and shut. There's an anxiety to the movement of these objects, and Anna has to resist the urge to turn the car around.

"You have a gun on you, right?"

"How'd you figure that out?"

"You're not as sly as you think. Come on, I'll show you where we get in."

They exit the car and make their way towards the backyard where the cellar window is. The plywood Anna had kicked in hasn't been replaced. It's easy access inside.

As she bends to crawl in, Anna doesn't bother to see if they're being watched. If the police are called now, there's hardly a chance they'll show up.

"Alright." Anna shimmies so her legs are through the window. "You got a flashlight?" Anna asks Justin.

He slings off a small backpack and opens a pocket. "I've got everything. Band-Aids, flashlight, batteries."

"I just need the flashlight."

"You got it." He clicks it on and hands it to her.

She slides herself through the window and plops down on the floor. "Get in here. And get that gun out."

She gets to her knees and starts trying to pry one of the loose bricks out from the floor. Justin trips on his way down but catches himself just before he falls. "Jesus . . ." He looks around. "This is quite the décor."

"Spiderwebs and mold? Yeah. Can you help me with this?"

"What are you trying to do?"

"Lift one of these." Her words become mumbled as she sticks the flashlight in her mouth in order to use both hands. Justin sets his long fingers on one side of a loose stone while Anna holds the other. They lift slowly, and the brick scrapes against the others as it rises.

Below it, there's isn't an empty space like Anna had hoped, just rocky soil. With the one brick removed, it's much easier to get their hands under more bricks to lift them. After the fifth brick, Justin stops, while Anna keeps removing them at a feverish pace.

"Anna." She keeps removing stones until he sets his hand on her wrist. "I don't think there's anything here."

She stares down into the dirt and pants. “Then let’s get out of here.”

“Come on, Anna. We’re here. I want to see the rest of this place.”

“Then let’s be quick.” She starts towards the stairs but pauses as Justin doesn’t follow. He’s looking at something on the floor.

“Is this what barricaded the window?” he asks, holding up the piece of plywood that Anna had kicked out of the frame a couple days ago.

“Yeah.”

“Did you look at this?” He turns it over in his hands and shows the inside to Anna. It’s made of two plywood sheets that have been screwed together, and there’s a middle.

“It’s stuffed with soundproofing.”

She walks over to take a closer look and pulls out a handful of black foam.

“You really didn’t see this?”

Anna wants to yell. “No. I was in and out. I took some pictures and bailed. It was literally right after everybody left.”

“Okay.” Justin sets the plywood down. At first, Anna thought he was giving her a hard time for not searching thoroughly, but now she thinks it’s because Justin is a little skeptical of her all around.

Maybe he doesn’t trust her. Just as she’s thinking it, he pulls a small handgun from its holster.

“What?” he says while Anna is staring at him. “You wanted me to keep this out, right?”

“Yeah,” Anna says, but her eyes linger a moment longer on the little black pistol before she starts up the stairs.

The first floor of the house is just as she’d found it on Friday and just as quiet. She should hear the wind roaring in the street, but the house is silent.

“These boards . . .” Justin walks to the barricaded windows that line the living room. “They all have to be soundproofed same as the one downstairs. Did the police ever mention this?”

“I don’t think they know. The girl I talked to who trespassed here and found the body said that one of the plywood sheets was missing. That’s how she got in. Nobody found it lying around. The police don’t know this place is soundproofed yet.”

“I find that hard to believe. I can hear my heartbeat in here.”

"There was probably a lot more commotion when the police showed up. And they kept the front door open, so you didn't have the same kind of silence we're getting now."

"Hmm." It's all Justin says. He approaches the pipe that hangs down from the ceiling close to the wall in the living room. He pokes at the squishy patch of rotted wood with the toe of his shoe.

"God, that reeks. What is this? Mold?

"Yeah, black mold or something."

"It smells like . . ." He sniffs loudly. "It kinda smells like . . ." He gets down on his knees and puts his nose closer. When he takes another sniff, he recoils away. "It smells like piss. Ammonia." He looks at Anna like this means something.

"Yeah?"

"What if that's what it is?" Justin shines his flashlight on the pipe. "Someone painted this pipe." He shines his flashlight on the walls and trims and runs his thumb on them. "Nothing else has new paint. Here." Justin holds his gun out to Anna. "Can you take this for a sec?"

She hesitates and then grabs the pistol. "What are you doing?"

"I'm trying to answer a question. I mean, why would someone paint a pipe, of all things?"

Justin takes a pocketknife out and flips it open with a quick click. Then, he starts cutting at the paint on the pipe. It's been lathered on in thick coats, and the shavings fall to the floor.

"Shine the light close here, would you?"

Anna shines the light right where Justin is cutting. After half a minute, he folds his knife and blows on the area. "You see this?"

Anna bends closer. "The metal?"

"Yeah, it's all scratched and dinged."

He crouches and starts cutting another area on the pipe. This time much lower. "It's the same," he says before standing again. "Someone was trapped here." He points at the floor. "Right here. And the stain. This is where they'd piss."

"Come on," says Anna doubtfully with a chuckle. Part of her laugh comes from the fear that she missed something so critical again. "Where'd they shit, then?"

"Well, maybe our captor cleaned that business up. Do the toilets flush?"

"Yeah, the place has water."

"There you go. Hannah was alive for years, and I'd be willing to bet this is where she spent most of it."

The thought threatens to send Anna into a panic attack. It was one thing to have her friends be murdered, but to be kept alive in a hell such as this dark, silent house . . . She shivers.

"How can we find out which Robinson bought this house?"

"Well, I know the mom, Clara Robinson, purchased it, because she made a big stink about not being able to renovate it. But it's possible any number of family members or even friends used this place after word got out it would be left to rot."

"Justin . . ." She holds his gun back out to him, and he takes it. "We're going to have to break into that office."

He sighs. "There's just one problem with that."

"And what's that?"

"Come on, Anna. It's on Battery Street. There's bound to be a bunch of cops around there still."

"We don't have a choice, do we?"

"Maybe you don't."

"What?"

"Can you blame me?" Justin says louder. "You want me to risk my whole career because your mom wrote a letter to the Robinson family? This all feels like a stretch."

"A mummified corpse was found in this property. And you just said you think a girl was kept here for *years*. Now you're suddenly not sure it's the Robinsons behind this? They own the house."

"Why would someone shit where they eat?"

"Because serial killers all itch to be caught."

"I'll go with you and I'll stand as casual look out, but I'm not breaking in. There's a curfew, and that's a felony."

"Fine."

"But this story . . . I still want equal share."

"Oh, for fuck's sake. You'll get it. I don't care about the glory. I want to solve this."

"I'm just a little concerned for you, if that's your aim."

"Why?"

"Because if your theory is right and he wants to get caught, then you solving this is exactly what he wants. Am I wrong?"

Anna is quiet. "Come on. Let's search upstairs and get out of here."

She shows him to the master bedroom, where Sylvie's body was found. The tea table and chairs are set up the same as they'd been. The place seems untouched from the last time Anna was here.

Justin shines the flashlight on the riddle and reads part of it. "I am had by all but not by some. Called a name, but not my one. The apple of my eye, and it is there where one can find me. What am I?" He turns to Anna. "Any guesses?"

"What do you think?"

"I suck at riddles." The house creaks from the wind, and Justin whirls around with his gun drawn. "Let's just go, yeah?"

"Yeah." Anna walks past him down the hall.

They don't speak on their way out. When they crawl from the cellar, they're both still brushing the dust off of themselves when they slip around from the back and onto the street.

Anna sees it first, and she stops in her tracks without even thinking. Justin keeps walking several steps before he realizes she's not following him.

"What?" He spins to look at her and then follows her gaze.

At the end of the block is a long black sedan. It's a Mercedes, just like the one Anna had almost been run over by.

"Sweet ride," says Justin. "Not sure that'd be my storm-chasing choice, but—"

"We need to go." Anna walks around to the driver's seat of her car.

"What? What's wrong?"

She didn't include the bloody footprints and her encounter with this car when she told him her story. "I've seen this car before. We need to go."

"Is this Terry?"

"No. It's not the cops. Get in the car."

"What if it's the killer, then? Anna?! Anna?!"

She says nothing while she fumbles with her keys. Anna gets the door open and starts to get in the driver's seat when she notices Justin is not waiting by the passenger seat. To her horror, he's walking down the sidewalk towards the car.

She rolls down the back window to talk to him. "Justin!"

He stops and points. His right hand gently rests on his holster. He thinks he's being sneaky, but anyone with a knowledge of firearms would be able to see he's getting ready to draw. "Is this him?"

The wind is howling now, and the anxiety is eating Anna alive. Something feels very wrong. The tops of the palm trees sway, panicked. "This isn't a clue, Justin. This is a trap!"

"Anna . . ." He lowers his voice and mouths, "I've got the gun."

"Justin," she says and pauses. "Get in the fucking car."

He grimaces and looks from the Mercedes to her Taurus, as if torn whether or not to listen to her. He relents and gets in.

The second he shuts the passenger door, Anna pulls from the curb. For the first block before she turns, Anna's eyes are glued to the rearview, but the black car doesn't move.

"Maybe there's no one in it." Justin says as they turn left. "Come on, Anna. We should search it."

"Are you some kind of killer, Justin?"

"Excuse me?"

"I don't know if you're just young or an idiot or both. This man, he's *murdered* people. You want to walk up to his car on an empty city street?"

"Fine, can we just circle back? See if it's still parked there?"

"Already on it." In a couple more blocks, Anna takes a second left so she can loop back. They creep slowly towards the intersection with Church Street, leaning forward in their seats to see if the car is still there. The spot it had occupied is empty. He must be following them.

"Fuck." Anna says quietly while her eyes flicker back to the rearview.

"Is he back there?" Justin turns to look out the back windshield.

"No, I haven't seen him."

"What do we do?"

Anna is quiet, thinking. She's scared, but she's sick of looking for clues. She has no interest in going to Battery Street.

This is her chance. He's here, and with a car and a gun, Justin and Anna have just as much of a chance of winning as he does.

"He's hunting us."

Justin cranes his neck to look behind them again. "Let's find a cop. Give them the vehicle description and tell them he's a murder suspect. It's not exactly a hard car to miss."

Suddenly, Anna sees the black car cross an intersection a few blocks ahead of her. "There!" she says and steps on the gas.

"What are you doing?!"

"Give me that gun if you're not going to use it."

"Are we certain this is even him? I'm not shooting at a random fucking car, Anna!"

"It's him. Give me the gun."

"You know what? Let me out. I'm done with this."

Letting Justin out will mean bringing the car to a stop, and Anna is doing no such thing.

She takes a hard left to follow the black car, but the street she'd seen it turn down is empty.

"You're kidding. What is this thing, the Batmobile?"

They drive slowly, and Justin points out the windshield. "He's got to be behind that bus."

Two blocks up, on the left side of the street, is a parked coach bus. It's too wide to see what is parked directly ahead of it, but there's certainly space for the black car. Anna slows as she approaches.

"What's the plan?" Justin asks. But Anna doesn't have one. She'll ram the car if she has to.

She drops the speed to ten miles per hour and then slower than five. As they begin to pass the bus, it's clear there's no one parked in front of it.

"Maybe he's not trying to follow us," says Justin. "Maybe he came to the mansion not expecting us to be there."

Anna considers the possibility that she caught him off guard. "It's possible."

Suddenly, the Mercedes spits out of the mouth of an alley on their right. It pulls up right next to them. Again, her instinct is to run.

She hits the gas to escape, but she's not looking at the road.

The street ahead is blocked with construction. She'll have to go in reverse.

"Anna," Justin says calmly. "Just stop the car."

"I'm not stopping the fucking car!"

She puts it in reverse, but he puts his hand on top of hers as it rests on the gear shift, and they stay stopped.

Justin has his gun held just below the passenger window, and he starts rolling it down. "If what you've said is true, and if this man wanted you dead, then you would be."

Anna's hands are white knuckled on the steering wheel. Something in her head is screaming that Justin is wrong, but she keeps her foot on the brake pedal as the black car rolls up next to them.

All of its windows are up, and the glass is so tinted it's impossible to see so much as a shadow within.

"Justin."

He holds a hand up to quiet her. He has his finger on the trigger, ready.

Suddenly, the black car's driver side window begins to roll down. All of Anna's good sense is gone. She's staring, transfixed.

This is it.

The reveal she's been after for years.

The glass suddenly stops. It's almost halfway down but still too high to even see the head of the driver.

"Hey," Justin says. "Can we help you?"

Anna thinks whoever drives the Mercedes must either be short or sitting low in their seat in order to still not be seen, when suddenly the glass vanishes.

There's an explosion, and Anna is peppered with glass and something warm. She screams and covers her ears with her hands.

When she looks back up, she's staring at the smoking mouth of a muzzle resting on the black car's windowsill. There's a hooded figure in the driver's seat. Before Anna can get a look at them, the car begins to roll in reverse.

It takes her several seconds to figure out why she's suddenly so wet. Justin is slumped over in his seat, and blood leaks and leaps as if flowing from geysers from half a dozen holes in his head and neck.

"Justin!" She pats his cheek and says his name again. Even though it's clear he's dead, the shock won't let her act like he is.

"Justin! Come on." She pats around, searching for his gun. When she finds it on the floor, she holds it in her lap. Then she calmly undoes her seat belt and steps out of the car. The open-door alarm sings as she stares back at the street.

The black car is a block away already. "Hey!" She points the pistol at it and pulls the trigger, but the gun doesn't fire. She looks at it and can the see the slide by the ejection port is bent; the gun had been hit by some of the buckshot.

It's as good as useless. She watches helplessly as the Mercedes keeps driving on. It drives slowly, calmly. And even uses its blinker to take a right and disappear from sight.

Fate

It would've been as easy as pulling the trigger one more time for them to have killed her. Justin was right—they wanted her alive . . . and alone.

She holds her phone to her ear after dialing 9-1-1, but it doesn't even ring—she still doesn't have service.

And so what if she did? Anna wonders. She'd be put on hold or told to sit tight. She ends the call.

Then she walks to the passenger side of the car. The glass is all broken, and the wind gently moves Justin's hair.

As the shock leaves her system, she starts cry. She's in too deep, and it's all her fault.

She knows the answer to what she should've done is easy—she should've been done playing this game days ago. She doesn't have what it takes to get a step ahead, and now, someone's dead because of it.

She has to get to the police. She snaps to it, gets back in the car, and drives west towards James Island and the Scarborough Bridge.

At every intersection, she slows to look both ways, but there are no more military trucks or school busses loading civilians. Nor is there a black Mercedes. The storm is closer now. Anna starts to hyperventilate. She's close to a panic attack and reaches over to turn on the radio.

"This curfew applies to all residents of Charleston who are found outside of their vehicles. If you are still within the city or choosing to try to weather this storm, then you should be hunkered down. Anyone caught on the streets will be arrested and evacuated by the South Carolina National Guard. It doesn't matter if you're taking pictures of the storm or breaking into a liquor store. The punishment for being outside of your home is the same."

When Anna starts driving on the Scarborough Bridge, she's the only car. She drives with the windows down because the minerally scent of Justin's blood is making her nauseated. To her left, she can see Charleston Harbor. Already there are six-foot swells, but what catches her eye is the ocean beyond.

The storm clouds above it are as black as night. She can see it now. The clouds out there are the outer rings of Hurricane Charlie.

She stops on the bridge. There's another checkpoint ahead. From what it looks like, they're not stopping people who are driving out of the city, only in.

She's far enough west to connect to a working cell tower, and her phone buzzes a half dozen times as it's lit up with notifications. She stops completely and looks at the screen. There's a message from her landlords asking if she's evacuated yet and a handful of government alerts about the storm and curfew, but the only thing that catches her eye is a new message from an unknown number.

It's an 843 area code.

Local.

With the car stopped, the scent of blood is nearly nauseating. Anna gets out of the car and stands in the open wind.

She opens her messages. There's a picture of a young woman with her mouth bound. Her bangs are bunched together, as if she's been struggling, and they hang in front of her face.

The text below reads:

Why couldn't you find me?

She looks back to the picture. Even with her face mostly covered with hair, she knows it's Tess. The picture, however, has to be old.

But what if it's not?

If Hannah was kept alive for years, could Tess still be breathing? The thought gives Anna a new kind of vigor.

She could drive up to the checkpoint and give the cops the car description and the phone number as well as the letter her mom wrote to the Robinsons. Whoever this person is, they'd left enough clues to now be caught, at least by law enforcement.

Anna tries to think ahead. If she does all that, then this game is over. She can wait on the sidelines while the cops track this psycho down.

She was always going to lose. She's been playing a game that the other player makes up as they go.

Anna glances to Justin's body and then back to her phone as it dings with another text.

Don't leave me twice.

Tess. Alive?

Anna doesn't quite believe it. She starts typing.

Enough games. You want me? Tell me where you are.

She hits Send and suddenly flinches as her phone violently vibrates in her hand.

It's not another text. An emergency alert warning takes over the screen while the sirens begin to wail on either side of the Ashley River. She looks at her phone.

ALERT

A hurricane warning is in effect for this area. Winds of 180 mph and storm surges of 25 feet are expected to cause severe damage to life and property.

EVACUATE INLAND IMMEDIATELY.

Her mouth gapes open as she suddenly understands part of the riddle. "The apple of my eye," Anna says aloud. "And it is there where one can find me."

It's in reference to the eye of the hurricane. The killer has expected all of this. Anna is right where he wants her. To leave is to win.

And yet, she can't say no. Not to all those years of curiosity finally coming to a close.

She puts her phone in her pocket and looks at the skyline of Charleston.

Its steeples stretch into the gray sky. All that history, hours away from erasure. And Anna doesn't care if she ends up among the rubble.

The sirens sing their eerie howls in the empty city, but this time, they don't feel like a warning.

They're a starter pistol, Anna thinks.

Let the games begin.

Soaked

Anna's not going to take her car. She needs Justin's body to be found. If she leaves it on the bridge, she's sure some of the last evacuating National Guard will find him.

It might make more sense for her to drag his body out and lay it on pavement so she can still take the car.

On foot, she has the dual threat of being stuck in the storm and being arrested for curfew, but the thought of taking him out of the car and putting him on the pavement seems too disrespectful.

She takes out a packet of wet wipes from the center console and starts vigorously scrubbing the blood off her face and arms. When she's mostly clean, she leaves the driver's-side door open so any passing vehicles can clearly see Justin's body inside and starts walking back to downtown.

She only makes it about three steps before the wind slams her car's door shut. She trots back, opens it, and then kicks the door towards the hood. The old door snaps and bends farther than its hinge allows. Now it won't shut at all.

She's proud of her work and about to start off again when out of the corner of her eye, she sees something coming towards her from the other end of the bridge near the checkpoint.

It's a police car that's left the barricade to come and investigate. They're driving slow with their lights on but sirens off. She doesn't know what to do. She's got about a fifth of a mile of bridge to run down before she even reaches the streets of Charleston, where she might be able to find an alley to disappear down.

Anna's wasting time staring at the oncoming headlights. She breaks into a run.

She hears its siren turn on and the engine rev as they accelerate.

Even with an Olympian's speed, there's no chance Anna makes it to the mazey streets of Charleston.

She's going to spend the night in prison trying to explain why she's driving around with a dead body in the passenger seat. She hears the car at her heels and stops and climbs the concrete barrier so she stands over the river. As far as bridge jumps go, it's not that far. Forty feet. A high dive.

Even so, Anna is terrified. There's a marina below the bridge. A dock stretches out into the water and branches off to make boat slips like words on a Scrabble board.

The cop in the passenger seat opens his door. "How about you step down from there?"

The police are taking advantage of her indecision and getting closer. They could pull her back over the edge.

At this point, she's forced to move. She closes her eyes and jumps. She has enough time in the air to notice her mistake. In her fear, she hadn't focused on where she'd land in the water. She could hit the dock and break both legs.

Thankfully, right when she's level with the shore and expecting a burst of pain, she plunges through the water.

The only thing she notices is how cold it is. The water is as cold as the ocean. The storm is already pushing the cold waters of the Atlantic deep into the harbor.

She pushes for the surface and takes a gasping breath. She only missed the marina dock by a few feet. She swims to it and rests her arms on the wood before pulling herself up.

As she drips on the dock, she glances back to the bridge. The two cops are staring at her over the ledge.

One waves.

Anna realizes they had sped by her car too quickly to look inside. They don't know about Justin's body. Right now, she just looks like a crazy person—one they don't have enough interest in to pursue. They're probably just glad she didn't drown.

Anna nods back to them and starts trotting down the dock. She has a minute, maybe two, before the police drive back towards the barricade and inspect her car.

Then they're going to realize she is, indeed, worth their time.

She climbs a fence and looks both ways. The office on Battery Street is to her right, but the police will expect her to run that way. Instead, she's going to loop around to get there.

She runs under the expressway bridge, leaving a trail of water drops on the ground, but as strong as the wind is, she prays they evaporate before the cops come looking.

She keeps sprinting north towards Cannon Street. By the time she's panting for breath, she hears the sirens.

She drops to her knees and crawls under an SUV that's been left parked on the street. Four police cars have left the barricade to come looking for her. Two go right, one stays straight, and the last takes a left and heads right towards her.

She's not completely hidden, but the cop assumes she's made more ground than she has, and it flies past her.

She stays underneath the car and catches her breath. She curses her stupidity.

She's made this more difficult than it should have been, but there was no way she could've revealed Justin's death to the police and not been brought in for questioning.

She's freezing cold now. She didn't even consider hypothermia, but in her drenched sweatshirt and jeans, the threat of hypothermia feels real. The strong wind chills her to the bone.

It's September in the south, and while she might not freeze to death, she already feels sapped of her strength as her skin prickles into gooseflesh.

She has to get dry.

She sprints across the street away from the river. She's several blocks from a residential neighborhood. This area is all hospitals—VA, Children's, University.

She darts through the empty campus. It's creepy in this darkening light. The power is out, maybe for the entire city, and what is typically a bustling complex of thousands of workers and patients has been turned into a ghost town. The wind howls through it. The only things that cross her path are plastic bags and palm leaves. There are no police.

By the time Anna reaches houses, her teeth are chattering.

She picks the first one she sees, goes around to the back, and throws a rock through a ground-floor window. Then she takes off her soggy sweatshirt and uses it to clear all the shattered glass from the frame.

She crawls inside and tries a light switch, but of course, the power is out. Even though it is still only afternoon, the house is gray and dark.

"Hello?" Anna says aloud, even though it seems clear this house has been evacuated. There are baby pictures on the fridge and kids' toys littering the floor.

If there was a family here, they wouldn't be silent.

She walks farther into the house cautiously. The broken window acts as a flue, and the wind is sucked inside. It flutters the curtains and blows over picture frames.

Even with the house shuddering and creaking from the coming storm, Anna finally feels safe.

Unseen.

She can regroup and get warm here. After all, she has time. The storm surge is still nearly twelve hours away from sweeping into the city.

She's itching to get to Battery Street, but she'll have to wait for nightfall. She's too exposed on the streets and the police will be looking for her until they're forced to evacuate the city.

She's not going to be any help to Tess if she's in a holding cell.

She needs to cool down. Compose herself.

Anna heads upstairs into the master bedroom and into their walk-in closet. She flips through their clothes and loses her own.

She throws off her T-shirt and spends a full minute wrestling off her wet jeans. She hasn't even thought of her phone until now. The screen is dark, and water runs from the charging port. If the man who had sent her pictures of Tess has responded, she'd have no way of knowing.

She takes off every article of wet clothing, ditches her bra and underwear, and wraps herself in a bath towel.

She finds an oak box in a drawer in the closet. It's rich, polished wood. For a moment her heart leaps, but when she opens it, she sees it is not a gun.

There are several watches inside—Rolexes, Omegas. Tens of thousands of dollars' worth of them. A pricey oversight for whoever evacuated. But what catches Anna's eye is a little electric Casio.

She picks it up and fits the belt strap to her wrist. Then she sets an alarm for three a.m.

That's when she'll have to evacuate in order to have a hope of making it to safety. There's a parking garage in North Charleston she knows of. It's new construction, several stories high. It would certainly withstand the worst of the storm.

At a pace of four miles per hour, she could get there in two. It wouldn't leave her much time, but she thinks it would be enough for her to reach safety before landfall.

She lays out a dry sweatshirt and pants and goes into the master bath. It's brighter in here. There's a big skylight that takes up half the ceiling, and in its own little corner is Anna's dream tub. It's a few hundred pounds of antique porcelain and sits on iron balls that are grasped by talons.

She walks to the tap and runs the water hot. Then she plugs the drain and breathes in the steam that rises from the bottom of the tub.

She sits there until the tub is half full and then returns downstairs to the kitchen.

She eats three granola bars, finds a pair of scissors, and starts back upstairs when she freezes by the front window in the living room.

There's an unmarked police car inching down the street. Just as it looks like the cop in the driver's seat turns to face the house, Anna drops to the floor. She curses her bad luck. She can't believe it. The cop in the car is Terry.

Of course he'd be looking for her too. He probably heard her description on the police radio. All the officers who are out looking for her might already know who she is.

She doesn't have a chance to run out the back—she's still only wearing a towel.

A minute passes and there's no knock on the door. But what if he's waiting for backup?

Anna crawls to the front window and pokes her head up. The car is gone. The street is empty. She could've sworn he had seen her when he turned, but he must not have. She feels like an animal being hunted. She bites her lip and draws the blinds.

Upstairs, Anna uses the scissors to cut a pair of women's pants she found to the same length as her ankle and tries them on with her belt. They're not comfortable, but they fit.

She loses the pants and goes back to the bathroom.

The water in the tub is scorching hot, but Anna couldn't care less. She tosses off her towel, turns off the tap, and stands in it while letting her shins adjust to the heat.

When she sinks into the water, she sighs with her eyes closed. She splashes her face and lathers her arms with soap, but after a few minutes, her movements slow. She gets lethargic as she feels her blood begin to warm.

Images flash in her mind's eye—Justin's corpse, Tess sucking air as water begins to cover her face—but she can't move. The hot water sits heavy around her shoulders, and before she can even sense it's happening, Anna's falling asleep.

Nightfall

Anna wakes in a panic. She splashes and gasps as she gets her bearings. The water she lies in is no longer hot. In fact, it's not even lukewarm. Sheets of rain and wind pound against the windowpanes.

She can't see a thing.

It's night now, and there are no shadows outside. There is no streetlight or moonlight. The power is out, and the city sits in darkness. Waiting.

She rises from the tub cautiously and puts one foot on the floor and then the other. Instinctively, she tries a light switch, but it's dead.

She doesn't have her phone light or a flashlight. She should've looked for one before taking a bath. She was being stupid, but then again, she had been so tired she could hardly function.

After a minute, her eyes adjust more to the dark. There's a meager amount of light coming through the windows, enough to paw around by. She opens the drawer to a nightstand and finds a little reading light that clips to a book.

"Please, please." Anna says as her fingers find a little button. It lights up as she clicks it. "Alright." She checks the time on the Casio: 11:24.

She'd slept for nearly six hours. She doesn't shine the light on her skin to see how pruned she is. She doesn't need to in order to feel the wrinkles in her fingertips.

When she's dry and dressed, she goes downstairs. The kitchen is wet and windy. The rain is blowing in through the open window.

Anna feels bad for a moment, until she realizes that with a twenty-five-foot storm surge, this entire house will be underwater in a matter of hours. The broken window hardly matters. It's a papercut compared to a plane crash.

Anna uses the reading light to look for a flashlight but doesn't have any luck. They were probably part of the checklist for the evacuating family who lived here. Everything that might be useful is gone. She doesn't find a weapon better than her folding knife.

She thinks about going to the next house on the block to look. This is South Carolina. Someone is bound to have a gun in their nightstand. The problem was that these emergency firearms were all in use, taken with the residents as they fled the storm and feared the riots.

Her knife is going to have to do.

She takes a black raincoat out of a hall closet and zips it all the way up. It hangs below her butt, and she has to roll the sleeves back to find her hands. Everything here is too big on her. The pants she's taken hang on only because they're strangled by her belt, and the rough-cut bottoms look like a fashion statement.

But her clothes are all dark. She'll be difficult to see. But no matter what she does, she's going to get wet.

When Anna opens the front door, it flies from her hand and knocks against the house. What must be a fifty-mile-per hour gust of wind roars down the street, tumbling palm branches and swaying the street signs.

She doesn't hesitate or wait for the wind to cease. She ducks her head and starts south, towards Battery Street.

The city is like she's never seen it. She walks through a nightmare. The streets are dark, and every structure is in shadow. It's hard to adjust to. She stumbles off curbs and into puddles but finds her way to Battery Street a little after midnight. She thinks it's brighter here, or perhaps her eyes are now adept in the dark. Either way, she can see fairly well.

The street is void of cops and the National Guard, though towards the waterfront, illuminated in halos of light, are the storm chasers.

Already, the harbor sloshes over the seawall—the first gentle inches of the surge. First, it'll be ankle deep and without current, like a minor flood. Though soon, as enough water is pushed inland, there will be no difference between city and sea. The waves will roll through Charleston in a scene akin to the sinking of Atlantis.

Anna starts walking with her head tilted up, squinting through the rain. When she gets near Limehouse Street, she looks for the window with the stencil that reads *Robinson A&T.*

After a block, she's found it. It's a little colonial two-story. The upstairs is an apartment, and the first floor is a tiny office space. The door is propped open with a few heavy law textbooks.

Anna takes the knife out quickly and steps in out of the rain. She's convinced the open door is another trap, but when she clicks on the reading light, she sees maybe that's not the case.

The entire back wall of wooden file cabinets has been ransacked. Loose cords hang off the back of a desk like dead snakes. The computers they were plugged into are all gone.

These things were all probably taken to be safeguarded from the storm. The door being left open is an afterthought. This business was on Battery Street, directly facing the harbor. Even if the hurricane predications were mostly wrong, this entire structure would still likely be leveled.

There are two big front windows, and neither has blinds. Her reading light is visible to the outside here. With the rest of the city so dark, it shines like a beacon.

She creeps towards the file cabinets and notices with a jolt of hope that not everything was taken. The cabinets to her left that are labeled *Financials* are looted, but others are not. The *Miscellaneous* cabinets on the far right look like they haven't been touched. She slides out the top drawer, which is nearly above her head, lifts it off its tracks, and sets it on the floor.

She puts the reading light between her lips and starts to flip through the files with both hands. None of it is interesting. There are budget sheets for weddings, funerals, birthday parties. Car lease forms and the deeds to multiple houses, but not the one on Church Street.

Maybe if she had all night, she could make sense of this. Find a connection or a clue. She takes the drawers out one by one. Nothing catches her eye until the second to last one.

She flicks through it with a sigh. It's filled with more or less the same, but her fingers pause on a folder tag labeled *The Experiment.*

She frowns and takes out the thick folder. When she opens it, she has to catch her breath. She's not sure whether or not this was something she was supposed to find. Either way, she holds in her hands what may just be the answer to everything.

Paperclipped to the inside pocket of the folder is a picture. It's of three little girls under an oak tree.

Each sits politely crisscrossed and smiles towards the camera. It's Hannah, Tess, and herself. But in this photograph, they're younger than they ever were when they knew each other.

Her heart beats faster as she opens the folder.

She mumbles, not quite believing what she's reading. The caption she sees is a lie. It has to be.

She reads a short paragraph, but she starts seeing stars halfway through and has to start over.

It's ridiculous. Absurd, Anna thinks. It's impossible. Hannah, Tess, and Anna were friends.

But these papers are saying they were sisters.

Correspondence

The folder starts with an exchange of old letters that have been kept, but the correspondent info has been blacked out with permanent marker. The first letter reads,

Dad,

I'm glad you were receptive to our discussion, but I would like to reiterate on the finer points. I'm telling you this is the kind of science you can't get in the real world. Social studies on human beings are wrapped in red tape and ethics bullshit. But tell me, don't you think this could answer vital questions related to human behavior? Don't you think the world at large is better off knowing the answers to these questions?

Also, the money was mine to do what I pleased. The endowment isn't just for this study to gain favor. The university is unlikely to play favorites anyway. I made it as an investment in our academic intuitions. God knows they need it.

Best,
James

Anna thumbs to the next letter. She's reading as fast as she can.

James,

None of what you are studying is controlled. Not the environment. Not the children. No academic would ever take this study seriously. No matter how surprising the results your experiment ends in conjecture. On the ethics, those barricades are there for a reason.

Many scientists have reached exciting conclusions only to find out that the public is more hung up on the methods they used to prove their hypothesis rather than the result.

I have a hard time believing you made a two-million-dollar endowment in nothing but good faith. Does Mindy know about this? This family's money is not a plaything. Nor is its name. That money should've lasted half a decade, and you're not getting more for at least that long. Consider yourself cut off. Delusional behavior. Ridiculous. If it wasn't for the risk of this going public, I'd get our lawyers involved.

The exchange reads like it's between a son and father. They're obviously from the same family. She picks up the next reply.

Ted,

Of course. It was never my intention to publish. You won't ever hear a peep about this. I'm not delusional and I understand the optics. But see it from my eyes, how rare is it to find three siblings who don't know about the existence of one another? They only share their father's blood—some deadbeat out in Beaufort—yet still, two of the girls are already best friends. Inseparable. There are a litany of other kids in the trailer park they live in, yet they sought out each other. Fascinating. No?

Could humans have a subconscious sense that can seek out family to trust and bond with? I think it's a question worth studying. Even if it's not one I can answer with any certainty.

The third girl I'm working on moving to the trailer park, as well. I already put in an offer on a house nearby. The money is going to their mothers, who in turn are able to provide them a better quality of life. They aren't aware of you, the trust or anything else. It's safe science. Sorry if I sound like a madman.

As for the money, that's fine. We will make do. Getting

the family name out there can't hurt, however. The university is open to giving their new study center the Robinson name. What do you think?

Also, Mindy is aware of it. It's a better hobby than spending my evenings in a bar.

Best,

James

There's no response letter. Anna pauses for a moment, trying to comprehend what she's reading. She, Hannah, and Tess. Sisters?

Her mother was being paid to live in Oak Grove. All of their mothers were. Anna suddenly doubts the existence of a wealthy aunt in Atlanta—their money was coming from the Robinson family. Some wayward, strange son conducting an experiment.

But which kid? She begins to understand that this was somebody she's probably never met before. Somebody who's been watching her from the shadows.

Once the girls grew and reached their late teens, the experiment was over.

Anna finally feels one step ahead. All she needs to do to figure out who's behind this is find out which Robinson made the donation to her university.

Geller would know. At the very least, he'd be able to make a phone call to someone who would. She can get out of the surge zone, get to Geller's mom's house, and hand this bastard to the police on a silver platter.

Her attention is taken to her legs as they suddenly grow cold. Then the folder begins to float.

She looks down to see water has swept into the office. She curses and stands and flaps the water off the folder. She starts walking to the desk to keep reading, when she sees flashlight beams bounce outside.

Heavy boots splash on the sidewalk.

Her heart leaps into her throat, and she clicks off her reading light, but not in time. Anna is suddenly blinded by lights attached to rifle barrels.

Prisoner

"Freeze! Hands! Let me see your hands!" Several men shout the same commands at once.

Anna drops the papers as her hands shoot towards the ceiling and cringes as they land on the wet floor. One of the soldiers slings his rifle over his back and walks right up to her.

He pulls both her hands down quickly and clinches her wrists together. Then he strangles her hands behind her back, cuffing them with a zip tie.

"You got any weapons on you?"

"Knife. Left pocket," Anna talks softly in defeat. It's over. Whatever answers she got just now may very well be the end of it. If Tess is still alive, there's no way to come to her rescue.

The solider takes the knife out of her pocket and tosses it into the water. "Let's go."

"Aren't you going to read me my rights?"

"This is a state of emergency and I'm not a cop. Schmidt, make sure to record the address."

"Already got it," says another soldier, then he turns to face them. "Hold up, hold up, hold up," he says and shines his flashlight in Anna's eyes. The hood of her raincoat is down, and already her hair is soaked and sticks to her face.

"Isn't this the girl CPD put an alert out on? The one who ditched the car with the dead body in it?"

"We'll let them figure that out." He guides Anna by the arm to the street and opens the back of a military truck. The door is solid metal, and its bed is lined with benches and topped with thick canvas that pops as it's pelleted by the rain drops.

Inside are three men.

All have their hands zip tied behind their backs like Anna. They each glance over her but then look back to their feet as Anna steps into the back.

The solider who cuffed her suddenly yells, "If that fucking hole is any bigger when I get back, you'll all be charged with eluding an officer of the peace. That's another felony, you got that?"

None of them says anything. Anna feels a little moisture being blown in from outside and notices there's a hole about the size of a baseball in the right side of the truck's canvas that faces the harbor.

When she takes a seat, the heavy door shuts behind her and the latch clacks into place. The inside is not all dark. On the back of the truck cab is a yellow light that casts them in a color like dark urine.

They're wet and dripping and quiet, apart from one of the men, who sobs silently.

"Cleo," he moans.

"Give it a rest, man," says another, sighing.

"Cleo," he cries again and makes eye contact with Anna. "It's my dog." The man is chubby and not dressed like the others. He wears a pink gingham shirt and wool trousers. "They arrested me for trying to save my dog."

She looks away from his eyes.

"If it weren't for you fucking *looters*, there wouldn't be a curfew! They wouldn't arrest people like me! Oh . . . Cleo. She's probably so scared right now."

"I'm sorry about your dog," Anna says quietly.

"It's the sitter. Can you believe it? I was out of town, and the sitter just left her when the governor gave the evacuation order. She said her parents wouldn't let her go back to get my dog. The bitch. If I ever . . ."

One of the other men turns to him. "I'm gonna headbutt your ass if you don't shut up."

He begrudgingly goes quiet, and Anna leans her head back against the canvas. She can hardly think. She's too pumped full of adrenaline from being arrested. The truck begins to move, but after only maybe a minute, it comes to a hard stop and they're all tossed towards the cab.

Anna can hear the guardsmen shouting outside.

"They're requesting backup at the Atlantic bank branch on Meeting Street! They've got robbers trying to get into the vault. Armed."

"Meeting is fucked. The wind blew a stoplight down, and we're not getting over it."

"Let's hoof it! It's only a couple blocks."

Someone bangs twice on the truck cab, and the driver's door opens. Then there's the sound of boots pounding away. The man who'd been crying about his dog begins to panic. "Are they leaving us here? Alone?"

No one answers him, and he begins to yell. "Hey! You can't just leave us! Hey!"

But as there's no response, he quiets.

The truck bed becomes completely silent as the four prisoners sit listening to the rain and the wind.

Anna keeps looking at the hole in the canvas. It's her only hope. "Do you guys really care about that felony threat?"

A young guy in a baseball cap with a goatee responds. "We didn't make the hole. The wind blew a branch through it. That canvas is some military-grade shit. We can't tear it. At least not with our hands like this."

"Have you tried getting these off? Like biting them?"

The man stands up and turns around. Anna can see the plastic of his zip tie is dimpled with teeth marks. "Also some military-grade shit."

"Shit," says Anna.

"Yep."

"It ain't fun to chew on either," says another man. He's thin and scraggly, and his pale skin shines sickly in the yellow light. "It looks like you're kissing the other guy's ass. But now that you're here, maybe we can try again for longer."

"I'll pass." Anna turns away.

The primal fear of being left alone with several strange men sets in. Even if their hands are tied, the glances they give Anna suggest they'd be using them if they weren't.

They're listening to the rain, resigned to their fate as prisoners often are, when suddenly, above the patter of rain on the canvas comes the crack of gunshots in the distance.

There aren't many, just a short spurt of half a dozen and then nothing.

It may have only been a block or two away, but the sound was muted by the storm.

The man in the gingham shirt perks up in fear. "Were those what I think those were?"

"They were probably itching to light up those bank robbers," says the man with the goatee.

They stay quiet, listening for someone to return, but five minutes pass without any sound outside other than that of the growing storm.

Then ten.

Then twenty.

The rain beats down harder, and the wind shrieks against the canvas. It's strong enough to rock the truck that is sitting vulnerable, broadside to the harbor.

By the time a half hour passes, it seems abundantly clear that something bad has happened. No one is coming back for them, yet none of them wants to be the first to suggest it.

Anna scoots towards the hole in the canvas and squints. It's still plenty dark outside, but she catches sight of something white flashing a couple hundred yards away in the harbor. The shapes fade and grow. Anna can't make sense of what she sees until suddenly, she tenses in fear. She's looking at the white caps on waves.

The swells rage ten, fifteen feet into the air, and already, the storm surge is a foot higher than when she was put into the truck. It's creeping up the tires.

"What's out there?" the man in the gingham shirt asks Anna, and she flinches.

She looks away from the hole and shakes her head. "Nothing." She takes a deep breath. "There's nothing out there."

Surge

Anna has to see how strong the canvas is for herself. She stands on the bench, turns around so the fingers of her cuffed hands can grasp on to the sides of the hole, and pulls.

It doesn't budge. She can't get that good of a grip—the canvas is wet, and her fingers are bunched together, but it's obvious this waxed fabric wasn't made to simply be torn.

"It's no use, lady."

Anna stops and sighs. "Have you tried biting it?"

"What?"

She kneels so her head is in front of the hole. "Like tearing it with your teeth?" She bites the canvas and pulls, but it slips, and her teeth clack together painfully. She cringes and runs her tongue across them.

"Just wait. They'll be back," says the skinny man near the door. "They ain't gonna just leave their hundred-thousand-dollar truck here."

Anna wants to explain that for a storm that is projected to cause billions in damages, this truck is merely a drop in the bucket.

She's thinking of ways they can combine their strength to try and get through the canvas, when suddenly there's a gust of wind strong enough to tilt the truck. Anna begins to slide forward and then drops back hard onto the bench as it rocks back.

"Everyone come sit on this side." Anna gestures with her head to her bench. The others seem to understand that she's trying to weight the side that the wind is hitting to keep the truck from tipping. They all sit scrunched together on the one bench.

"You really think the wind can knock over a ten-ton truck?"

"Easily," says Anna. The big canvas acts as a sail and with wind speeds of a hundred miles per hour, it's putting forty pounds of pressure per square foot. They don't have long before a gust comes along with the power to tip them.

Anna's taking deep breaths, trying not to panic. Trying not to picture drowning to death.

Minutes later, her eyes jolt open as someone bangs on the truck cab.

"Hey!" a soldier yells from outside. "Y'all still in there?"

"Yeah!" All the men start yelling. "Get us the fuck out!"

"Hold on!"

The truck door slams and the engine starts. They begin to grumble away. They all lean their heads back and sigh and laugh in relief, but after a couple blocks the truck slows and then stops again completely.

The cab door opens, and again the soldier's shouts are muffled by the canvas top. He yells at the top of his lungs so they can hear him. "The water has moved cars sideways into the streets! They're not passable! We've got a plow truck that can clear the roads for us! My radio's not working, I've got to find my unit again. Just sit tight!"

"Hey! Hey!" the man with the goatee shouts. "Just let us out of here, man! This is a fucking death trap!" But there's no response. "He's already gone, ain't he? Fuck!" He headbutts the canvas. "You've got to be kidding me! This is just like Katrina." He looks towards Anna and the others. "They let whole jails full of guys drown. Let us out!"

"He's gone." Anna nods towards the hole. "You want out of here, that's your one option."

He doesn't hesitate. The man drops to his knees and starts tearing at the canvas with his teeth. From what Anna can see, it does nothing.

She leans her head back and tries to make her peace. Hours pass like this. The truck keeps tipping on its tires. The wind is getting stronger. When her watch alarm blares that it's three a.m., still, no one has come.

The water is most of the way up the tires now. They can hear it slosh against the truck's underbelly.

"I don't want to die. Oh, God. I don't want to die." The gingham-shirt man rocks back and forth. The other two men are pulling and scratching at the hole, now.

"What if we both try to pull on one side with our teeth at the same time?" says one.

Anna watches them adjust so one stands above the other and bends his head low. Then they bite the canvas. Their eyes are wide and desperate, and their mouths are held in snarls, showing their sharp and crooked teeth. They yank on the canvas like dogs on a toy.

Men reduced to wolves.

Then, with hardly any warning, the big gust comes.

It's feels like gravity is lost immediately. They all begin to spin and tumble as the truck lifts and topples onto its side in little more than a second. There's a splash and then darkness.

They're sitting on the canvas that was the left side of the truck. The hole in the other side is now directly above them.

Anna stands. Her entire bottom half is soaked now. Water is pouring in and she sees near the back of the bed, the canvas has been ripped. They've fallen on a fire hydrant and it sticks into the truck with water gushing in from around its sides.

"We've got to do something!"

"Help! Help!" The men are all acting like animals in a cage. There is no coordination or real attempt to free themselves. Only panic.

Anna walks towards the truck's rear door but unfortunately finds it just as locked as before.

There's no way out and the truck is shorter on its side. It doesn't have its big tires keeping it off the ground. The water in the bed will be deep quick and without their arms to swim, they'll likely drown before it fills completely.

Anna leans against the door while the others scamper about wildly. In a half hour, everybody has exhausted themselves, but the threat of death lies closer. For Anna, the water is now neck deep.

"Not like this. Please. Come on, God." The gingham shirt man says with a thick, sobbing voice.

Anna is the first to have to start bouncing off the bottom to stay afloat. It feels like she's only delaying the inevitable, but she can't bring herself to not try to survive.

When the men can't touch the bottom either is when her fate feels sealed. The one in the gingham shirt kicks over to Anna and starts trying to rest his body on top of hers to stay afloat.

"What are you—" Anna says, but then she's dunked under his weight. She lets herself sink to the bottom, and then she kicks off of it in the opposite direction. When she resurfaces, he turns and starts pathetically kicking over to again try to use her body as a life preserver.

She's angry more than anything. Anna doesn't give him the chance to try to beach himself on top of her. She kicks towards him instead, gets her head up as high out of the water as she can, and brings it down with a crack right on the bridge of his nose. He screams until his mouth touches the water, and then he starts gurgling and coughing.

Gingham shirt is the first to accidentally inhale the brine of the Atlantic. He coughs helplessly, and unable to get the oxygen it takes to keep kicking and stay afloat, he sinks.

Anna's not far behind him. She can keep from sinking by kicking her legs. The problem is with her arms behind her back, she's unable to balance in the water. It's a constant effort to stay upright to get a breath.

She suddenly feels something wrap around her neck, and she sinks. The skinny man has put her in a choke hold with his legs to try to stay afloat for longer.

She wriggles helplessly. Anna can't turn her head enough to bite him. It feels like seconds before her vision blurs purple. Anna screams underwater, and just as she does, there's a dull metal bang. The skinny man's legs immediately wilt. She shrugs them off and kicks off the ground for the surface.

She breaches with a deep, gasping breath. It's mostly dark in the truck bed, and it takes her a moment to understand what she's looking at. The wind has blown a stop sign clear through the canvas near the top, and a sharp side of the hexagon has dug itself deep into the skinny man's head.

Anna kicks for the hole it's made. She's able to set her shoulder on the canvas so she won't sink. Then, when she has more strength, she wriggles herself out like a worm. As far as her survival chances go, it's out of the frying pan and into the fire. But the idea of dying in that canvas cage was too much.

She lies on the side of the truck and catches her breath. The raindrops are driven so hard by the wind that they pelt her like BBs.

When she kneels to assess her situation, she notices none of the men have made it out. The watery inside of the truck bed is silent. But she herself is still far from safe.

She's surrounded by at least six feet of storm surge on all sides, and the next strong gust of wind will surely throw her in. If she falls off the truck with her hands still zipped, she'll drown.

One of the sides of the stop sign sticks out of the canvas. The edge looks sharp. Or at least sharper than anything else in sight. Anna looks out towards the harbor. The storm surge is gaining inches by the minute. If not the wind, a wave will toss her into the water. She stands cautiously, leaning her weight into the wind, and turns so her back is lined up to the edge of the stop sign.

This is going to hurt, but there's no way around it.

She sticks her butt out as far as she can so her tied hands are more exposed. Then, without another thought, she jumps like she's going to start a back flip but stops halfway. She screams in agony as her lower spine collides with the sharp metal edge of the sign.

She missed the zip tie and writhes in agony until the waves of pain lessen. She stands slowly. There's a madness in her eyes. A determination to live she's never had before. She grits her teeth, screams, and jumps again.

This time it's a bullseye.

The metal meets the plastic perfectly, and with Anna's falling weight behind it, the zip tie snaps.

Still, the steel edge digs into her back. "Fuck!" she shouts. "Ow, ow, ow." She doesn't have time to take any satisfaction in her free hands. Her back burns in pain.

When she's well enough to stand again, she's only up for a moment before the wind pushes her to the edge.

She totters for a moment, trying to keep her balance, but it's no use. She plunges back into the water and is surprised to feel there's already a current. It's sweeping her into the city. The narrow streets are acting like funnels, and Anna is quickly sucked down one. She's speeding in the current until the pressure relaxes, and then it's more like a lazy river. She swims out of the center of the street towards where the sidewalk would be.

With the water so high, there are some second-story balconies that are only a few feet over her head.

She reaches for the first one but misses. The next one she manages to get her fingers on the ledge of, but the pressure of the water behind her slams into her shoulders, and again she's dragged into the current.

On the third, she pulls herself up quickly enough so she can get a foot next to one of her hands like a rock climber. With the extra support, she's able to lift herself up. She stumbles on the balcony and is relieved to see the door leading inside is glass. But before breaking it, she tries the handle. It slides open easily.

Inside is a bedroom. She doesn't know what she's doing. She has no phone. No flashlight. No weapon. Going back into the water is a gamble. Any second she could be pulled beneath the surface by an undercurrent or sucked into an open storm drain.

She comes through the door to the hall and sees the water swirling below. Soon the full force of the winds will come to rip the roofs off, but the thought gives Anna an idea. The house she's in has a third story, and there she finds another staircase that leads to the roof.

She's shielded from the driving wind and rain by a wall, and she's able to look north into the city to see if there's a path or street with less flooding. But she doesn't look for long before something else catches her eye.

Six or so blocks farther into the city, there is a building with light. It's a brick apartment on King Street. It's tall for Charleston, standing some ten stories high.

From its windowpanes comes the only light for as far as the eye can see. Though this isn't what has stopped Anna in her tracks.

It's that one of the windowpanes in the same building isn't just illuminated with steady light—it goes dark for a few seconds before brightening.

Again, and again, and again.

It doesn't look like someone is signaling SOS with the lights. No, even from this distance, she can tell what it is.

It's a camera flash.

Signals

Anna watches the flash for a while. It seems to be on some sort of timer, with one picture being taken exactly every five seconds.

She thinks she knows exactly what it is—a signal. He must've planned for this. In order to have power, he must be running generators.

He must've hauled fuel up eight stories and stockpiled enough to last for days. She can picture him staring out at the storm, a safe distance from the windows, whispering for his moth to come to the flame.

After the last few hours in the truck and her brush with death, all Anna wants to do is go home.

Of course, with the storm, that's not even an option. Her only other choice is to go farther inland, get to Geller's mom's house where she can hunker down and hopefully find out which member of the Robinson family made the donation. With that, she can give it to the police. To Terry.

One of the only things she can say for certain is that this monster doesn't want Anna to slip away. He wants her to come and try to exact her revenge.

She wants to scream. Landfall is two hours away, and by then the storm surge will quadruple. The currents that rip down the streets will be strong enough to drown her, and the wind will turn branches, street signs, silverware, anything and everything, into bullets.

She probably doesn't even have time to make it to Geller's mom's or the parking garage she'd planned on. Anna eyes the building again. She watches the flash burst in the distance.

She's walking straight into his trap. Nothing has changed since she first found the riddle written on the wall. She hasn't really made a single stride. Yet all this internal debate is for nothing. Tess *could* be alive. And Anna's known from the second she saw the flash in the window that she was going to fly into this flame.

She scours the streets below her. It's hard to see with how dark it is, but by gauging where the water levels are at the streetlights, she can tell that the streets to the northwest are less flooded than those to the northeast. But to get there, she'll still have to swim.

She goes back inside and down all the way to the ground floor. About halfway down the last staircase, she has to wade into the water. It's freezing, and she takes gasping breaths until the shock fades. It shouldn't be this cold. It's as if the storm has churned up the icy waters from the Atlantic seafloor.

The darkness, the salty smell of the ocean in an old colonial living room. To Anna, it all feels like some strange nightmare. The house shudders in the wind and creaks like a sinking ship as it takes on the weight of the water.

Before she goes back out into the street, she heads to the kitchen and takes a small knife from a holder on the counter. It's hardly a weapon, but it's better than nothing.

She fords floating furniture and is back in the quick current of the streets. Thankfully, it shallows out in a few blocks. She wades until it's waist deep then walks through the shin-deep flood.

The apartment building is just a few blocks ahead. Perhaps the worst thing she can do is go inside, but she can't walk past it. Death itself may be inside, it doesn't matter.

She's drawn through its double doors as if by a tractor beam.

Answers

Anna's first priority once inside is again to warm herself. Her clothes are drenched, and while she walked, the high winds sucked away her body heat like some sort of parasite.

She feels herself growing weaker as her body burns the energy to try to maintain her internal temperature.

The apartment lobby has a desk and back office for management. The doors here aren't locked. She hops over the desk, hoping to find a lost and found, and sighs in relief.

There's a half-zip sweatshirt, a flannel shirt, and two water bottles in a file box on the floor. She's not going to find another pair of pants, but this will do.

She changes tops and rubs her arms until she's warm, and then she begins to look for spare keys to apartment units. She opens cupboards and drawers, but no luck.

She wants an adequate weapon. Maybe the entire reason this killer feels comfortable inviting Anna so openly is because he knows she doesn't have a gun. If she could just change that, maybe she could have the upper hand.

The only thing she is able to find that is of use is a flashlight. She goes back into the lobby and turns it on. It had been dry when she came in, but now a great puddle of water has seeped under the doors. It expands out quickly, multiplying like a virus.

This may be Anna's only chance to get out of the city before the storm surge becomes too ferocious to swim in. She heads to the stairwell and opens the heavy fire door.

It's all concrete walls and concrete steps. She thinks she hears the groan of the wind here, but then she realizes it's something else above her: generators.

She keeps her hands on the door while it shuts so it makes as little sound as possible and then begins to walk slowly up the stairs.

From the noise, it's obvious that the seventh floor is her destination. She stands at the door and stares at the big number seven.

The knife is wedged in her belt, but she doesn't even bother to grasp it in her fist. Some of Justin's last words echo in her head. "If he wanted you dead, you already would be."

She depresses the big rectangle handle of the door and pushes it open, but she doesn't move a step. The moment the door opens, the sound of the generator dies.

The hallway in front of her is lined with Christmas lights. Two strings are stapled to either side of the ceiling. They're green and red alternating bulbs, and while they don't cast much light, they're enough to see by. Still, she keeps the flashlight in her fist.

She tries to think fast. The generators must have some sort of battery for these lights to stay on. She looks down to see if there was some kind of trip wire attached to the door, but nothing stands out.

How did the generators turn off, then? Unless she's being watched. She snaps her head back to the hall. It's a straight line to the other side of the building where there's a window and elevators. There are six or so apartment doors on either side of the hallway.

When she starts to walk, she grabs hold of the knife. One of these doors could open at any second, and she'll be snatched, killed, and stuffed, just like Sylvie.

She reaches the end of the hall. None of the doors bursts open, nor do the generators restart. There's no sound but the ever-present white noise of the wind. She's at the opposite window by the elevators and peers down the seven floors. The surge has made its way here.

White caps in city streets. It's what the news has been frothing over, and now it's here.

Something rumbles in the distance. Her gaze darts up just in time to watch the wooden spire of a church rip away from its base and explode in the wind.

She's about to turn back to the hall, but something keeps her at the window. Directly below the window is an empty space. Even though it's filled with water, she can tell it's a parking lot.

"Fuck," she says aloud. She knows exactly where she is.

She didn't recognize the building coming from the south, but now seeing the north face of this building, she remembers. She's seen it before. She's *been* here before. Outside, at least.

It's where her mother always used to come when she had errands in the city.

Anna whips around to face the hall. The doors are all closed as they were. But suddenly, there's a voice.

"I was wondering whether you'd remember."

Anna feels her throat close. The voice is not of anyone she knows. It's distorted. Electronic. Like it's being translated by a computer. It's clear and crisp and coming from the ceiling. From a vent nearby.

She walks to it, her head tilted up. Her mouth hangs open in shock.

"Your mother would come here to give me updates on you. She never spoke of you very fondly, I'm sorry to say."

"Yeah." It's all Anna can say. She's slightly in shock. None of this feels real.

"I was worried for a moment there that you weren't going to come."

Anna is slow to respond. Can she even be heard by whoever is speaking? "I'm here."

"And I'm so glad."

"How can you hear me?"

"Same way you hear me."

"A speaker?"

"I wish this voice could laugh. Yes, darling. A speaker."

Anna's coming out of shock. The word darling sparks her dormant rage. "Which door are you behind? You fucking creep."

"Ah. There you are."

"Tell me!" She sticks her hand on a doorknob, about to open it, but the volume of the voice is suddenly louder.

"I wouldn't do that."

"Why not?"

"You get a single guess as to which door I'm behind. Get it right, I'll let you do whatever you wish to me. Get it wrong, and well . . . end up like your sisters. And the rich bitch from Borough Street."

Anna takes her hand off the knob gently. She notices that instead of a number on the door, there's a letter. This door is L.

She twists her head to look at the other doors. All of them are the same. They have a single letter instead of numbers. She didn't even notice it walking in.

"What do the letters mean?"

"That would be too much of a hint, Anna."

She walks down the hall and recites all the letters to herself. There's eleven more, not counting the L. They're not alphabetical. There seems to be no sense to them. There's a J and a G and a T. Eleven letters in all, and none of them repeats.

Anna's anger is building at her own inability to make sense of the puzzle. If she relies on nothing but luck, she has a single digit percent chance to get this right. "How much time do I have?"

"As much as you like."

"If I'm going to die, I want answers. Why did you pick me? Why did you recreate the story I wrote?"

"It added a little fun to it. Did it not?"

"Fun?" Anna trots towards the ceiling vent and shouts, "You realize what a sick little *fuck* you are?!"

There's silence for several seconds.

"When I was nine years old, I picked a mouse apart with a pair of pilers. Piece by piece. It was a symphony I don't expect you to understand. Such is this."

Anna is speechless. She doesn't know how to begin to respond to that. "Where's my mother? Where's Tess? Is she alive?"

"I am not here to play twenty questions with you."

"Then maybe I'll leave. Are you going to run after me? Try to shoot me dead in the stairwell?"

The voice is silent in response, and Anna's anger grows. She speed walks towards the stairwell door and turns the handle, but it won't budge. It's locked.

"I think you'll have a difficult time rescinding your decision to visit me."

She sprints back to the other side of the hall and sets her hands against the window. A seven-story leap is essentially a cliff jump, but the waters below churn wildly. It's not quite a death sentence, but it might as well be.

"You've made it this far, Anna. Why not finish what you started?"

"Because that's only what you want. Tess is dead, isn't she?"

Again, there's a long silence. She wonders if they have to type what they want to say first before the computer turns it into this voice. "You would've come anyway, dead or alive, because you don't know the answer."

"And what's that?"

"You never figured it out on your own. It's black and white. It's all so obvious if only you thought, Anna."

"Well fucking enlighten me!" Anna kicks the wall. She's boiling now. "What does it matter if I did know? What good would understanding a fucking riddle be, because they're all dead! Right?!"

She listens to the wind roar against the windowpane in the pause before the voice speaks.

"I liked you not just because you were the prettiest, Anna, but because you were the smartest. You aren't going to jump out that window. So please, pick a door. You might be pleasantly surprised."

"How do you know I won't jump?"

"Because I know you. You really never put it together, did you? You never came close on your own."

"I know you paid for us to live at the trailer park. I know you took notes. Turned my sisters and me into your own serial killer experiment."

The voice is quiet for too long, and Anna shifts on her feet uncomfortably.

"Think, Anna." The voice loses its fake tone and instantly becomes familiar. "My girl. Do you really believe I happened upon such a coincidence? That I found three girls who were sisters? Who somehow just didn't know about one another? How could I have possibly done that?"

Anna's eyes search the floor. The voice . . . It's Geller. But as shocked as she is, this reveal of his identity is an afterthought as she begins to understand exactly what he's saying.

He continues and begins to read the riddle. "I am had by all, but not by some."

Anna's mouth creeps open in horror while her mind flashes back to the lunch table in middle school.

"Anna doesn't even have a dad!"

"Yes, I do, idiot. Everyone has a dad."

"Oh yeah? Where's yours then?"

Her eyes fill with tears. The hairs on her neck shoot on end.

"Called a name." Geller pauses. "But not my one."

Anna is standing still, yet the world begins to spin.

"Dad?"

Blood

"You're not actually . . ." Anna says, vehemently shaking her head. "You're not my dad. My mom took me to see him. He's a bum in Beaufort, just like you said in that letter."

"She told me about that trick. Picking the meanest-looking man at the bar and telling you he's your father. A little sick, but clever. Just like Allie."

"You son of bitch. You're lying."

"I don't think so."

"You're fucking lying!" Anna throws open the closest door. The apartment entrance revealed is dark. "Where the fuck are you?!"

There's a long, disappointed sigh from the speaker in the vent. "Wrong door, darling."

She spins around and crosses the hall. "You think I care!?" She throws open another door and then another. "Come out, then! You psycho, deadbeat fuck! I trusted you. I thought you were my friend!"

Anna is crying, and from the metal taste in the back of her throat, she knows she has a nosebleed. "Why?" She throws open door after door. "Why did you do this to us? *How* could you do this to us if we were really your own kids?"

"Anna. Sweetheart. I don't expect you to understand the thrill of seeing your own eyes stare back at you as you choke the life from them."

She doesn't respond to that. She doesn't know how. She feels dirty. Vulnerable. The thought of sharing blood with this man . . . It makes her want to vomit.

"I'll kill you," Anna says more quietly. "You hear me?!" She walks towards the speaker. "Come out!"

She kicks down door M.

Door E.

Door H.

There's nobody behind any of them. Geller doesn't respond from his speaker in the ceiling, and Anna stands panting, out of breath. She's out of doors. All twelve of them are open now, each to a dark apartment.

The drone of the generators begins to restart.

Lights flicker on.

Anna stands, waiting for them to come on completely before going into any of the apartments. She looks inside some of the units and sees they're just regular apartments. Some have picture frames of families and women's shoes by the door.

Geller doesn't even own all of these.

Anna goes to the apartment where the generators' hum is the loudest and steps inside. There are closed doors and tight corners. He can hide too easily.

She's cursing her disadvantage, when suddenly, she hears something shuffling quick and right behind her. Before she can even spin around completely, something cracks into her forehead and she hits the floor hard. She's lying in pain on her back when something is laid over her face. It's wet and reeks chemically of alcohol.

Anna feels hands hold down her arms. She's still too stunned to fight. The splintering in her head feels like one plate of her skull has slipped against another to make an earthquake of a migraine.

The wet rag presses into her nose and mouth, and she cannot help but take a burning breath. It's like a dream, and before Anna can even fear her death, she loses consciousness.

Eye Wall

Anna has a lucid dream. She hears shattering booms in the distance. Thunder. Artillery.

A bomb is detonated that was made of glass.

The booms come one after another but without pattern. They seem loud enough to wake her, but still she sleeps. She wants to wake and scream. She knows she's sleeping. She knows she needs to wake. But the sounds cease, and without them, her mind has nothing to grasp its claws of consciousness into. She slips back to thoughtless, dreamless sleep.

Sometime later, her eyes slowly blink open. She sits at a dining room table with her hands tied in hemp rope. This time they're bound in front of her.

The room is filled with pinkish-orange light. Sunset light.

Anna's eyes narrow in confusion as she looks out the window. There's a wall of clouds so straight and long that it looks like a mountain, and it burns with the same colors as the sunset.

Candles burn on the table. Dozens of them. Candles in the daylight?

She hears footsteps, and before she can turn her head, a hand is set on her shoulder. She flinches away.

"How are you feeling?"

"Don't touch me."

The hand lifts and hovers. Then Geller walks so he's in her line of sight. He stands in front of a row of floor-to-ceiling windows. He's in a navy wool suit with no tie. He's not wearing his glasses. It may be the first time Anna's ever seen him without them.

"Beautiful, isn't it? Not many people will ever see something like this."

Anna doesn't say anything. Her head aches along with her

heartbeat, like a throbbing wound. She must've been unconscious for twelve hours. More.

"You woke up just in time to see the end of this. The eye of the storm. Can you believe it? You're *exactly* where I wanted to have you." He turns and smiles.

"I swear to you—" Anna starts, but Geller interrupts.

"No threats. Please. This should be a nice evening. Dinner is almost ready. Ever had wagyu cooked on a Coleman camp grill? No promises I do the meat justice, but it should at least be edible."

She stares at the china plate that's set on the table in front of her. There are little yellow lilies painted on the rim.

Geller looks back to the window. "The second side of the eye wall . . . It's the strongest part of the storm. Isn't it amazing how calm it looks now, even from just a few miles away?"

Anna can tell from the tops of landmarks in the flooded city below that this apartment faces east. The wall of clouds she sees is coming towards them from the sea.

"You slept through quite the whirlwind."

Anna jumps as the bells from an old cooking timer start to rattle.

"Ah, excuse me a moment." Geller walks through a doorway to what Anna presumes is the kitchen. When he comes back, the smell of cooked beef wafts in with him.

He plates it for Anna. The sliced steak sits on top of watery blood.

"The sides are fingerling potatoes and some sautéed broccoli rabe." He doles them out onto her plate. "Also, there's chocolate cake for dessert."

He arranges his silverware so it's perfectly straight. Then he takes a revolver from a holster under his suit coat and lays it next to his steak knife, facing Anna, as if it's just another utensil.

Anna stares at her plate with wide eyes and looks back to Geller, meeting his gaze for the first time.

"You really think I'm going to eat like a pig at a trough?"

"Nonsense, I'll feed you one bite at a time."

"What's wrong with you?"

"I'm just being polite, is all."

"Polite?" Anna says quietly while he picks up his steak knife and begins to cut. She watches him chew and swallow.

"Wow." Geller wipes his mouth. "Seventy-eight dollars a pound, and worth every penny."

Anna is hesitant to speak, and when she finally does, her voice is weak. "What are you going to do to me?"

"Oh. Patience. That is something you'll have to wait and see, but if you have any other questions . . . I'd be happy to answer them."

He wears a slight smirk, like he thinks he's some sort of genius. Anna almost doesn't want to give him the satisfaction of a question, but she needs to know.

"Why did you do that thing to Sylvie's body?"

"You mean why I stuffed her? Like an animal?"

Anna cringes and turns away.

"I'll tell you why. I wanted to practice, for you. Sylvie was a fighter, believe it or not. I kept trying to break her like some wild bronco, but she'd always bite and kick and scream. I didn't keep her alive long. Unlike your sisters, who both played much nicer."

Anna's regretting her question already. She tenses her bound hands, but it's hopeless; the rope has zero slack.

"Hannah tried to act like she loved me. Like I'd let her go. She was smart that way, but I was smarter. Hate isn't something you can hide from your eyes, and hers *glowed* whenever I wrapped my hands around her neck."

"Shut up!" Anna drives her knee into the bottom of the table. It bangs and glass clinks.

Geller wipes his mouth calmly. "You asked."

"Tell me, how much of it is lies? Do you even have a wife, kids?"

"Of course. I married Lily Robinson, and she took my name. What better way to blend in than a family?" He chuckles. "I have three sons. Only one from my wife. The other two were . . . mistakes. Byproducts of you and your sisters' conceptions. It took a few tries to get three girls."

"Did you kidnap those women?"

"No, no, no." He smiles and runs a thumb on his chin. "I was a lot more handsome back then. I dated them. Tracked their cycles. Bought them fancy dinners. And that was that."

"Why didn't my mom come for more money?"

"Oh, she did. They all did. But kill a girl's dog and threaten her life, and suddenly that fourteen hundred dollars a month doesn't seem so bad. It was just enough to keep them alive. To keep them stuck in that trailer park I picked out for them."

Anna looks past him out the window. The sunset glow is gone, and the eye wall has darkened. It's close now. Eerily, there is still no wind.

There's no sound of a storm at all.

"I hope you realize how special I think you are. Do you remember that November when I took your picture?"

Anna can't make eye contact with him. She stares at the wall and starts to cry. "I was going to do it then. This." Geller gestures all around him. "I was going to have you, but then you went back to Sylvie's house. And it was just so . . . clever," he breathes heavily. "I saw myself in you at that moment. I played by the rules of your stories. I went for Sylvie, not you, just like you wanted."

"I didn't want that."

"No? You didn't want to live?"

She shuts her eyes tight, squeezing a tear out of each. "I hate you."

"Oh, Anna." He reaches across the table, and she recoils as he wipes the blood out from under her nose with a napkin. "Don't say that. You hate the man who's done so much for you? Who has sacrificed hundreds of thousands of dollars just to be close to you? My father in-law cut me off from the Robinson family trust. Do you know what it cost to buy myself into your university? To convince them to let a man with a master's but no teaching experience lead an undergraduate class?"

"Shut up." Anna starts shaking her head. "If this is happening, just shut up and kill me." Her voice gets louder the more she speaks. "You pathetic piece of shit! Because I'll kick and scream, and I'll bash my head into the wall until I have a brain hemorrhage if you don't."

Geller looks at her fondly. "You are something, aren't you? Those other girls weren't so smart. They took after their mothers. But you? Brains and a fighter." He leans forward in his chair. "Ah. You don't care to be doted on. So . . ." He claps his hands. "No food. But what about wine? I have a Rothschild here." He picks up a bottle of wine from the table and plucks out the cork with a pop. "Ever wonder what a seventeen-hundred-dollar bottle of wine tastes like?"

"Not once."

"Hmm. Well, I suppose when you grow up in a trailer park, you keep your trailer tastes."

"Something like that."

His hand trembles as he pours it, and the wine splashes in his glass unevenly. He puts the bottle down but keeps his hand firmly on it, as if it's still not steady.

Anna squints at him skeptically. There's something she's missing. Geller seems nervous. Scared.

He takes a long sip then tilts his head back and finishes the whole glass. "Excuse me," he says, and pushes back in his chair. He heads into the kitchen, leaving Anna alone at the table. It's already darkened considerably in just a few minutes. The candles cast shadows. The wind begins to blow against the window again.

She stares at the gun placed across from her.

Her feet aren't bound. She can stand, but her hands are tied so firm that she doesn't have use of even her fingers. She looks around and under the table, and then she sees it.

The table has metal arms that fold up the collapsible ends. The arm to her left is jagged. The edge looks sharp and has corroded holes that make it look like a sawblade.

It's dark under the table, so she doesn't know for certain if it's sharp. She places her forearm against it and swipes it away. She's never been so excited to see blood in her life. The metal bar is sharp enough to cut her.

Anna's heart begins to pound. She places her bound hands against the metal arm and moves the rope back and forth against it. It saws quickly. The rope is already loosening. She has all but the last few coils cut when Geller comes back in the room holding an entire chocolate cake.

His eyes lock on to what Anna's doing under the table. They widen for a second in interest, and then he quickly looks back to the cake.

She blew it, she thinks. There's no way she didn't. But Geller is only smiling at the cake.

"This . . ." He sets the platter on the table. "This may just be the very last cake ever made at Mary's Famous Bakery. I had it custom ordered. They told me it was the last thing that came out of their ovens before they shut down for the storm."

"Where's Tess's body?"

"What's the matter? Don't think that picture I sent you was recent?"

"I know it's not."

"I thought you might ask about your mother."

"I don't care about my mother."

"Fair enough. You were supposed to find Tess. But I suppose Jeffrey wasn't the most reliable source to pass on a clue. She's below your mother's trailer, just like Hannah was in hers. I figure you ended up at her apartment instead. But she kept clues, too. Didn't she?"

Anna looks away in response. The rope is loose enough to where she doesn't need to saw the last bit. She gently begins to thread her wrists free.

The wind shakes the windowpane. And Geller's hand trembles violently as he pours another glass of wine. Anna suddenly wonders if he's dying. He could be sick. This last little treasure hunt of his could be a last hurrah.

"The storm . . ." He sits down and turns around to face the glass. "It's going to come on quick."

Already the palm trees shake below. White caps appear on the water that floods the city. Geller turns his chair away from Anna so it faces the window and begins to eat his cake and sip his wine.

In another five minutes, the hurricane rages at full blast, and Anna's hands are free. Her pulse creeps all the way up to her throat. She can't speak without giving herself away. She couldn't even be looked at. She has an amateur's poker face and the best hand on the table.

"I'd do it all over again," says Geller. His face is somber, and to Anna, it feels like he's talking to himself. She's about to reach over the table for the gun, when there's a crash from below. She gasps and tucks her hands as if they're still tied.

There's another bang. This one seems closer. It's the same shattering boom from her sleep. Breaking glass.

"It's the glass on the floors below," says Geller. "It's only a matter of time before the wind throws something up here, and then . . ." He doesn't keep talking. He finishes his wine instead.

He sighs, rolls his shoulders, and then positions himself so his back is directly facing Anna.

"You were always your father's favorite. I wanted years to enjoy you, but you'd fight like Sylvie."

Anna watches some of the candle wicks reflect in the window as she slowly reaches across the table. The gun is inches away now, and her fingers find it silently. She doesn't snatch it. She doesn't risk a sudden movement.

Her eyes widen madly as she holds the gun in her palm. She has him, but something feels wrong. It all feels too easy.

Could he have been so sloppy?

Geller is staring transfixed out the window, and Anna takes a risk and opens the cylinder of the revolver. Her breath is ragged with fear as she takes one of the bullets out and rotates it in her fingers.

It's not a blank or a dummy round. It's a real, heavy bullet. She shuts the cylinder with a click, pulls the hammer back, and aims it at the back of Geller's head.

His ears twitch at the sound, and after several seconds he half turns over his shoulder. "Anna?"

"Yeah?" she says shakily. Tears roll down her cheeks, and she blinks them away quickly to keep her vision clear.

"Put it *down*."

Anna stands up from the table. She walks towards the center of the room with the gun's barrel homed on Geller.

"That's your pitch? Put it down?"

He sets his plate of cake down and raises his hands feebly in front of him. Anna thinks she should shoot him already, but something just feels off. She can't quite put her finger on it, but after days of being led down this maze as if on a leash, she can't help but sense this is just another trap. The gun will blow up in her hand or honk like a clown's nose when she pulls the trigger.

Geller takes a deep breath. "If you're not going to put it down, then what are you waiting for?" Anna doesn't respond, and he suddenly bursts up from his chair but doesn't charge her. "What are you waiting for?! Do it, then! Kill your father, you ungrateful bitch!"

She aims it at his chest and starts to depress the trigger, but she stops halfway. He doesn't rush her or try to save himself, and then she sees it.

He's still holding his hands up, and from where his left suit coat and sleeve wilts from his arm, she can see a red scratch running down from his wrist.

It's bright red. Infected. And it all comes together.

Terry was telling the truth.

"Sylvie, Hannah, Tess," Anna says. "Were they the only girls you killed?"

"No." Geller takes the time to smile. "Eight."

"You've killed eight girls?"

"Oh yes. Would you like to know how they begged?"

He's egging her on, but what he doesn't know is that Anna is finally a step ahead. Otherwise, he would've kept his mouth shut.

"Have you been to Orangeburg lately?"

Geller's eyes flash with fear.

"They've got you, don't they?" asks Anna. "DNA. Dead to rights. You're done."

He looks at the wound on his arm, realizing what has outed him, and lowers his hands. "I have money, Anna. Lawyers. Whatever they throw at me, it won't stick."

She knows he's lying. "You don't believe that. The suit. The steak. The cake . . ." She briefly points the gun at the table. "Nice last meal. You don't think I've seen you shaking, too? You're afraid of death. But not as afraid of it as spending the rest of your life in prison, right?"

There's panic in Geller's eyes, and Anna thinks he's going to rush her, but suddenly he snatches the wine bottle from the table, turns to the window, and hurls it.

But Anna's just as quick. In the same second, she lowers the gun so it points at his knee and pulls the trigger.

The bangs are simultaneous. The entire floor-to-ceiling window shatters as the gun bucks, but there's a third sound. The wind tunnels violently through the glassless frame. Hundreds of pounds of pressure bursts in, and the dozens of candles are extinguished in a single second.

It knocks the gun out of Anna's hand and sends her stumbling into the wall. Plates soar off the table, and the chairs topple and hurdle so Anna has to dodge them.

When Anna is able to see again, Geller is on the ground. He crawls against the wind towards the open frame. She hit her mark. His knee bleeds. Anna can see droplets of blood run on the floor in the wind, but it's not enough to stop him.

The open frame acts as a sluice gate for the winds, making them even stronger. Anna can't even walk upright. She can hardly see. All she knows is that she cannot let Geller die.

His death is the final step in his plan, and she burns to see him fail.

She drops to the floor and begins to crawl after him.

With the use of both legs, she's quicker. Anna catches up to him before he can plummet seven stories down. She grabs hold of his leg but is stunned as he kicks her shoulder.

He's gotten his arms onto the empty frame. He can pull himself over the edge now. Anna grabs on to the back of his suitcoat and pulls with all her weight to try to keep him inside, but she's losing ground. In order to keep him in, she needs the strength of her legs.

Anna moves so her feet are planted on the ground and stands into a low squat, her entire body acts as a sail for the wind. As the wind runs into her, it helps her grip on Geller.

She watches his hand begin to bleed as he grasps a piece of glass in the window frame that's pointed sharp like a tooth. Then he throws it at Anna's face.

She can't help it. It's instinct. She's not even thinking as she lets go of the back of his suit. The wind tosses her to the floor hard, and when she recovers, Geller is gone.

"No!" Anna shouts and scampers to the window. The waves below roll and crash into the base of the apartment building. Falling looks like almost certain death, but for the first time in her life, she isn't frozen by flight. Before so much as a second passes, she's already jumped headfirst into the tall black waves.

Undertow

She sinks more than ten feet below the surface before she's able to regain buoyancy. When she starts swimming up, she opens her eyes underwater, but it's hopeless. She can see nothing but dark shapes.

She gasps for air as she surfaces. She feels herself rise and get tossed as she rides up the crest of a wave and down into its trough.

Geller is nowhere in sight. She thinks he must've sunk. He got his wish after all, and now she's going to die, too. She breaststrokes to her right, away from the apartment building, where the waves don't break but keep rolling down the streets. As she's pushed into this open water, she sees debris everywhere. Stuffed animals, couches, the debris from power lines, and palm trees, and among this mess, she spots a head.

It's only for a moment. He's twenty yards ahead of her in the current. Face towards the sky, eyes closed peacefully. She swims furiously with the current, and after a minute, she's dangerously exhausted and perhaps only halfway to him.

She dog paddles while riding the current, catching her breath. When she looks towards Geller and the direction that the water leads, she panics.

The street they're on ends in a T intersection, but there's a narrow alley at the top that some of the water is sucked into. All the debris that goes into the alley disappears from sight, and Geller and Anna are headed right for it.

She tries desperately to swim away from it, but it's hopeless. Geller's head disappears first, and a few seconds later, it's her turn.

She times it well and takes a deep breath just before the undercurrent yanks her down.

She's spun around. Collides with something metal that digs into her already bruised back. She kicks and paddles as hard she can, but she's not in control. She's stuck in the center of thousands of pounds of whirling water.

Again, the water throws her into something, but this time it's soft. There's an obstruction she's pressed up against. She's stopped. Anna is able to pull herself up to the surface and breathe.

She can understand what's happening by feel alone. There's an iron gate swung open that lets the water pass through the space between the bars, but Anna's caught against it, and she's not the only one.

The softness she feels is Geller, but his head is under the water. She takes a breath and goes under. His face is just below the surface, and she pulls on the collar of his shirt until he's visible.

He takes a deep breath, and there's amusement in his eyes as he looks at her. "Decided to die with me?" But he frowns as Anna smiles. He's alive, and she'll do whatever it takes to keep him that way.

Anna doesn't waste time. She can tell he's stuck through the fence somehow and dives under to figure out how. She quickly finds it's his left arm. His wrist has been wedged between the narrow bars and behind his back.

When she comes up for air, he shoves her with his free hand. The push is enough to send her back into the full strength of the current, but she catches onto the other side of the fence. The rapids hold her sideways like a flag against the wind.

"Goodbye, Anna." Geller leans his head back and closes his eyes. The water level is rising in the alley, and it quickly runs over his nose and mouth.

"No!" Anna shouts, but then the water sloshes over her face, too.

She lets go of the fence, and just before she's swept away, her hands grasp Geller's wrist. She twists with all her strength to get it unwedged.

He fights back, trying to keep his wrist from bending, but the angle at which it's twisted doesn't allow him to apply much strength.

Anna screams under the water and rotates her entire body. There's an audible crack. Geller's wrist straightens, and she pushes it out from the bars as the undertow drags her down and away. She bounces off the bottom of the alley, but then she's twirled around. She can't swim up. She doesn't even know which way it is. Her vision is all saltwater sting.

She doesn't know how much time has passed, but her lungs burn and her brain screams for air. To take a breath would be a death sentence, but just as violently as the current took her, all the pressure around her is suddenly released. She's spit up at the surface and coughs for breath.

She goes to kick but finds her feet meet ground. She's been channeled into another street, where the water is only above her waist. As she stands, she looks towards the river pouring from the alley. The street she's on runs north and south, and she's sheltered from the worst of the wind.

Above her, terracotta tiles fly from roofs and over the street like flocks of birds. Water sloshes in the street.

Something catches her eye away from the mouth of the alley. Geller stands with his back to her, clinging to a streetlight. The current must've carried him quicker.

Anna looks around for a weapon. With the storm as loud as it is, she doesn't have to worry about him hearing her splash around.

She jogs and picks up a blonde wood board that must've been blown out of a window it tried to cover. It's four feet long, and she holds it in both hands underneath the surface as she walks towards Geller.

He turns when she's only feet away. "A broken wrist, a shattered kneecap." He reaches around to his pants and struggles as he undoes the button to one of the back pockets. "Think it's a fair handicap?"

When his hand is back in sight, he holds a small knife with a blade of maybe three inches.

He doesn't know Anna has anything in her hands. When he lunges forward, she bursts from the water with the board already pulled back, ready to swing like a bat. Geller doesn't have time to react. It cracks against his jaw and the knife falls gently as his grip goes limp.

Bloody drool hangs from his mouth, and as he looks at her, Anna speaks. "You should've just slit your throat." She brings the board down again, this time on the crown of his head, and he slumps in the water. His dumb eyes search the sky, and Anna tosses the wood. Then she puts her hands under his armpits, so he doesn't sink in the street.

Rise

Anna pulls him towards a three-story house, just to her right. Its front door is broken in from the water, and inside the entryway, it's just as deep as it is outside. It takes all her strength to pull him up the first flight of stairs one stair at a time. At the top, she drops him on the floor and sits down hard. The water swirls below, rising.

Anna will have to make it to the third floor, but for now, she has some time to catch her breath. She leaves Geller where he lies and crawls to the other side of the hallway. From the way he had to cling upright to the streetlight, Anna doubts he can even stand with his shot knee. Still, she watches his chest rise and fall with each breath as the wind and rain beat through the broken windows. It's funny how little she thinks. She can hardly hold a thought. Twenty minutes pass like this, her body slowly recovering from all the physical shock. She stands and walks back to the banister to look down to the first floor.

The water has swelled immensely, and already it licks and sloshes near the top of the stairs. She puts her hands under Geller's armpits again and drags him up another shorter staircase.

He mumbles and groans but does not make any conscious attempt to thwart her grasp. At the top, she drops him down again. If the water rises eight more feet, they'll be in trouble.

The storm surge predictions were twenty-five to thirty feet. She tries to estimate what that looks like but has no idea. Even though the third floor of this house is stunted with low ceilings like an attic, the whole thing has to be taller than thirty feet.

The floor they're on now is little more than an old servant's quarters. What few rooms there are under the low ceilings are mostly used for storage. She has to clear a space of big plastic tote bins and cardboard boxes to reach the bathroom.

Anna's beyond thirsty. She hasn't had a drink of water in nearly a day. When she turns on the tap, a brown sludge of brackish water rushes out. She curses and looks at the toilet. She lifts off the back and sets it on the floor. There's no ring of algae in the toilet tank. It looks mostly clean. She scoops handful after handful to her mouth until she's bloated, and then she begins to go through the boxes and bins.

She doesn't find food or a first aid kit. Or a gun or a radio. The two things she finds that may be of use are tools.

There's a power drill, a box of six-inch deck screws, and a hatchet.

She clicks the trigger of the drill a couple times, and it spins and whines. The green lights on the back indicate full battery.

"You awake?" she asks Geller, and he rolls his head on the floor to look at her. She keeps the drill in her hand and puts some screws in her soaked back pocket.

"That night you nearly ran me over . . . Whose bloody footsteps were those?"

He chuckles. "That lowlife you dated. You can't say I never did you a favor."

Anna's more clearheaded. She's annoyed. "And why do you want to protect me? What have you been keeping me alive for all these years?"

"Because then what would I have to look forward to? You were the climax, Anna. I know that gives you no pleasure, but it should."

"You're pathetic."

"Do you want to know how your sisters begged?"

Something cracks on the floor below them and splashes. Anna goes towards the narrow stairwell. The water is already on the second floor. It pools and swarms at the foot of the stairs like something alive. A predator coming for its trapped prey.

It's rising so fast, Anna swears she can see it inching up. Their odds aren't good. She picked the wrong house. In what time they have left to live, she wants to inflict a lifetime of suffering.

"You don't think you'd beg, too?" She walks to Geller and steps on his broken wrist. "Because you seem like a coward." He screams in pain as she applies more pressure. "Maybe it's your blood in them that begged so badly. Their pathetic father. A coward too afraid to face the music."

"Death is the music! Not a prison sentence!"

Something crashes into the house. She hears water, hundreds of gallons of it, pour through the second-floor windows. The waves are hitting the house.

"Dying isn't a consequence good enough for you," she says, but Anna thinks it'll have to do. Maybe the water will stop before reaching the ceiling, but keeping Geller afloat until they'd be rescued isn't an option. She didn't find rope or duct tape. There's nothing to keep him bound either.

The water glugs and sloshes in the stairwell, and Geller strains his head to try to see. "This was just death with some extra steps, darling. Maybe you can move me up some stairs when I'm hardly conscious. But you can try with all your might, you're not getting me to stand now."

"Mind if I hold you to that?"

"What?" He frowns, and Anna smiles. "You know what, maybe we are related, because I'm going to enjoy this, *Dad*."

"Anna . . ." He stares, his eyes wide in fear at the drill in her hand. "What are you doing?"

Anna drops on top of him. She pins one knee on his neck and the other on his good arm. He struggles, but he's weak and his free arm with the bad wrist is hardly any use.

She snatches a screw from her pocket. The drill bit is magnetic, and the screw head is deep. She's able to keep the screw balanced on the bit as she guides it towards his hand.

He screams and balls his fingers into a fist, but it's little help. Anna pulls the trigger and keeps her hands pressed into the back of the drill.

Once the first threads take, the screw sinks through his hand like putty into the hardwood floor below.

Geller screams in agony and tries to pull his hand free, but it doesn't budge. "Please. Oh, please."

Anna rolls off of him and catches her breath. "Okay," she says with a sigh and bites her lips while she digs into her pocket for another screw. "Time for the next one."

She pulls the drill trigger twice, and this time, blood spins off the bit.

Axed

Geller moans and mumbles to himself. He bleeds steadily from the holes in his hands, but Anna doesn't think it'll be enough for him to bleed out. The water has breached the top of the stairs and races in a steady pool across the third floor. Anna jumps as Geller suddenly screams in agony as the saltwater washes into his wounds.

Despite the danger of death, with Geller bound, Anna relaxes. She sits on a plastic container and leans against the wall to stay out of the water.

It doesn't matter how long she had been unconscious for earlier; again, she's exhausted.

At times the wind sounds like it's going to take the roof off and the water could start drowning her in minutes, but she leans her head back and closes her eyes. Her body is simply out of adrenaline. There's no fight or flight. There's nothing she can do now but pray.

She's tilting her head back, trying to think of nothing at all, when Geller speaks. "Extra steps, Anna. That's all this is. Extra steps."

He seems to have calmed himself from the pain and is getting ready for death. The water is halfway up his ears now. Anna just looks at him, dejected. Everything she's fought for in the past hour has led—what almost feels inevitably—to failure.

She keeps watching the water. It takes several minutes to rise another inch, but then it seems to hover just below his ears.

She's skeptical it will stop. Then again, storm surges don't grow and grow. They level out.

When a half hour passes, Geller seems to realize this, too. Anna watches him turn his head so his nose and mouth are in the water. She panics and stands but then stops short of him. If they do survive the storm, they'll be here for hours. Days.

She's not going to be able to hold his head out of the water the whole time.

She watches the bubbles escape to the surface, trying to feel some pleasure from the fact that this monster is dying in front of her eyes, but it's what he wants.

Just as the bubbles are beginning to come up less frequently, she's splashed as Geller pulls his face from the water with a giant gasping breath.

He curses and tries to slam his head into the floor, but it's not hard enough to render himself unconscious.

He doesn't have it in him, and Anna's heart soars. He thrashes in the water and again puts his face under, but this time he comes up for air even sooner.

They lock eyes, and Anna says nothing. Her expression is telling enough: coward.

It's why he went through all the trouble of setting Anna up in the first place. He needed someone else to kill him.

She grabs the hatchet she'd found from its plastic bin and walks so she's standing over him.

There's fear but also relief in his eyes as he stares at the hatchet. He nods gently, indicating that this is what he wants. "Do it."

Anna swings the little ax back over her shoulder and then heaves its head into the wooden ceiling. She swings again and again and again, until she can hear the wind whistle through. The hatchet is strong and sharp enough to break through. If she survives this storm, she'll be able to chop through to the roof to be rescued.

She looks down at Geller, and a strange feeling begins to bubble out from her gut. It's not anxiety or guilt or anger. As she watches him on the floor, she can't help but feel a child-like excitement.

She's proud of herself.

Sunbathe

The water doesn't get any higher. In fact, it decreases quickly over the next few hours, perhaps as more streets flood inland and suck more of the surge away. Anna slept sitting on top of a plastic bin and was woken by silence.

The wind no longer roars. The little attic upstairs is silent, apart from a few drops of water that fall from the ceiling.

Geller has exhausted himself from trying to hold his face under, but he hasn't come close to drowning himself. His eyes are closed, but Anna knows he's only asleep.

Hatchet in hand, she goes slowly to the hole she'd started in the ceiling and begins to chop. It's not long before sun beams filter in. Geller says nothing but flinches away as bits of wood and plaster fall onto his face.

When the opening is shoulder-width, she throws the hatchet towards where the staircase was, and it sinks.

She grabs on to either side of the hole and pulls herself onto the roof. For several seconds, she's blinded by the sun and blinks, letting her eyes adjust. Then she looks out over Charleston.

The churches that marked the geography of the streets the same way skyscrapers do in other cities are all headless.

The Holy City has lost its steeples.

Smoke rises in the distance. Other survivors who stayed in the city dot rooftops in the distance. While the wind has gone and the waves of the storm surge calmed, the water remains.

Twenty feet of it sits in the streets. Anna's eyes widen a bit in wonder as she sees the stealthy shape of a shark muscling its way through the water. It's a hellish scene and, at the same time, Anna thinks, it's beautiful.

With the fear gone, her mind can finally wander to her sisters.

To Sylvie. Anna wants to mourn. To dress in black and take a vow of silence, but that is not what they'd want.

They'd want her to live, for all of them.

It's a conscious effort, but Anna hops back into the house and goes to the bathroom, paying no mind to Geller.

She yanks a towel off a peg then returns to the roof. She kicks off her soaking shoes, peels off her socks, and spreads her toes on the hot shingles.

Then with the towel laid out, she takes off the rest of her clothes.

There's no one around to see, and Anna wiggles her shoulders into the roof and tries to smile, but it doesn't quite take. Her thoughts can't be taken from the past. She's able to relax more on the roof as the sun soaks into her skin. She feels herself warm and the humidity rise as the flood water evaporates around her.

In a half hour, helicopters begin to pass overhead. Dozens buzz and hover over rooftops like pollinators as they rescue people.

Anna isn't all that noticeable by herself. She has not written *HELP* in big letters, nor does she wave a shirt overhead like a flag in distress. She's fine waiting her turn.

An hour passes. She's begun to doze as the pounding blades of a helicopter are suddenly closer than the others. She stays on her back and opens her eyes, expecting it to pass directly overhead, but the sound grows deafening and stays steady.

Her hair dances in a whirlwind as she sits up to see.

There's a Blackhawk helicopter hovering behind her. It's enormous and gray, and the word *NAVY* is painted in black letters on the tail.

The door to the cabin is open, and two men are crouched there, staring at Anna with open mouths. They look at her naked body, but their expressions are not aroused. They seem stupefied by the sight of a naked woman sunbathing in this hellish aftermath.

She doesn't bother to try to cover herself. It seems ludicrous to care about being naked while the world is destroyed around her. She smiles awkwardly and attempts to wave them away. There are plenty of injured people who need rescuing, and Geller can wait.

"I'm okay! I'm not injured!" She doubts they can hear her, so she gives them a big thumbs-up and a beaming smile. The helicopter just hovers. The men all too shocked to move. "Go help others!" She gestures towards rooftops in the distance. A third face appears in the cabin. The three Navy men all look at each other bewildered. One turns to talk into the cockpit, and the helicopter slowly starts to fly on. Then they all wave to her with big grins.

She waves back and starts to laugh, and they all do too. All through the day and night, they will be lifting bodies and the injured from these rooftops. She's happy to provide a moment of levity for a misery-filled day of work. It's this that she hopes they remember, not the corpses that float through the streets.

The helicopter shrinks in the distance, and she thinks of what Hannah and Tess would say. Even serious Sylvie would get a kick out of this. Anna's still laughing, or at this point, crying. She can't quite tell.

Maybe it's both.

Aftermath

Anna spent two days in a tent hospital set up in a strip mall parking lot before she was transported to an actual facility in Charlotte. Then it was four days there. She had a fracture in her left arm and another in her collar bone. The doctors would've just sent her home right away, if it weren't for the fluid in her lungs they wanted to monitor.

She's been back in Charleston for almost four weeks already.

The city is done mourning. After the first day of sunshine, a gloom moved in. Rain and clouds came in off the Atlantic for weeks as if the ocean was sorry for what it had done. Now in the middle of autumn it's been nothing but blue skies and seventies.

Anna's been helping clean up the neighborhood around her apartment. She can't do as much as she'd like with the sling and cast around her left arm, but she acts as a helper. She fetches tools, gives her input when she can, and more than anything, she cracks jokes.

The team she works with thinks she has probably always been a funny, carefree girl, and she's glad she can have a fresh start like this.

They still don't recognize her, at least not yet. Her story was not lost in the news of the storm. It's gone national and the nation wants more. Locally, people still only know her as a name but not a face. A lot of Charleston still doesn't have internet and those that do are too damn busy picking up the pieces to follow the news.

Even so, things still sometimes feel out of hand. Somehow the media got her phone number and her address. She's started dumping her mail in the recycling before looking at it and has gotten a new number.

She has an agent to field the requests who's currently putting together her media strategy. She's not sure she wants a book deal or a six-episode docuseries, but the idea of having life-changing money at her fingertips is alluring.

Right now, she's just trying to figure out who she is.

The site she's working at is a block of single-story homes near the riverfront that was wrecked by the high winds. Most of what they're doing is clearing debris—picking up glass, cutting out sodden carpet, ripping out ruined cabinets.

It's nearing the end of the day, and Anna has sweat through her clothes. Yet she thinks she might be as happy as she's ever been.

The entire city has come together as a community. They work hard during the days and at night, someone, a bar owner, or group of neighbors, will have a bonfire and they'll stay up drinking and talking. She's made more friends in the last weeks than what feels like her entire adult life.

Anna is in the trailer that is parked on the street. She's organizing the tools as the other volunteers bring them in to be put away for the night.

"You coming out tonight, Anna?"

"Don't you know it."

It's only been a couple weeks since she first heard it, but it's a voice she's already grown very warm to.

It's Marcus. He sets a sledgehammer down and leans on its handle. Then his eyes travel from it to her. "Can you even lift this thing with one hand?"

Anna bends over, grasps it close to its head, and heaves the sledgehammer up and onto its peg.

Marcus shakes his head with a smile. "What am I opening your beers for?"

Anna grins. "Because that takes two hands. And . . . I like it."

Marcus is tall, funny, and like Anna he had a rough time growing up that he doesn't let hold him back. He runs his own construction company with five employees and got a contract from the city for hurricane clean-up. When he smiles, his teeth light up in his face like fireworks.

Love was the last thing she expected to happen to her in the last few weeks, but she's rolling with what life throws at her.

Marcus grabs a shop towel and inspects it to see how clean it is before wiping the sweat from his forehead. He talks while he pats himself dry. "Sammy's is having a one-dollar beer night. They've got some stock they haven't been able to sell that's about to be expired so . . . fire sale."

"Great, I'll bring a twenty."

"Cool." Marcus acts like there's something else on his mind. He scratches his head uneasily. "Would you want to go there together?"

"What do you mean?"

"You know, instead of meeting at Sammy's, I meet you outside your place and we walk together. It's on the way for me."

Anna's face betrays her ability to play it cool. "I'd like that. Yeah."

"Okay," Marcus smiles. "How's eight thirty sound?"

"Perfect."

He knocks on the side of the trailer and steps out. "See you then."

Anna keeps putting tools away, but she's giddy and in her own head, and she laughs at herself when she realizes she's been putting everything in the wrong spots.

Anna's lucky enough to be able to shower. Most of the neighborhood still doesn't have their water back on. She's fresh and light and even her fractures don't ache like they often do. She and Marcus walk to the bar together, holding hands for the few blocks it takes to get there.

She enjoys herself for most the evening, but nights are harder for her than the days. Her thoughts drift to Geller.

The county prosecutor promised her his trial and conviction would be a priority despite the hurricane and the crimes and deaths that came with it.

They're trying him for the murders of Justin and Joyce Fox. The prosecutor said those would be the easiest cases to get a conviction. What happened to her sisters will be more difficult to prove. They'll try to stack those convictions for the sake of justice after he's already behind bars for life.

Anna sometimes has the urge to try and visit Geller when she's angry. She'll wake up mad and want to drive to the jail to tease and taunt him. She'd make crude jokes about what happens in prison showers and what fellow inmates do to men convicted of killing little girls.

He made a game of her entire life, but perhaps she's the better person by not trying to do the same of what is left of his.

Marcus has run into some friends who he hasn't seen since the hurricane, and they're all busy telling each other animatedly about how they weathered the storm.

Anna is sitting by herself on the patio, her chair is pushed a little further back from a circle of others. It was a longer day than usual for the team she works with and most people still at Sammy's are strangers now.

A man walks past quickly, one who has been getting louder by the beer. He stops and does a double take. "Holy shit. You're the girl." He points at her like an idiot and before Anna can even respond, he shouts to a friend. "Yo, Ronnie, it's The Flash Girl!"

There's the sound of a chair screeching on pavers and another man, perhaps even drunker, comes stumbling over. He finds the same words his friend did. "Holy shit."

"Look. Um. I'm not doing autographs." Anna tries to sound joking but she's sure she just sounds annoyed.

Both are too drunk to notice.

The original pointer starts talking. "Your dad *taught* my brother's best friend in 2019. He said he seemed like a normal-ass guy." He pauses like this is something Anna should respond to.

"Well . . . he wasn't."

"Yeah. Yeah. Course not. But I actually have my minor in psych and this whole thing feels fake. Hear me out. The news, you, you've mentioned that it wasn't a sex thing for him. Like he was playing a Jigsaw game. I don't think that's true. Even if it was a game for him, its root has to be in sexual satisfaction. If it wasn't that would be rare. A super rare thing."

Anna starts touching an empty beer bottle on the ground. The county prosecutor has been kind. They've all but figured out she was the one that broke into the coroner's office but mentioned it's not an investigation they're going to pursue.

She shouldn't try her luck by launching a beer bottle at this moron's skull. There's a simpler solution. She tilts her chin up at him. "Do me a favor and fuck off."

"Oh," The man begins nodding his head in long arcs. "So, The Flash Girl's a bitch."

Screw it, she thinks, and her hand goes back to the bottle, but just then a deep voice shouts from behind her.

"Hey!"

The men look to its source. Their eyes widen and then find the ground and Marcus comes up to Anna's right. "Everything okay?"

She's not used to having someone fight her battles for her. She leans back in her chair. "Yeah, these idiots were just leaving."

They don't give Marcus a challenging look, they wave their hands, mumble and walk inside the bar. There are some big men that guys of shorter stature might still size up thinking they could take in a fight. Anna looks up at Marcus with a smile. He is not one of them.

She pats his arm. "OK, my savior," she says somewhat sarcastically. "Thank you, but you can get back to your friends."

"Yeah, saving you from jail. I saw you messing with that beer bottle." He points at it. "They're not worth it."

"I know. I know." She stands with a big sigh. "I think I'm going to get home, though."

"Alright, let me walk you back."

"No, that's okay. You walked me here. It's three blocks. I want some time to myself."

He looks at her for a moment but doesn't argue. "Okay. I'll text you."

"I'll see you at *nine* in the morning."

"I meant to make sure you got home."

"You're sweet." They hug and say their goodbyes and then Anna is walking down the empty streets of Charleston. There was a crime wave in the week after the storm, but the police cracked down quick. If anything, everybody is saying they're safer now than they were before.

Her mind goes to her sisters the way it often will when she's alone in the dark. She thinks of what they would want her to do with all the media deals at her fingertips. She knows the answer. They'd tell her to get that money.

Still, she feels guilty. She didn't want to be her father's favorite, even if it saved her life. When she gets close to her apartment, she looks up from her feet, suddenly alert.

She can tell something is off, and then she sees it.

It's a car. A boxy 90's sedan is idling with its lights off. She thinks it could be a journalist trying to catch her for an interview, but it's far too late for that. They'd assume she was asleep in bed.

Maybe it has nothing to do with her, she thinks. Her paranoia is still something she's trying to kick.

She had started to walk slower, but she picks up her pace again and has halved the distance to the door to her building when suddenly, the car pulls out from the curb.

It doesn't speed but cruises.

Anna hasn't felt fear in weeks. Her heart beats so hard her broken bones hurt. She's trying to see who's behind the wheel when suddenly she's blinded. She throws her arm over her eyes as the car flashes its brights at her for only a moment—the length of a camera flash.

It keeps driving off while she stares at it wide-eyed. The shadow of its headlights is burned into her corneas. She's too terrified to chase it. She can only watch the car get smaller in the distance before it turns and disappears from sight.

Was it a prank? Some sick joke? Or a warning? She can't make up her mind. She might never know.

She may be looking at a happy life now. A boyfriend and a fortune might wait for her, but no matter what she does, the past will try its best to haunt her.

She will always be a Flash Girl.

From the Author

Thanks for reading my first book! I hope you enjoyed.

It took me years to go from writing short stories to novels and because of readers like you, I've been able to make writing my full-time job.

I'm more grateful than you know.

-J.M.

About the Author

J.M. Cannon lives in the Northwoods of Minnesota where there is plenty of darkness, trees and strange sounds coming from them to keep the writing ideas coming.

About Embla Books

Embla Books is a digital-first publisher of standout commercial adult fiction. Passionate about storytelling, the team at Embla publish books that will make you 'laugh, love, look over your shoulder and lose sleep'. Launched by Bonnier Books UK in 2021, the imprint is named after the first woman from the creation myth in Norse mythology, who was carved by the gods from a tree trunk found on the seashore – an image of the kind of creative work and crafting that writers do, and a symbol of how stories shape our lives.

Find out about some of our other books and stay in touch:

X, Facebook, Instagram: @emblabooks
Newsletter: https://bit.ly/emblanewsletter